PRAISE F~~..~~ ~~~~~~

Once I started reading, I did not want to stop. The action was well-paced and kept me turning the pages long after I should have gone to sleep. And, of course, the dog, Surge, was a scene stealer. This is one of my favorite reads for 2024.

Surge is another great book in A Breed Apart Legacy series! If you like MWDs, excitement, and romance, this is the book for you!

This story will fill you with a surge of non-stop adrenaline! It grips your attention from the start and will not let go until the end! I love how the characters grow and develop to overcome their own past and fears, learning to fully trust on God. This is one of those books that stays with you long after you've finished! A definite cannot afford to miss book!

This book has lots of action, amazing dog feats, and lots of romantic sparks between Garrett and Delaney. Surge could be a fierce warrior and also a playful sidekick.

SURGE

A BREED APART: LEGACY || BOOK 5

RONIE KENDIG

VONI HARRIS

sunrise
PUBLISHING

Surge
A Breed Apart: Legacy, Book 5
Published by Sunrise Media Group LLC
Copyright © 2024 Ronie Kendig and Voni Harris
Print ISBN: 978-1-963372-33-5
Ebook ISBN: 978-1-963372-34-2

For more information about the authors please access their websites at roniekendig.com and voniharris.com.

Published in the United States of America.
Cover Design: Kirk DouPonce, DogEared Design

DEDICATION

Surge is dedicated to Mr. Incredible, my hubby who knows nothing but support, nothing but love, nothing but service, nothing but strength in family, nothing but faith. I love you, Rich, and I'm so glad our lives are interwoven with Christ.
"A cord of three strands is not quickly broken."
Ecclesiastes 4: 9-12 NIV

Leah and Ephraim, Rhode and Zarya—there is nothing but love and support from any of you. I am so proud of you, so honored that we are family.

For it is by grace you have been saved, through faith — and this is not from yourselves, it is the gift of God — not by works, so that no one can boast. For we are God's handiwork, created in Christ Jesus to do good works, which God prepared in advance for us to do.

Ephesians 2:8-10

PROLOGUE

SOMEWHERE OVER DJIBOUTI

"THE CHANCE WE'VE BEEN WAITING FOR IS FINALLY HERE," NAVY SEAL Master Chief Garrett "Bear" Walker said as Charlie team huddled in the hangar. "According to COMINT, Sachaai terrorists have been training in their homeland for a purported large-scale attack on America, but they were spotted boarding a C-17 to return to their Tadjoura workhouse early tomorrow morning and will effect that attack."

Communications Intelligence hung slightly below Human Intelligence on the intel ladder, but that was harder to come by in Djibouti City and especially with these terrorists—cowards, who poisoned the air and people rather than facing their enemy head-on like real men.

Petty Officer Third Class Blake "Zim" Zimmerman—the newb on the team with a couple degrees in chemistry—let out a low whistle. "They deal in some nasty stuff."

"To put it mildly," CIA operative Bryan Caldwell said as he strode across the hangar. Leathered skin spoke of many hours in the sun. Gray hair at the temples spoke of stress. Probably because the guy didn't have friends. He slid images—satellite photos, pictures of men, structures, an aerial shot of a village, and a picture of a container—onto the table. "Sachaai is Urdu for *truth*," Caldwell said, "and their goal is to make Pakistan the world hub of Islamic truth. They will stop at nothing to remove all obstacles in their way."

The *thwump* of rotors and engine whine of the Black Hawk powering up on the tarmac fought to dominate the air.

"Hold up." Senior Chief Petty Officer George "King" Kingery scowled, his thick red beard twitching as he frowned and took in the spook. "This op is vetted by *him*? The guy who burned us in Burma?"

Petty Officer First Class Beckett "Brooks" Brooks tapped his heart and pointed at King. "Truth!"

"I didn't—"

"And we're going to believe he's giving us everything and *not* risking mission success?"

Grunts of agreement skidded around the hangar from the rest of Charlie team.

Caldwell huffed. "I'm giving you everything you need—"

"*Need*? That's a load of—"

"Bury it." Garrett didn't bother to hide the growl in his voice. Nobody was happy about operating on intel from the operative. "We've been champing for a chance to get these pukes, and now we have it. The chemicals they're using are lethal. I'm going to hand it over to Zim for a quick brief, but the second thing is that we need to get in and out before first light. We aren't exactly American Idols here. So, we have a few hours to get in and get back here." He nodded to Zim. "Brief them on the chems—but fast. Helo's waiting and the clock is ticking."

"When we head in there, we'll be looking for metal lockboxes with an indicator like this," Zim said, holding up his phone with an image of a red-and-black panel. "We've all heard about sulfamic acid and potassium cyanide—not a big headache, but the Sachaai love to make hydrogen cyanide gas with those chems."

"Symptoms?" Garrett asked.

"Nausea. Vomiting. Temporary blindness. Heart palpitations . . . or heart attack. Shortness of breath . . . or no more breath—but if this stuff disperses into the air, we have seconds. If that." His dark eyes were wide.

"Their chemist has found a way to stop it from doing that," Caldwell said, "so if we can get hold of him, we could possibly shut down the Sachaai for good. Or at least long enough to decimate their infrastructure."

"We know who that is?"

Zim sagged. "No, but this guy is a genius. Being able to do this and keep these chemicals—"

"See your nerd coming out," King teased in his deep Southern drawl.

"Which is why we're all going in with chem gear," Garrett said, not willing to be turned into a blistered corpse. "HAZMAT will be on standby to come in behind us to secure the site, if we find anything."

"Okay," King said, stroking his beard as he stabbed a thick finger at the image with the white buildings. "Djibouti City?"

"SATINT tracked Sachaai to a neighborhood a klick inside the southern border of Tadjoura before signals got scrambled, impeding analysts from narrowing the target location any further." Garrett grunted. "That's a quarter mile of potentially unfriendly territory to sort through. HUMINT has an informant describing their headquarters as a small white building."

Laughter filtered through the space.

"Reckon it'll be a challenge to find the Sachaai's 'small white' HQ in that sea of white structures," King said, eyeing the device with the SAT imaging of their target location.

"Doesn't matter," Zim said, pointing to the MWD team. "We've got the Mal to sniff 'em out."

All eyes turned to Petty Officer Third Class Sam "Samwise" Reicher and his military working dog, Tsunami M501—also a petty officer, but Second Class, one rank above his handler.

MWDs were force multipliers and morale boosters all wrapped up in one aggressive package.

Samwise patted Tsunami's tac vest. "Tsunami has all the training of a military working dog with the added special forces training. On top of that, she is the only MWD with specialized training to rout the signature lipid that's unique to the Sachaai."

"So make sure the dog lives," Garrett said. "We'll chopper in, hit the beachhead a klick outside Tadjoura. Hoof it to the sector defined by intel. Let the MWD do her thing and sniff out the workhouse. Then Sensitive Site Exploitation: Secure the site. Document the site. Search the site to learn what the terrorists planned against the US. All to rout that lipid. Any questions?"

"Negative," came a chorus of replies.

"Lives are depending on us. We fail, thousands die. This time, it's our own—Americans." He skated Caldwell a glare. "This mission can't fail, or we fail them. Let's move out."

The team checked their gear. Garrett clipped his M4A1 to his sling harness, double-checked his Sig, then set the comms piece in his ear. He started toward the hangar doors.

"What's this?" King taunted as he snatched something from Samwise.

"Hey!"

Garrett looked over his shoulder and saw the big guy angling away from the handler, which amped Tsunami.

King whooped. "What?" The big guy whipped out a huge smile. "How did you get a beauty like this to marry your ugly mug?" He looked closer. "I need one of Zim's microscopes to see the diamond. Cheap, man. Too cheap."

Samwise snatched it back and, over the rotor, shouted, "Because unlike you, I have style."

King barked a laugh and headed out to the tarmac.

Eyeing the picture his friend held, Garrett saw him start to tuck it away. "You asked her."

Grinning, Samwise nodded.

They fist-bumped over Tsunami's head. "Finally. Good job."

But why did this feel like a bad omen? Every mission they went on was one they might not come back from. And Sam wanted to put a wife through that? Too much risk . . .

In the helo, the MWD team sat across from him, the fur-missile stuffed between both Garrett's and Samwise's boots.

Jutting his jaw at his buddy, Garrett dropped on the net seat and felt his back pop. A dozen years as a SEAL had battered his body. Broken fingers, twisted ankles, a few bullet wounds, whiplash . . . This was it. His last mission. Time to get out before he came back in a pine box or sans a limb. He wasn't signing the reenlistment papers. Not that he had Samwise's attractive reason waiting back home.

Home . . . They had to do this mission right, or thousands of Americans would die.

That's why he'd become a SEAL—for the people, the innocents. No re-upping meant he couldn't help people in the only way he knew how and was skilled at. How could he not sign the papers? This was his life's purpose, even when a pre-mission briefing meant listening to CIA operative Bryan Caldwell. When Zim crowded in around him, Garrett felt the gas mask providing tension. He shifted it . . . and his thoughts went to the mission in Burma. Caldwell had been a jerk then too, but the HUMINT he'd brought to the table had been flawless.

Garrett narrowed his eyes. Okay, mostly flawless. He could admit that . . . Either way, a threat against the good ol' US of A wasn't one he'd take standing down. No way he'd sit on the bench while terrorists attacked his country. It was the only reason he'd listened to the man's lecture about the Sachaai and the political landscape fueling them: America was friends with the "westernized" Pakistani president, whose politics stood in direct opposition to the Islamic terrorist cadre's goal.

Garrett refused the headache trying to take over his brain. *God, help us.*

Hand still on the mask, he scanned Charlie team. Felt the buzz of adrenaline as the chopper zipped them closer to target.

These were the best of the best. Warriors. Hunters. SEALs. His men.

Warmth pressed against Garrett's calf, and he eyeballed Tsunami. In the dark, the pure-black Malinois looked more like a phantom than a dog. Soulful brown eyes squinted at the terrain, blurring a hundred feet below. Her pink tongue dangled, and she shifted her position, those keen eyes sweeping up to him. When she noticed him looking at her, she jammed her snout up under his hand and thrust upward with that powerful Malinois neck, insisting he pet her. This hard-hitting Malinois and her snout were the key.

"You help us do this, and I'll buy you a steak," he muttered, knowing the Malinois could hear him over the thunder of the chopper and elements. When Garrett didn't immediately pet her, she nudged his hand again.

With a quirk of his lips, Garrett gave in. Always did like a girl with attitude. "One day," he said in a quiet tone, "that attitude will get you in trouble." A double pat to his shoulder drew his gaze to the flight chief, who held up both palms.

Garrett nodded and keyed his mic to Charlie team. "Ten mikes out."

Tsunami stood and her tongue disappeared, ears up and trained on the beachhead. The four-legged warrior was ready for action.

Garrett looked out at Tadjoura. Home to around 45,000, it was the third-largest city in Djibouti and had a smattering of white houses that all looked alike.

The flight chief held up three fingers.

"Three mikes out," Garrett announced to Charlie as he shifted to the edge of the nylon seat. Brought his M4 around in front of him and lowered his NODs.

The helo descended, dust and dirt swirling in a cloud as it held station over the tiny sheltered beach they'd mapped out one klick north of Tadjoura.

Garrett hit the beach and rushed forward, dropping to a knee to provide cover as the rest of Charlie deployed behind him. He scuttled up to a six-foot wall and pressed his shoulder against the concrete. He scanned up and down the beach as the rest of the team dropped in. Zim patted Garrett's shoulder, giving the ready signal, and he pushed up, his boots digging into the sand. Eyes out, ears alert, and heart steady, he trekked down the deathly quiet street that paralleled the gulf.

As they reached the outskirts of the neighborhood intel had targeted, lit by the moonlight, Garrett pulled aside and motioned the MWD team ahead. The neighborhood was empty and quiet. He looked over at Samwise. "Go."

The handler caught Tsunami's collar. "Tsunami, seek-seek-seek."

Garrett trailed the duo, who were checking shadows, windows, doors, rooftops, the hard-working nose taking in scents.

With all her spunk on full display again, Tsunami charged forward to do her job, towing Samwise as they took point. Just like Charlie, the dog ran toward the trouble, anxious to seek it out. Ears swiveling, the Malinois rushed onward, sleek snout drawing in long, puffing breaths as she zigzagged up the street. She hugged the first row of structures, sniffing out each door and moving on to the next.

Keeping pace, Garrett patrolled the street, monitoring the dog's progress and the comms chatter, anticipating trouble. Which would come. He could feel it in the air.

Tsunami hurried to a house, passed it. Lifting her head, she took in long draughts and circled around. Took more time sniffing a corner of the building. Paced the scent trail back and forth. She angled toward Garrett and brushed against his leg. He'd swear she did that on purpose, almost as if telling him to give her room to work the scent cone.

He backed up. Samwise had once explained that the scent trail started wide and narrowed—like a cone—as it got closer to the scent source.

Tsunami planted herself in front of a door.

Attagirl.

Samwise glanced at him and gave a nod, then drew his Malinois aside.

Shoulders taut, Garrett stepped up to examine the barrier and spotted a digital lock. *Well, that's different . . .* He visually traced the jamb for tripwires or plastique. If the dog said the lipid was here, then the lipid was here. He just didn't want to get blown to kingdom come proving that. "Zim, you're up," he subvocalized to their communications specialist as he shifted aside and saw Charlie holding watch.

The five-nine SEAL hustled up, phone in hand as he eyed the digital lock. In what felt like seconds, Zim overrode the electronic lock, then snapped up his weapon and stepped back.

"Send the dog," Garrett said.

Samwise caught Tsunami's lead and unclipped it. After a nod from Garrett, he sent the black Malinois into the white house.

M4A1 up and tucked into his shoulder, Garrett glided left, checking the corner, then swung right along the wall. Amid a series of *clears*, he caught the winey smell of cookstove ethanol with a hint of mold that permeated the tightly packed space. The four-legged operator trotted down a long hall, ducking into a room and out of another.

Garrett navigated the plaster home. Around a wobbly table, a threadbare cushion lazily tossed in a corner. Soda bottles and cans littered the dirt floor.

"Clear," Zim comm'd just before he reemerged, moving methodically to the next room, weapon tucked firmly against his shoulder.

Ahead, Tsunami emerged from a back room and headed for the stairs.

Stairwells were notorious for creating an incredibly risky fish-in-a-barrel scenario. Garrett nodded to the handler, who sent the dog up.

Tsunami vaulted from every third step till she reached the

top and rushed to the left and an open door barely visible from the lower level. Spine to the wall, Garrett swept his weapon up as he climbed the stairs, expecting contact any second.

On the second level, he peered around the corner.

Tsunami was hauling in scents as she headed down a narrow hall straight to the farthest door on the left. The Malinois sniffed at it. And she again planted herself with a double thrust of her snout at the door. Ears pricked, she stared at the barrier, then shot a glance to Samwise as if to say, "Right here, Boss."

After Zim swung to his right on the top stair and readied himself, Garrett took up position. King and Brooks lined up behind them on the stairs. He'd learned long ago to trust MWDs. The team had to breach this location. But what was on the other side? Explosives? Was the door rigged? Wouldn't put it past Sachaai.

Unexpectedly, the door jerked inward.

Garrett snapped his weapon up as a tall, lean man jolted at the sight of the dog.

"Hands, hands!" Garrett shouted in English and Urdu.

Samwise lunged at him as the man's hand went up—revealing a small round device.

Without warning, Samwise and Tsunami dropped like wet blankets, bodies convulsing violently . . . then . . . went still.

No! Instinct pushed Garrett forward even as he smelled . . . nuts? What was—

Thud! In a blink, the local was laid out on the floor too. The device tumbled from his hand and slid across the hall.

Was the guy dead? Garrett moved in to check—

A hand slapped his chest—Zim's. "Masks!"

The shout was enough to jack Garrett's heart into his throat. He snatched his chemical mask and stuffed it on, quickly securing the straps. He gave Zim a nod of thanks, then glanced back to the team.

King backed down the hall to the stairs, grabbing his mask off his belt, Brooks doing the same.

Backstepping, Garrett aimed for the stairs and eyed Tsunami and Samwise. "Eagle One, this is Bear. Possible chemical agent. Samwise and Tsunami down. Local male down."

"Copy that, Bear. Advise immediate exfil and head to rendezvous site."

"Good copy, Eagle One." Garrett darted into the invisible chemical fog and caught Samwise's drag strap. Hauled him back.

Zim shifted a now-limp Tsunami around his shoulders and snagged the man's odd device and started to exfil.

Hiking Samwise onto his shoulders, Garrett hoofed it down the suddenly cold hall. The floor shifted—and he collided with the wall. Oh no. Dizziness. He'd been infected! A fog edged into his mind, but he forced himself on, away from the bitter almond smell. "Charlie team, clear out!"

Ahead, Zim began stumbling.

Garrett hooked his arm up around the nerd and shoved them both down the hall toward the stairs.

At the stairs, Zim whispered, "I'm okay now, Boss."

Taking in the area, Garrett wondered about that scent. Where'd that come from? Didn't matter. Men were down, the dog was down. Samwise's weight made him take care as he hustled to the first level and rushed out the front door, where the team waited. He rolled his shoulder, releasing Samwise into the capable hands of the corpsman. "Chemical. Passed out." They laid him out and Garrett shifted aside.

Brooks went to a knee, bent over Samwise. "Unconscious. Breaths are light and fast. Pulse is normal." He huffed. "We need to get him to Lemonnier and their medical team. And a decon team for all five of you, considering that chemical effect."

"How's Tsunami?" Garrett asked.

"Same."

He turned and spied Zim still up and moving. Then he took a long draught from his CamelBak and caught one corner of the tactical litter Brooks had deployed.

"Chopper's en route to rendezvous," Zim announced.

"Let's go," Garrett called as they quick-stepped through the shadows with King bringing up the rear, monitoring their six.

Hoofing it through the city, they stayed alert, grateful for no contact. And for the helo waiting for them once they reached the beach extraction point. They slid the litter onto the deck and climbed in. The chopper lifted and whisked them away from the site.

Grateful his dizziness had faded, Garrett glanced at his swim buddy next to him. Something about the way Samwise was lying there, unmoving . . . "Sam!" Garrett lunged. Checked for breathing—nothing. Shoved two fingers against his buddy's throat—again, nothing! "Sam, c'mon!" He dropped to his knees and began CPR.

From the back, Brooks counted out loud to keep him steady. "Check his pulse."

Garrett did. "Nothing!" And he started CPR again.

"One man down, chemical inhalation. Unknown agent," King comm'd, shouting above the rotor noise. "Not breathing, no pulse. En route, three mikes out."

Garrett kept up the rhythmic presses on Sam's chest. "Live for Catherine, Samwise. Catherine!" he yelled over the chopper noise.

"Check pulse," Brooks said again.

"Nothing!" Despite the pronouncement, they kept working. Compressions. Breath. Compressions. Breath.

Garrett bit back a curse as they landed at Lemonnier hospital. A medical team swept forward and set Sam's litter on a gurney. A doctor climbed on and continued resuscitation efforts as they rushed into the facility. Brooks followed, providing Sam's medical status info.

Garrett pounded the side of the helo, then spotted a team loading Tsunami onto a gurney. He rushed over to her.

"Animal hospital. Now!" a corpsman barked.

Medical staff moved toward Zim.

"I'm fine," he snarled, and the woman backed away, eyes wide.

As they hurried toward a vehicle, Garrett ran his hands slowly up and down the sweet, hard-working Malinois as she was transferred to another gurney. His gut tightened as she let out a keening whimper beneath raspy, difficult breathing.

The nurse pulled out her phone and called the vet clinic as he climbed into a waiting ambulance with Tsunami.

Garrett stood on the tarmac, the team hurrying in one direction or another to take care of the injured. Didn't look good for Reicher. Iffy for Tsunami. All because of . . .

"The chemicals were weaponized," Zim huffed. "They didn't tell us that. I mean, it was a possibility, I guess—but . . ." Face sweaty and pale, the newb looked up at him. "They'd tell us if they knew that. Right?"

"Caldwell," he growled.

This was Caldwell's fault. No way the operative didn't know . . .

An hour later, Garrett threw open the door to the Tactical Operations Center and strode up to a CIA analyst, whose hair was tied in a tight bun at the back of her head. The remnant of Charlie team gathered behind him, battle faces on.

"Where's Caldwell?" Garrett demanded.

"B-break room," she stammered, finger pointing to the rear.

Garrett pivoted toward the hall, feeling the team snake behind him. He punched open the door that reeked of burned coffee and frozen dinners.

At their intrusion, Lieutenant Commander Taylor swiveled from the counter as he heated some food, licking his thumb. His gaze seemed to automatically slide to the far side of the room.

In that back corner, Bryan Caldwell smacked his laptop shut and rose. "Problem, Walker?"

"You could say that." Garrett stalked over and got into Caldwell's smug CIA face, and the team circled behind him. "You knew the chemicals had already been weaponized and didn't tell us!" He clenched his fists at his side. "Tsunami's sick, snapping at Hell's gates, and Reicher's dead."

The operative held his gaze as he processed the news. "My condolences." He scratched at his long nose like that itch was more important. "Sorry to hear that."

"Condolences? This is your fault! You withheld vital intel and killed Reicher."

"Now hold up." The man's face reddened. "There was no way to know they'd made a weaponized form already. And your team should have exercised more caution consid—"

Garrett's fist swung on its own. Connected with Caldwell's nose. *Crack!*

With a strangled shout, Caldwell shoved away, cupping his hands over his blood-gushing nose. "What the—" His eyes widened. "Walker, you're through!"

"Through with you? You bet your sorry six I am!" He didn't step back, hoping Caldwell would try something so he could level him.

Silence strained the air between them. Caldwell spat to the side, then stormed out.

"He'll press charges," Taylor warned from behind. "That was . . . dangerous—he's powerfully connected to the brass. Could get you discharged."

Behind him, Garrett felt the hot eyes of Charlie team.

"I'm not re-upping anyway."

1

SIX MONTHS LATER

NEW BRAUNFELS, TEXAS

DELANEY THOMPSON STOOD IN THE CENTER OF A MIDDLE SCHOOL gym—one that was a blasted twenty-seven years old, complete with the usual aluminum bleachers, multiple basketball hoops. The usual must of sweat and body odor. This was obviously a torturous middle school just like the one she'd attended.

At her side, Surge pressed his shoulder into her thigh.

"Yeah, sorry about the smells . . ." She grinned down at her jet-black Belgian Malinois boy and stroked the thick coat around his neck.

Okay. Technically, he was Heath "Ghost" Daniels's A Breed Apart dog.

She buried her hands back into his fur. "You've got this, bud. When the students get here, you'll show them your awesome scent skills. This'll prove your recovery to Heath too."

Heath. She sniffed. He'd been her mentor since high school— five years. Now he was her boss.

The vein in Heath's neck had throbbed when he'd found out about the eight grueling weeks of counterconditioning training she'd been doing with Surge. Behind his back. And Crew's.

15

Crew Gatlin had procured Surge for the ranch, but both men were considering retiring the four-legged hero because Surge was a tough nut to crack. But Delaney knew this maligator well and believed he had more work in him before being relegated to Fort Couch for the rest of his days.

Unbelievably, Heath was letting her continue to work with Surge, despite her clandestine training.

She sniffed again, stood to check the setup of her video camera. Then glanced at Surge and—oh man. Black fur stuck to the white pants she'd stupidly chosen to look all professional for the scent discrimination demo today.

She brushed off the MWD's fur, then gave Surge an ear rub. "You've got this. I've got this." She stepped back and grinned. "This is your first ever solo demonstration. Are you ready?"

Surge leapt into her arms, and she laughed, hugged him before he jumped back down.

If he was ready, she was. And she wouldn't get fired. She hoped.

The school bell rang.

Surge stood and turned toward the gaping gym doors, panting as his ears swiveled toward Mr. Finch's social studies students pouring into the gym.

"Good boy," she whispered, burying her hand in his fur. "We're here to show Heath and Crew that you're ready to work again, right?"

Surge's post-traumatic stress after the death of his sister, Tsunami, had relegated him to the ranch, where he'd excelled. Except with certain sounds. The school shouldn't be a problem, since the bell's tone was deeper, resonant. Not high-pitched. The one that bothered Surge was a frequency so high most humans couldn't hear it—the alarm that had gone off in Djibouti when his littermate Tsunami died after exposure to toxic gas on her mission.

Delaney scratched behind Surge's ears as the flood of preteens and teens clambered up the bleachers. The noise level rose as they mingled and teased and chased and called out for each other. The kids shifted around, each trying to get the best look at the working dog. Murmurs and whispers carried easily across the gym floor.

"Look at those eyes. Intense."

"All black—so pretty!"

"Did he kill anyone?"

"Can he smell drugs?"

Saving the answers to all those questions for later, Delaney appreciated the way Surge remained steady and focused, ready to work. Ready to deal with any issue, yet compliant enough to keep his black KONG in his mouth. She grinned. A few weeks ago, Surge would've been too panicked for a situation like this. And if they could pull this off, she could prove to Heath that she had counterconditioned the Mal well. She did regret not telling him about this, but she had been sure he'd reject her request.

Mr. Finch's black shoes squeaked as he approached slowly. "Good morning, Miss Thompson."

"Easy," she murmured to Surge, then smiled at the teacher who'd invited her to come. "Good morning. Thank you for letting us do a demonstration."

Surge looked up at her with those bright golden-brown eyes, KONG dangling from his mouth like an old stogie.

Again the bell rang, signaling the start of the class period.

"Okay, boy. Leave it." Surge dropped the KONG and readied himself, clearly detecting it was time to work.

Delaney pocketed the rubber toy. Movement pulled her attention to the bleachers, where a male student held something aloft.

Yelling "Victory," he yanked a string at the bottom.

Pop-pop-pop-pop!

Body tense, Surge snapped his snout shut, eyes trained on the boy even as the students applauded the chaos the party popper launched.

RONIE KENDIG & VONI HARRIS

Whooping, the boy produced more poppers, passing them to his friends.

Surge let out a keening whine. Excited. Eager to work.

"Easy. Heel," Delaney said, patting her leg, which brought his black hide against her pant leg. She glanced around, anxious for Mr. Finch to take charge before this went south.

"Steven Eagen!" Mr. Finch pointed at the boy, then to the floor. "I am so sorry, Miss Thompson."

"Aw, come on, Mr. Finch." The youth climbed down the bleachers. "We won the football championship yesterday. We're celebrating!"

Finch motioned him out the door and confiscated the rest of the poppers.

"Ooh! You're in trouble," the others called.

With an unrepentant grin, Eagen hung his head and walked out.

Mr. Finch quickly texted. "Letting the principal know he's on his way," he muttered as he joined her at the front. "Are we still good for this exhibition, Miss Thompson?"

She looked over at Surge. Seated, keen eyes on the kids, and tongue dangling, he was calm. Man, he'd come a long way. "Yeah. Looks like we're good."

Mr. Finch introduced her as Surge watched over the crowd, the soft push of his muscular body against her leg. Delaney kept her posture relaxed, a cue this eighty-pound Malinois would no doubt mimic.

"They're all yours," Mr. Finch said as he took a seat on the second row.

She moved to the center of the gym and put Surge in a heel. "Hello. I am Delaney Thompson, an intern trainer with A Breed Apart ranch, and this is Surge L724, a six-year-old Belgian Malinois," she told the group. "He's a former military working dog—or MWD—who is now a contract working dog. That means a *working* dog. All work, all day. For every period of work and training, he earns this reward." She held up the roped

KONG, and Surge's eyes snapped to the dangling toy. "As you can see, even when he wants to play, he is one hundred percent intense. That's what made him such an outstanding MWD. Keep that in mind—because to Surge, work is play. He loves it. So never approach or try to pet him unless I tell you it's okay, because he is trained to respond and protect me. Everyone understand?"

She waited until heads were nodding. "For our demonstration, Surge is going to search for shallow scent tins. I have ten of them."

A nod to Finch had him passing out the scent packs to the students. She played a short working-dog video as the tins made the rounds through the bleachers. At the end, she resumed her spot at the center with Surge. "Anyone ever smell birch before?"

One hand raised.

"What does it smell like?" Delaney asked.

The girl pursed her lips in thought. "I don't know . . . kind of like root beer, maybe." She shrugged. "My mom loves it."

Delaney laughed. "I have to agree with her and with your description. Some people say it's minty." She motioned to the side door that led to a bit of lawn. "I'm going to take Surge outside for a moment, and Mr. Finch will let those of you holding the scent tins hide them. Then Surge and I will return to let him do his job." She started to walk away but turned back. "And do me a favor? He has to earn his KONG time, so don't make it easy for him, okay?"

"Yes, ma'am," they chorused.

She headed out to the grassy area. After he did his business, she let him sniff around for a couple minutes, played tug with him. She turned and put him in a sit, then waited for his eyes to meet hers. "Let's show Heath we can do this." When his tail wagged, Delaney ruffled his ears.

The door opened and Finch nodded. "We're ready."

"Okay, Surge," she said with a breath for courage. "Time to work."

His pace slowed to a drag as they returned to the gym, and she fought the clench in her gut. Heath's admonishment to her over the last eight weeks as he'd begrudgingly allowed her to continue counterconditioning Surge rang in her head. *Emotion travels down lead.*

She grinned, stood, and signaled a jump—his favorite trick. He leaped into her arms. "Are you ready? Are you ready?"

Surge gave her a sloppy kiss across her face and jumped back to the ground, his tail practically causing a breeze.

"Let's do it." She pulled the door open, and the roar of the kids smacked her. They sure had ratcheted while they were waiting. She could handle it. So could Surge.

This was going to be fun.

She ruffled his ears again, then slipped her hand around his collar, a move that sent anticipation through his muscular body, making his black fur bristle. "Surge, seek!"

Lunging ahead, Surge dropped his nose to the ground, trotted to the right, hauling in scents. He turned his head side to side. At the trash can, he got a hit. Planted himself in front of it.

"Good boy!" Amid the kids' applause, she got him back to work looking for the others. When he'd found them all, she'd give him some KONG time. He quickly located two more, and she felt exultant. She'd known he could do it—she could do it!

Amid the squeal of someone's phone—earning a quick remonstration from Mr. Finch—Surge's behavior shifted. He wasn't as eager.

Stomach tight, Delaney clicked her tongue, diverting him to the wall, trailing her hand along a rack of basketballs. Redirecting and guiding him.

When he followed and sniffed the trail, she felt the knot in her stomach loosen. It'd worked.

For two seconds.

Then it happened again. This time, he went lower . . . then down, as if trying to sink into the floor. She pulled out his

KONG. *God, please.* Again pointing, again clicking her tongue, she tried to inspire him.

No response. Not even to the KONG.

Great. Middle school was the perfect place for embarrassment, right?

His ears flattened back against his head. His panting ramped up to sixty miles an hour.

Stressed. Overwhelmed.

Just like before. Delaney winced, feeling her own gallons of stress and being overwhelmed, especially when he pressed his belly to the floor and sank his snout onto his paws.

He was done.

"Is he scared?" someone asked.

"No, dummy, he's tired," another kid scoffed.

"You're right," Delaney said, her face hot, "that does happen, even to the toughest dogs. Or they have a bad day." She wanted to shake some confidence into Surge, but it wasn't his fault. It must have been the frequency from that crazy phone. "Anyone ever have a bad day?" she asked, breathing a little easier when several hands went up. "Well, so can even the most hard-hitting working dogs like Surge."

Nods around from the kids.

To see him shut down killed her.

Her brain scrambled through ideas, what might have triggered him. It had to have been that phone that made the particular sound that triggered Surge. After all that progress, maybe he hadn't been ready. Her fault.

But the one thing she knew right now was that she had to get him out of here.

HILL COUNTRY, TEXAS

Three things kept Garrett rooted in this middle-of-nowhere area: wide open spaces, no military, and sweet-tang barbecue.

He whipped his F150 into the restaurant parking lot. His mouth watered, and his stomach grumbled as he thought about the spicy, smoky flavor of their pulled pork and brisket. The Foxes had owned this place in the Blanco County for four generations. The only legit barbecue in the world as far as he was concerned. He'd globe-hopped enough to vouch for that.

He opened the restaurant door and just stood there, soaking in the rich smokiness of the mesquite they used to slow-cook the meat. Loud country music reverberated against his chest, making conversation almost impossible.

Perfect.

Add to that the fundraiser the Foxes held every year to benefit the Navy SEAL Foundation—they gave the foundation all their profits from that day—a guy started to feel like God actually existed. Especially when he could stuff his gut with barbecue while supporting his SEAL brothers.

"Hey, Boss!"

Stunned at that voice, Garrett stilled. Turned. He barked a disbelieving laugh at who stood there with a wide smile and big hands propped on his hips. "Zim! What on earth?" He pulled the guy into a shoulder hug.

"Wow. Looks like freelance contractor biceps aren't anywhere as big as Navy SEAL biceps!" He flexed.

"Maybe. But my perfectly trimmed beard is ten times cooler than your baby face."

Zim rubbed proudly at his hair-free cheeks.

"What're you doing here? Haven't seen you since . . ." Garrett swallowed at the memory.

"Yeah." The same heaviness hit Zim's face. "It's been too long, Boss."

"I'm not your boss anymore, remember?" He punched Zim's shoulder.

He rubbed his shoulder like he'd been hurt. "You'll always be 'Boss' to me."

Pulling out his wallet, Garrett shook his head.

Zim pointed at the cashier as they ambled over to order. "I already ate, but yours is on me tonight."

"Nothin' doing."

"Hey." Zim jutted his jaw. "You saved my life. It's the least I can do."

The reminder silenced Garrett's argument. With a smile at the hostess, he ordered the pulled pork sandwich basket from the menu. "With fries and a Dr. Pepper. And banana pudding." It was fundraising day, after all. As she rang it up and loaded a tray, he leaned on the counter and eyeballed his buddy. "You saved my behind too. But I won't argue a free meal." He stuffed his wallet back in his pocket.

"Good. Because I got your six. Always."

"It's what we do." Garrett took the tray of food and soda. "What're you doing in Hill Country?"

"Visiting my great-grandpa. We don't expect too many more summers with him. He has some of the best Iwo Jima stories. He was craving some Fox's brisket, so I came." Zim grinned. "A friend of mine told me you live here, so I hoped you'd drop in on the first day of the fundraiser. You were always complaining there was no good barbecue around Coronado."

"Ain't that the truth." Garrett lifted his tray of food and thanked Zim for it. "Tell your great-grandfather 'hey' from your Navy brother, okay?"

"He'll love that."

Garrett looked for a place to sit.

"Uh, Boss, have some time to chat?"

He raised his eyebrows and shrugged. "Do I get to eat first?"

Zim lifted his palms in surrender. "I'd never get between you and your barbecue."

"You always were the smart one." Garrett stopped at a trough that served as the condiment station.

"I was glad to hear you still have my back."

Garrett piled pickles and onions on his pulled pork and peered sidelong at his buddy. "That sounds like a setup if I ever heard one."

"We need help." Zim motioned him toward the back of the restaurant.

We? Garrett had a bad feeling about this, but he trailed his buddy. They'd negotiated some tables when his gaze collided with a man sitting in a booth. Unmistakable long, crooked nose. *Son of a . . .* He stopped short. "Caldwell."

Lounging like he had all day and owned the place—that alone was enough to tick Garrett off—the CIA operative gave a cockeyed nod. "Walker."

Garrett glared at Zim. "What is this?"

Caldwell stood and extended his hand. "Nice to see you." The man's narrow, arrogant face made him look like he was in pain.

Not trusting himself to play nice, Garrett clenched his jaw and declined the handshake. Reminded himself he was holding a tray of food and a soda. Which he badly wanted to shove in the guy's face.

"Walker, please." Caldwell motioned to the booth. "We need to talk."

"Boss—G-Garrett." The stammering betrayed Zim's nerves. He shifted his weight. "Remember the device we brought out of Djibouti after the . . ." His buddy's rushed words were almost inaudible.

Garrett dropped his tray on the table and shoved it over, then he slid onto the bench across from Caldwell. "What about it?"

Zim sat next to the spook. "Brass told us to give it up, but Caldwell and I kept digging. There was residue on that device—"

"We tied it to another incident," Caldwell inserted quietly.

24

"The Agency recovered a similar device in the Pakistani presidential building when the secretary of state was visiting last month. It had the same manmade lipids as the device from Djibouti. Those lipids?" He seemed way too giddy about this. "Only one terror cell uses them when they process their chemicals for transport."

"Sachaai is done," Garrett bit out, ready to walk. "Fahmi Ansari died setting off the toxic gas in Djibouti. Killed Reicher too. And Tsunami." He glowered. "Remember?"

"His son took over the cell," Zim said.

"Hakim Ansari?" Garrett's gut tightened.

Zim nodded. "Hakim's dad hated their 'westernized' Pakistani president and America. Hakim triply so, he's so galvanized. HUMINT shows they still have a stash of chemicals that indicate the unique lipid."

"In Singapore, where Hakim relocated the cell." Caldwell's smug arrogance was resurfacing.

"What're are they doing in Singapore?"

"He likes the cell's ability to blend into the culture there."

"And Singapore is a leading hub for the chemical industry," Zim added.

"Jurong Island. Easy access," Caldwell said. "COMINT suggests they're planning to infect a food supply to bring into the US."

Okay, they had his attention now. Garrett pushed aside his food and drink. Wished he could do the same to these two thugs. He'd walked in here for barbecue, not mission talk.

"I've got COMINT on this, and they ferreted out info that Sachaai plans to hit America. Big plans," Caldwell continued. "They have an entire load of sulfamic acid and potassium cyanide—enough to wipe out half the population of the US."

"Which they use to make hydrogen cyanide," Zim reminded him.

And that's what'd happened in Djibouti. How Sam had died.

"But they're planning poison, not hydrogen cyanide gas now.

We've learned their chemist is Tariq Sayyim." Zim clenched and unclenched his fists. "I'd like to get my hands on him. Besides the lipid, he has invented an oil spray that will prevent hydrogen cyanide from dissipating. So it's a liquid that will infect whatever food they put it on to send around the US. It'll kill hundreds of thousands of Americans, if not more."

Garrett wanted to be in Singapore now. He squeezed his eyes shut. He was no longer a SEAL. "This is the government's problem. Not mine. Task Alpha or Bravo to take care of it."

Shifting in his seat, Zim took a deep breath. "DOD shut Caldwell down, even with the intel. No mission will be sanctioned."

"Why?"

"'False chatter' is the official answer," Caldwell said, his expression tight for the first time. "But I'm certain about my intel—this source has never been wrong. I've confirmed it. The intel is inarguable."

Nope. Gaze locked with Caldwell's, Garrett shook his head. "But maybe not complete. Even good sources can withhold necessary info. Like when you didn't tell us the chemicals were weaponized in Djibouti? The intel *you* withheld that got Reicher and Tsunami killed?" He clenched his fist under the table. Better leave or he'd light into that man. Yet . . . the spook's unwavering intensity kept him seated.

Letting the new intel soak into his brain, Garrett reached for the Sriracha Smoke Sauce, slathered it on his food, then returned it to the metal rack on the table. "This intel of yours isn't actionable. Get more and the DOD will give in."

Caldwell dropped his head to his chest. Then he popped it up and leaned forward, looking into Garrett's eyes.

As if Garrett had missed something. Couldn't the guy just tell them, stop holding everything so close to the vest? "What? What's going on here? Do I need to shake the info out of you?"

Caldwell sighed, roughed a hand over his jaw. "What we

have *is* actionable. But the one who shut us down at the DOD is compromised."

"You know this has to be addressed, Boss," Zim broke in quietly. "We've talked with Damocles—"

"Chapel's team?" Garrett couldn't help but be impressed. Tyson Chapel was no cheap meat, and his team—Damocles—was revered across the industry. "What'd he say?" He nearly cursed himself, because now he was listening with more than half an ear.

Caldwell smirked. Knew he had him. "He wants it addressed, but they're tied up with a couple of other ops. When I asked for recs, he suggested you." He cocked his head. "When I said I'd already been considering you, he said to get it done, that we have their backing and funding."

Tyson Chapel recommended me? Garrett choked a little that the legend not only knew who he was but had an awareness of his skill level . . . Wait. This . . . this didn't make sense. He reached for his Dr. Pepper and took a swig, then thudded it back on the table. "Why? Tell me why me? After all this time?"

"Like I said, we need you."

"Didn't answer my question." Garrett hated this guy. "There are hundreds of operators out there who can do what I can do." He scratched his beard. "And what I can't figure is why Chapel would give you the time of day." *Yet, he had . . .* So, what had Tyson seen that Garrett was missing?

A heavy, awkward silence settled between them before Caldwell finally huffed. "Look, you don't have to like me—"

"Good."

"—but I think we can both agree this needs to be done." His pocked face reddened. Anger? Irritation? "As for why Damocles? Because Chapel is the best at what he does, and this mission demands that skillset. Just like we need yours."

"My skills only go so far. Greasing me won't make me sign on."

"I told him about what happened in Burma." Caldwell

cleared his throat. "Damocles has identified one of the Sachaai's low-level guys in Singapore that we can buy a sample from. Chapel suggested you go in undercover as a buyer, get the sample, and then track him to the stash of chemicals."

Garrett couldn't help but roll the idea through his head. "Track him? And what—end up sniffing that stuff again and dying like Samwise and Tsunami? I'd go if you had positive confirmation that the chems weren't mixed, but if I lost him—I can't track him. You'd need a specialized search dog who can find that 'unique lipid.'" He stabbed a finger at the spook. "Your words. And since you told me in Burma that Tsunami was the only dog with that training—and oops, now she's dead thanks to your, once again, bad intel—you are out of luck and this convo is over." He stood.

Caldwell smirked. "Tsunami wasn't the only one."

Stiffening, Garrett stared at the spook. "What?"

"Tsunami wasn't the only dog trained to rout the Sachaai lipid," he said with way too much calm and smugness. "There's another. He's here, about an hour away at a ranch."

Garrett cursed himself—he'd walked right into that one. "A Breed Apart."

"That's it." Caldwell spoke quietly, too confident he'd ensnared them in this op. "Chapel put in a call to the ranch's COO, Heath Daniels."

"Yeah," Zim said. "I've seen him—a gorgeous black Belgian Malinois named Surge."

Surge. Wait . . . Garrett remembered Sam showing him a picture of Tsunami's littermate. But what were the chances this one had been trained in scenting the same lipid? The memory of watching Tsunami collapse beneath the gas hit him hard. "Hold up." He swallowed. "That chemical killed Tsunami. What's to stop it from killing Surge?"

Zim reached into his pocket, pulled out two clear two-inch plastic medical vials. He glanced over at the spook, then back at Garrett. "Caldwell, um, visited a Sachaai building on Jurong

Island and stole—er, found a few oral vaccine medicine vials. Like these. Twist-off lids. I tested Caldwell's find, positive for potassium cyanide and sulfamic acid. Also processed with Tariq's lipid." He held his hands apart, each holding empty plastic tubes. "The vials aren't harmful until"—he smacked them together—"they're mixed." His hands burst apart, and he let the vials fall into his lap.

Garrett squinted. "Or it becomes toxic gas. Like in Djibouti."

Zim shook his head, returning the tubes to his pocket. "I hacked into Sachaai messaging—"

Caldwell cleared his throat loudly.

Zim bit his lip. "Well, anyway, they want to put poison in our food supply—kill more people at the same time. And Surge is an MWD. Like Tsunami, he won't eat anything not given to him by a team member."

"What do they want to do with it?" Garrett asked.

"That, we're not one hundred percent on yet," Zim said with another shrug. "We know they're developing it into a liquid spray, but whether they'll put it on a food source being imported or ship it here for us . . . is unknown."

"And not our problem," Caldwell asserted. "Because we're going to stop them before they can do anything with it." He leaned forward. "Daniels has agreed to contract Surge to us for this op. He and Thompson are ready for action."

Garrett took a deep breath, feeling like he'd been caught in a volatile undertow. He owed Zim a listen. "So Sachaai is threatening a major chemical weapon attack on the US. We have to intercept those chemicals well before they get here . . ." Something . . . wasn't quite right. What was he missing? He glared at the operative. How had he convinced Chapel to underwrite this mission? No paramilitary firm had unlimited funds, so what had he bought this favor with? "Is there more?"

The man held his gaze for several seconds. "Isn't there always?"

Zim shifted in his seat. "Okay, look—Caldwell is going. Chapel likes the efficacy of his source on this."

Not him. Caldwell, of course, was holding something back. Same as in Burma and Djibouti. Why on earth would he trust the man a third time? *Fool me once, shame on you; fool me twice, shame on me. A third time?*

"I'm out." Throwing a glance at the food he no longer had an appetite for, Garrett stood and dropped a ten on the table for a tip. "Thanks for lunch, Zim. See you the next time you're in Hill Country."

Zim shoved to his feet, blocking his exit.

Garrett scuffed his beard. "Don't waste your breath, man. It's not happening." He let the growl fill his words.

His buddy held up his hands. "Damocles wants justice for Reicher—Sam. His brother is one of theirs."

Garrett frowned, digging through his memory. "Kane," he realized. "Kane Reicher is with them?"

"That's right," Zim continued. "Kane remembers you were his brother's buddy. It's why they suggested you." The short, wiry guy glanced at the spook, then back at Garrett. "We all feel you're the one with the fire to stop this."

So Kane wanted justice for Samwise. *As do I.*

But this still involved Caldwell.

Garrett tilted his head toward Mr. CIA. "No."

Zim's face fell. "Come on, Boss."

"I'm not going to work with someone who withholds intel and throws their own under the bus, lets innocents die."

"Why?" said Caldwell from behind him.

Garrett turned. "Burma. Djibouti."

"I told you my Burma HUMINT was simply wrong. Didn't know that the sniper chasing you was killing civilians."

"And people died because you didn't do your due diligence, nor did you inform me as the op continued. If it hadn't been for Zim, I wouldn't be standing here. More would've died." He leaned into Caldwell's face. "Oh, wait. They did—in Djibouti! Sam and Tsunami!"

"I told you I had no way of knowing the chemist had weaponized it."

"You are the intelligence officer. That means you get the intelligence before sending people out on some rushed job to die." Garrett stepped forward, ramming his shoulder into Caldwell's. "I'm done with you."

"You'd really let innocents die, just so you don't have to work with him?" Zim's voice hardened. "This isn't you, man. You're better than this." He edged in and lowered his voice. "Have you ever thought maybe Caldwell is trying to make things right after Djibouti?"

"Never crossed my mind," Garrett snarled. He headed toward the front door.

Zim paced. "At Reicher's funeral, you vowed to make those responsible pay for what happened." He swiveled around in front of him "This is it, Boss. This is your chance to make it right. To make sure it doesn't happen to anyone else."

Definitely wanted to pull Hakim Ansari's kidneys out through his mouth. Maybe if Garrett focused on that, not on the spook . . . Jaw tight, he stared out into the bright Texas afternoon. "When's it happening?"

Zim pulled in a quick breath of hope. "Intel suggests they plan to have the poison on American streets a week from Friday—the six-month anniversary of the death of Hakim's father."

Gripping the security bar of the door, Garrett worked through this very bad idea.

A voice cleared from behind—Caldwell. "My source says the chemicals are leaving Singapore Wednesday. We have to stop them before that."

Wednesday. A week.

Garrett slid his gaze to Caldwell, who had the good sense to look contrite, if not a little hardened. Curse it all. If he took

Caldwell out of the equation, he could do this. There was a reason he'd become a SEAL—to protect those who couldn't protect themselves. Even against men like Caldwell. Not acting now would lower him to the spook's level.

He had a chance to stop them. To stop the men responsible for Reicher and Tsunami and save countless other lives.

"Fine." He drove a hard glare to the spook. "But my rules, my way."

2

A BREED APART RANCH, BLANCO COUNTY, TEXAS

OUT IN ONE OF THE TRAINING FIELDS AT THE RANCH, DELANEY stopped tugging the dog agility obstacle. She stood with her hands on her hips, chewing her lip as she scanned the yard hemmed in by cinderblocks. Should she leave this double-combo obstacle in the agility course? Tire jump on the left attached to the window-shaped jump on the right. Crew had created the behemoth to level-up the challenge of the course. Surge would commit to whichever she signaled him through. But *should* she?

Delaney jogged to the front of the training yard, where Surge waited in a "sit" for her next to the eight-foot chain-link fence. She leaned against the chain-link fence opposite him, taking in the earthy, fresh scent of the newly mowed grass. This place reminded her of hot football afternoons back in high school.

Surge leaned his shoulder into her thigh, ready to play—which meant working this course.

"You goofball," she said. "Yes, we're going to do the course. I promise. Gimme a second."

Two hurdle jumps. Of course. Then the A-frame. Simple up

and down for Surge. Weave poles. Surge was superfast weaving between the poles. Dog walk. Up one side, across the bridge, down the other side. She'd have to sprint to keep up with him on that one. And lastly, his favorite—the tunnel run.

After what had happened at the middle school, she had to restart his counterconditioning. Okay, the double-combo jump was fine, but the point was to ensure Surge's compliance and focus on her. Simplified, this course would be a good bounce-back for them.

Before Heath found out about Surge's nonresponse yesterday and fired her for doing the scent demo without asking him.

"Surge, stay." Delaney jogged to the double combo and finished dragging it off to the side. She hustled back to the beginning of the agility course and patted her left leg twice. "Surge, heel."

His silky body rippled with taut muscles, his eyes and ears trained on the hurdles. She held his collar, barely restraining the raw power of the Malinois, who barked excitedly.

Praise God for eagerness.

Delaney chuckled. "Surge, go!" Releasing him, she was already moving with him. She signaled Surge to the hurdle and ran beside him as he flew over. Then the next. She rushed to keep pace with him toward the A-frame. He raced up and down it.

She signaled him to the weave poles, and he wove through them as fast as ever. They headed to the dog walk. He ran up one side and started across the bridge. Happy he was doing so well—he enjoyed it as much as she did—she trotted backward, grinning as he sailed off the bridge.

"Send him through the double combo . . . the tire, not the window."

Delaney's breath hitched at the intrusion of Heath's voice from behind her. Great. She probably should've added it to her course. Why had she doubted herself? Heath knew the Mal preferred the window side to the tire side. But they'd be okay. Surge was paying strong attention to her today.

Surge raced down the other side of the dog walk, and she signaled him to the double combo off to the side of the yard. She was throwing in a wildcard here. Would he do it?

Don't think about it. Don't stress. Just keep going.

They approached it, and she signaled him through the tire side.

He correctly ignored the tunnel but, thick-skulled, he started for the window half of the double combo.

No! Please please please.

She held her breath. At the last minute, he diverted—and sailed right through the tire. Though she wanted to reward him with a "good boy," it was important for him to learn to obey without verbal commands in the middle of a course.

That's right, buddy. Let's finish this thing. She signaled the opening to the tunnel. He shot through it, then spun back around, dropped down to his belly in the grass. Lying there, ears straight up, pink tongue dangling by a mile, Surge stared into the tunnel.

Her stomach fell. *What the . . .* Why was he signaling a hit? Wait . . . With her nerves bouncing, knowing Heath was watching, she jogged to the tunnel and peeked in.

And smiled. She pulled out a scent tin from the tunnel and lifted it in the air so Heath could see.

"Good job, Surge! Good job." She held out her arms.

Surge leaped into them, then hopped down.

She tugged out his KONG.

His head swiveled around, and he was in motion even as she sent it sailing. He jumped up and snagged it from the air. Proud of himself, he trotted around the yard, then came back to her as she produced the KONG tug. He ditched his other KONG and pounced on the tug. He jerked her shoulder so hard she flipped around to see Heath just outside the gate. With someone else.

Crew. Of course.

But they'd seen this—right? They'd seen that Surge had made the course even with the change-up. That he still had it in him, right?

Oh, wait. There was a third guy she didn't know—and he was watching her. Lifted his jaw in greeting to her. She nodded in kind.

Who was this guy with the scruff beard?

Delaney started to walk over and see who it was, but Heath entered the yard like an incoming storm. Ballcap shielding his eyes, he parked himself right in front of her.

"You found out," Delaney said, thinking about what'd happened at the school as she clipped the lead onto Surge. "I—"

"Yep."

She felt her career careening toward the brick wall. "I . . . I know I messed up." She'd never been good at listening to the small voice of her conscience. "But you said I could train him. And we'd made progress."

Heath's expression stayed blank as he zeroed in on her.

She pointed at him, immediately regretting that. "You said we made progress."

Going into a conversation with Heath on the offense . . . *Yeah, real smart, Delaney.* Knowing she was likely digging her own burial hole for him, she shut her mouth.

Surge gave one of his nearly-under-the-breath whines, tail wagging as he looked at the men outside the yard.

Heath smoothed a hand over Surge's head, and the traitorous Mal pushed into his legs, demanding more love. Then Heath pierced her with a look. "The school was too soon with too many unpredictables. Too dangerous with kids."

Oh snap. Her time here was up—he was going to fire her. She'd crossed too many lines. But she wouldn't cry. Not in front of the others, but especially not in front of Heath. What, was he going to fire her in front of Crew and the stranger? She glared at her judge and jury, her fingers playing with the hem of her jacket.

This was the job she didn't want to lose. Ever.

Though she wanted to defend her position and what she'd done, contrition went further with Heath Daniels. "I'm sorry I got in your face about Surge's progress. Sorry I pointed at you."

Heath waited.

She rocked back and forth for a minute, like Dad did when their Jeep got stuck in the mud during their off-roading. "I shouldn't have set up the scent discrimination demo at the middle school without your permission."

Heath grunted. "Do that again, go outside my purview, I will fire you."

She gulped. Wait . . . so he *wasn't* firing her today? "Thanks for trusting me—"

Heath arched a knowing eyebrow. "Surge wasn't ready for that, and it's your job to know the difference between his abilities and his history."

She found no condemnation in his eyes when she opened hers, yet he also didn't move. "H-he shut down. I shouldn't have taken him. It was too soon, like you said."

"A: you're right," he said. "It was too early for Surge to work a crowded environment. Going around me is a totally different problem we'll talk about later. B: Surge wasn't the problem."

Delaney frowned at him. "What?"

"You missed the tells—at first. You got it together, but it was too late—he'd triggered. You've trained Surge and he trusts you—better than I've seen him trust anyone," he said quietly, firmly. "But if you want out, then you know where the front gate is."

She hadn't missed any of Surge's tells. Over the weeks she'd been working with him, she'd been steadfast for Surge, and she didn't want to back down now. But she wanted to earn Heath's respect more than anyone's, to learn from him, so she bobbed her head. "I'm listening."

"You tried to pump him up on the way in rather than stopping to find out where Surge's problem was. You were focused on showing off. You were more concerned about proving you could do it. We know he can."

"No. I was trying to show off A Breed Apart."

"No. You weren't." He took a step toward her. "I know because we've had this same talk since you were sixteen. Your arrogance killed your attention to Surge. He was near overwhelm. Then when I used my phone to set off the tone—"

She gasped. "You?"

"—and Surge reacted. You missed it because your focus was on yourself, not on what he was communicating to you." He angled in closer. "It's your job to read the dog to protect the dog."

Her eyes started to sting. "So, I'm fired?"

His gaze hardened. "Do you want to be?"

"No!" She balked. "This is the most important thing I've ever done, working with these dogs. It's my dream—"

"Then quit being an idiot and pay attention to your dog." He scowled. "I believe in you, Delaney, but Surge demands your focus be on him, not yourself. If you can't do that, I'll find someone else—"

"No!" She had some growl in her voice this time. "I can."

"—for the mission."

It took a second for her brain to catch up. Then her jaw went slack. She eyed Crew and the scruffy guy. "Mission?"

Heath crossed his arms and shouldered in. "You trained Surge to scent the lipids the same way you did Tsunami, right?"

She blinked. Lipids . . . "Yeah, I wanted to give him a mental path other than nonresponsiveness. He took to it really well." Like Tsunami. She lifted the scent tin and eyed it. Was this—

"Good." Heath waved a hand. "I have something I need you to do, but we have some questions about your readiness."

She blinked at him. Surely he didn't mean . . .

"A mission. You'll go with a team and work him."

She looked back at the stranger. "Go where?"

"I'll explain inside, but it'll be out of country."

"You want to take Surge . . . on a mission?" Thoughts assailed her, but she connected the dots. "To search for these"—she widened her eyes at the meaning—"lipids."

"With SEALs."

Search for chemicals. With SEALs? "I don't understand. A legitimate *mission*?"

"Yes."

Cold washed through her. "I'm not cleared for operations—you've told me that many times." Why was her heart thundering? "I'm not a soldier or operator. I train dogs."

"Would I send you anywhere if I felt you weren't qualified?" His eyes narrowed.

"No, but . . ." She didn't want to let him down, yet . . . "I'm not really sure I even want to go." She eyed Crew and the other guy, who were edging closer. "You need guys like them, not me."

"Missions need operators, yes. But to work Surge, they're useless." Heath stood in silence, scrutinizing her. "You were the one with the instinct to bring him around. Surge does well with you, and we need Surge's nose. You need to be there if he shuts down again. Normally, I wouldn't send a dog who hasn't done the quals, but this is a special circumstance, and I trust you to handle this and him."

Okay, so Heath believed in her. She rubbed Surge's ear. "How long will it be for? Because I can't leave my dad for an extended period, as you know." When Surge pressed against her leg, she dug her hand into the thick fur of his neck, appreciating that he always sensed when some comfort was needed.

"Unknown." Heath then seemed to relax. "This is John we're talking about, so I know he'll be good. And we'll check on him."

"And Surge will have protection gear too?"

"Without a doubt."

Delaney nodded her head slowly. "Okay . . ."

"I need your promise you'll play by the book."

She'd often gotten that same look from Dad when she was

RONIE KENDIG & VONI HARRIS

growing up. "Yes." She would. She planted herself in the training yard grass and gave a nod of assurance.

"Thank you, Maverick. I know I'm asking a lot, but I wouldn't if I didn't think you could handle it. Too, I didn't want to mention this until you agreed, but there'll be a nice bonus." He inclined his head. "It'll put a big dent in your costs with John." He set his hands on his belt. "Briefing here tomorrow at nineteen hundred. You leave Friday zero-five-hundred."

"Can you tell me the country?" She squinted at him.

He hesitated, then nodded. "Keep it quiet, but Singapore."

Whoa. Not just another country that was close, like Mexico, but in Southeast Asia.

The scruff man edged in closer.

Heath pointed between them. "Garrett Walker, Delaney Thompson."

"Hi. Nice to meet you," she said. She tilted her head to her black fur-missile. "This is Surge."

"Wow," Walker said. "He's more beautiful than the picture Sam showed me."

Oh, that's right. She remembered now . . . "You were the chief for the team Sam was on."

He smiled. "I was."

"This boy may be a working dog, but you can pet him. He loves being petted."

Walker clicked his tongue, and Surge responded. KONG dangling, he popped up and came toward the SEAL, who smoothed a hand down the Mal's spine, then gave him some solid chest rubs.

Heath clapped her shoulder. "Maverick here will be at the briefing tomorrow, so y'all can get acquainted between now and shipping out."

Walker jerked, his gaze snagging hers. "Wait, *this* is Maverick?" He scowled. "She's a woman!"

"Yes . . ." She glanced between him and Heath. "That a problem?"

"Yeah, it's a problem—I mean, no—" He huffed, then turned to Heath. "No way, man. I thought Maverick was some operator you knew."

"That right?" Calm and controlled, Heath reached over and took Surge's lead.

Delaney frowned and tensed. But something in his gaze told her to trust him, so she released it.

He shifted to Walker and extended the end of the leash to him.

Walker took a step back. He'd spent time with Sam and Tsunami, so he likely was well aware of what these dogs were capable of, how one wrong move could mean a gnawed-off limb or worse. "I'm not—"

"Exactly. You're not." Heath's jaw muscle jounced. "But if you can get Surge to go through that tire side and not the window, I'll reconsider."

Walker's angry fists were like rocks he was about to throw at her. He snatched the lead away.

First mistake . . .

And stalked over the yard.

Second mistake.

"Emotion travels down lead," she murmured, seeing the way Surge closed his mouth and trotted alongside. "He's tense."

"Both of them," Crew muttered. "Think Surge will eat him alive?"

"Let's hope our boy takes a chunk out of the SEAL's pride." Heath folded his arms, then cupped his hands over his mouth. "Put him in a sit, then send him."

The guy walked him over to the last obstacle and faced it, his shoulders still bunched. "Sit."

But Surge glanced back at her, as if asking why he got stuck with the jerk.

"Hey. Sit." Walker's commands were louder.

Surge watched Delaney and finally lowered his backside to the grass.

"Now . . . do it! Go!"

Surge rushed forward, then diverted to Delaney.

The explosion of relief in her chest almost made it hard to breathe as Surge came to a heel at her side. She secured his lead and tried hard not to gloat at the SEAL. And failed miserably.

"Okay, okay, point made," Walker said as he came back to them. "But you have to admit, the odds were stacked against me here."

Seriously, who was this guy? "No wonder they call you Bear."

"She's going," Heath said in that quiet, authoritative voice of his. "You need Surge, and that means her too. Unless you're suddenly qualified to handle a contract working dog . . ."

Walker lifted his hands in the air, then dragged them over his head with a growl. He eyed her again, and his irritation seemed to wash out of his expression. "Sorry."

Not the best apology ever. But she'd give it to him. She held up the scent tin Surge had found. "I assume you hid this and it's the specialized lipid scent?"

"I did. It is." Walker took it and slid the tin into his pocket. "So . . . Maverick, huh?"

"Pretty sure I'm the only one who calls her that," Heath said.

Walker nodded, his jaw set tight. "Saw you work him on the course." Another, smaller nod. "Nice job."

He was likely the only person on the face of the planet who could say those two words and make them mean something entirely different.

Heath cleared his throat. "Mav, Walker will be the team lead on the mission. Whatever you need, talk to him. He'll take care of you and Surge." There was more than a little warning in Heath's tone as he rammed his gaze into the SEAL.

Another tiny nod from Walker.

Though she felt a thrum of exultation—this mission meant she could buy her father the leg prosthetic upgrade—Delaney felt another thrum, this one banging against all her old fears.

But for Dad she'd do it.

Maybe this was where Dad's slogan—*a little nice goes a long way*—fit in. "It's good to know there's a SEAL taking charge."

"Former SEAL." The way Heath said it seemed to be about putting the man in his place. "It's a paramilitary mission—so private contract with the government to work this."

"Like you're a *former* Green Beret, and she's not military, yet she's going, so I'm not sure what your point is, Ghost," Walker responded and slid a glower in her direction.

Was he blaming her for what Heath said? She tried to get along with him.

Do not get in his face. Walk away. Leave, before you say something stupid and get yanked. "You're high-handed, Walker."

Yeah, like that. She shouldn't have said that.

Walker's gaze stabbed her. "What do you mean *high-handed*, Ms. Thompson?"

She arched her eyebrow. "That your attitude earned you the nickname Bear."

His jaw dropped. "How on earth—"

In her peripheral vision, Delaney saw Heath smirk. She couldn't help but do the same.

First, she'd gotten in trouble for going behind Heath's back with Surge. Deserved.

Now, she was put with this bear-man for a mission—a real one. To Singapore. With a grizzly-sized SEAL. *Former* SEAL. What had she gotten herself into? Nerves quailing, she considered rescinding her agreement to do this. Let them figure it out on their own. But . . . the chance to get Dad that new prosthetic and prove to him—and Heath—that Surge still had what it took. That this four-legged hero wasn't ready for retirement.

That's what she'd gotten herself into, and she wasn't going to back out.

"See you tomorrow at nineteen hundred, Master Chief."

Garrett shook his head, watching Thompson high-five Crew. The two chatted as the beefy guy escorted her and Surge back to the kennels.

You are high-handed . . .

That your attitude earned you the nickname Bear.

That olive green jacket and her swingy caramel-brown ponytail matched her sass. When he'd first shown up with Crew to watch the demonstration, he'd noticed the woman and wondered where Maverick was. Should've put it together before Daniels blindsided him. Might've saved him from sounding sexist. He'd heard her snappy replies when Daniels was chewing her out, then saw her stab a finger at the guy—all moves that would've earned disciplinary action had she been in the military. Even he had been the target of her snark.

She was a massive recipe for trouble in his book, and he did not want to work with her. Period.

"You were comfortable around Surge," Daniels said as he started toward the gate and motioned him to follow.

Garrett hooked his thumbs in the back pockets of his jeans. "Spending time on ops with Sam and Tsunami taught me a lot. I loved tossing her the KONG while Samwise grilled for the team when we were back inside the wire."

Daniels's deep laugh radiated across the field, then he sobered. "How're you since Sam's death?"

How best to answer that? "Being strong."

"Staying strong in the faith?"

Of course. Yeah. Except . . . no. He looked down. "It was good to see you at Sam's funeral."

The bypass of answering didn't get past Daniels. "Sam was a good person and a skilled handler. I appreciated how he integrated Delaney's work to develop the necessary skillset as he prepped for a mission. She went several times." No doubt another warning to not discount her because she was a woman. "Clear?"

"We are." He'd muffed that one up. "Look—it just caught me off guard that she was Maverick. I'd expected a guy, someone with training, ya know? Not a . . . newb who doesn't even have basic training under her belt."

Definitely making a point about Delaney, wasn't he?

Daniels stopped and angled toward him, a fist against Garrett's shoulder. "When I contract out our dogs, I meet what's requested—bomb, patrol, scent." He dipped his chin and glared from beneath his ball cap. "But you don't get a say over the handler. That's my job. End of story." He gave a nod. "We clear?"

"Crystal."

"Good. You're not the first to make the mistake." Daniels started walking again and eyed him. "What have you been up to since you got out?"

"My former warrant officer contracted me some freelance jobs." He shrugged as they headed back to the main building. "I'm making rent."

"Barely?"

He pushed up one sleeve, then the other. "It's not the same kind of teamwork as SEALs, but it pays the bills."

Daniels nodded. "I hear that."

"I got to see Rocca Guaita in San Marino last month. I'd never seen it before that mission. What's been going on with you?"

"Besides Surge, Crew obtained a few dogs that are taking my time. Delaney's too. Going to be a dad soon."

Surprise made Walker jerk. "That's great."

"Yeah . . . if Darc doesn't kill me first. Nothing like a mama protecting her pup." He chuckled.

Garrett's thoughts ricocheted to his complete failure in getting Surge through that tunnel and tire. "How'd Thompson get him to do the tire side, not the window side?"

Daniels shrugged. "She's good at what she does. The

45

window is his running fave, so diverting him was a challenge. But he listens to her." His gaze bored into Garrett.

"You made your point—very well. I'm not sure I'll get my man card back after that."

"Maybe you shouldn't."

Garrett felt the lipid scent tin in his pocket and pulled it out. His gaze shifted to the legend in tac pants and a black shirt.

Son of a gun . . . "This was more than a lipid scent test."

Daniels held his gaze, resolute, silent.

"You were testing her—and me."

Daniels pulled his ballcap low over disapproving eyes. "Wasn't testing her at all. I know what she can do."

Huh. "Guess this means I passed?"

Daniels gave a cockeyed nod. "For now."

Garrett folded his arms across his chest. "I barely know you, Daniels." He shifted his gaze to Daniels, who'd nearly reached the gate. "Can I trust them out there in the field?"

The man stopped, stood silently, squinting at the smear of red across the southern sky.

Garrett waited.

"Surge had issues after Tsunami's death, yes. Dispositioned, yes." Daniels's hard gaze could cut steel. "I'm satisfied those issues are behind them." He sized up Garrett. "Chapel told me exactly what was needed for this mission. Surge is my dog. Delaney is his trainer. I know them. They're ready."

Logically, Garrett knew it should be fine. But he felt like this was Samwise's death in Tadjoura all over again. "But I don't need a show-off on this mission." He cringed. "Look what happened at the school."

Daniels considered him. "Don't recall mentioning that."

"I heard you chewing her out."

"Correcting her," Daniels said, not missing a beat.

"You're not going to convince me?" Garrett jutted his jaw, tossed the scent tin from hand to hand. He put it back in his pocket. "What happens out there on the mission?"

"As an operator, you know that can never be fully known."

That was the ABA owner's answer? Garrett shook his head. "I think this is a bad idea. What kind of training does Thompson have? Is she really qualified?"

"You're ticking me off, frogman." Daniels tightened his mouth. "I've already told you what you need to know."

"How am I going to protect her?"

Daniels laughed. "Same thing I told her. You're a SEAL. Zim's a SEAL. If the two of you can't handle it, Surge will."

"But her attitude concerns me."

Daniels stared hard. "Kind of like yours does me."

Man, he hadn't meant to insult the guy, or tick him off.

If it weren't for those blasted lipids, he'd already be out of here. But he needed Surge, or civilians could die.

The girl—guess she came with the dog. And Daniels had Chapel's rec. That told him A Breed Apart and their Legacy dogs were top-notch. "Okay."

Hands on his belt, Daniels eyed him up and down.

Erasing the distance between them, Garrett swallowed his pride. "I overstepped."

"You did."

He extended his hand. "Truce?"

"Depends on how you treat my people, both the two-legged and the four-legged kind."

"Understood."

"Do you? Because it seems you're trying to pull weight you don't have. I'm doing this because Chapel talked you up." His gaze raked over Garrett. "Never second-guessed the guy before."

"Harsh."

"Yeah, you were." Daniels adjusted his ballcap and angled in. "I get the concern. But it's unfounded. Either you trust ABA teams or you don't. No skin off my back. Just know, word gets around. Chapel vouched for you, I agreed. Now you've questioned my call about my dogs and trainers, neither of which you know anything about, Walker. This business has a long memory. And so do I."

"I hear you. Didn't mean any offense. Just want to be sure they both come home."

Daniels adjusted his ballcap again. "If they don't, that's on you. So make up your mind, frogman."

Left standing there in the parking lot, Garrett knew what he had to do at the briefing tomorrow. The dog was vital to mission success. The girl . . . Guess they needed to have a stiff chat about how things would go.

3

CYPRESS SUGAR CREEK, HILL COUNTRY, TEXAS

"This makes me feel like i'm twenty!" Delaney's dad called over to her from the driver's side of the Jeep Wrangler 4x4 as they approached Cypress Sugar Creek. It was the perfect spot to go four-wheeling, with its creek beds and rivers and the rare large cypress trees.

"No wonder you're obsessed with off-roading." She laughed. She was glad she'd agreed to this birthday Jeep trip for Dad. She had more to say than happy birthday, though. About the mission. But she'd think about that later when the moment was right. "It's been too long since we've been."

"Definitely." Dad stopped the 4x4 and switched to four-wheel low. From inside his helmet, his longish gray hair peeking out the back, he gave her a one-sided grin. "Ready?"

"Ready!"

They lurched hard as he drove slowly down into the creek. Feathery needles of the bald cypress trees brushed against the Jeep windows.

Delaney snagged the grab handle. Her grin turned into laughter, water spitting high on their windows. Dad flipped on the windshield wipers and steered around the huge rock in the middle of the creek.

The other bank he steered toward was even steeper.

"You got this, Dad!"

"If you could do this when you were seventeen, I certainly can too." He wrinkled his nose at her and pressed hard on the accelerator.

She wrinkled her nose back at him. "Age doesn't have anything to do with this. But be careful—you're driving like an old man!"

"Old, huh? I'll show you old." He sent them crawling up the other bank, taking the most challenging paths possible. At the top, their tires started to spin, and the Jeep slid backward . . . right into a mudhole.

They rocked back and forth between first gear and reverse as Dad tried to get the vehicle out of the mud.

Still stuck.

Dad looked down at the tennis shoe on the bottom of his prosthetic leg. "I've got boots in the back."

"I already have boots on, so I've got this." She twisted in her seat, reached in the back to get Dad's boots, and handed them to him. She hopped out into the mud and walked to the back of the Jeep, then pulled out the vehicle recovery boards.

Delaney slopped down in the mud and slid the recovery boards under the tires, stood and waved at her dad in the mirror, then stepped aside.

He accelerated forward, spraying mud all over her.

Clearing her face, she noticed the vehicle hadn't moved. "Jeep's not going anywhere," Delaney shouted.

He quit hitting the gas.

Scraping the last of the mud from her face, she grabbed the tree strap from the back, then trudged up to the driver's side window and knocked.

He lowered it. "You're a mess, girl!" Then he flashed an unrepentant grin. "Not sure I got enough mud on you."

"Ha. Traction boards clearly didn't help, so I'm going to use the winch." She slogged over to a nearby pine—the cypress trees had shallow roots, so that wouldn't work—and wrapped the strap around it. Back at the Jeep, she engaged the controller and plugged it in. Then she caught the winch anchor and struggled back over to the pine tree and hooked it up. At the Jeep, she grabbed the controller and started winching until it was taut.

Surge hopped out and had a good mud bath, making sure every inch of his sleek black fur was covered.

She groaned. "Oh, you goofball! You're going to need a bath." She'd have to do that before Heath saw the mess. Still couldn't believe he'd allowed her to let Surge have a romp pre-mission. That very word—*mission*—sent a jolt of nervous excitement through her. How was this her life?

Surge bounded out of the mud. On the bank, he shook his fur out, slinging mud everywhere.

Delaney waved at Dad. "It's ready," she shouted, holding the controller.

Dad waved back. "All right. Let's do it!"

She turned the winch back on. Very slowly.

He hit the accelerator, spewing mud again.

"Ease up on the gas, Dad!"

"Not sure any slower will get us out of here, but I'll try!"

The 4x4 started moving forward and slowly made it out of the mudhole. Which was now red with power steering fluid.

Dad hit the brake as she walked up to his window again. "What's up?" he asked.

"Power fluid in the mud. Enough it looks like blood."

"Well, that's that." Dad steered the Jeep up to the dryish part of the trail and pulled over. He got out and sat down on a large cypress stump. Took off his prosthetic leg.

"You're always adjusting that leg of yours . . ." This was her opening . . . but she just wasn't ready for that convo yet.

"I know, right?"

Delaney leaned into the Jeep for Surge's collapsible silicon water bowl and her five-gallon water bottle. She poured some for him, and he slurped the water bowl dry, so she poured him some more.

Dad buckled the prosthetic in place and tapped it hard. "It works, though, and that's what matters."

"Yeah, it works, but you'd do a lot better with a new titanium prosthesis."

"You keep bringing that up." He smiled gently at her, then sighed. "You're right. The titanium leg would be a significant improvement, but they're expensive, and this leg is fine for me."

But guilt harangued her, even after all these years. "If I'd stood up to that robber in our family store before he shot out your leg . . ." Her eyes burned at the memory. "If I'd run out to call 911, get a police officer. But did I?" She huffed. "No, I just hid in the next aisle."

And she was going on a mission? What had possessed her? Probably more than a little anger at the SEAL who basically insinuated she couldn't hack it because she was a woman.

"You know what I would say to that, Delaney."

"'You were only eight back then.'" She quoted him.

"That's right. You've got to let this go. Losing my leg was not on you—it's on the guy who shot me."

Didn't matter. She could've stepped in. Should've. She hadn't been help back then, but she would be now. She dove back under the 4x4 and shone her phone flashlight around. "Found the leak! You got duct tape, don't you?"

"You know I do."

She got out from under the Jeep.

He handed it to her. "Anyway, this leg will last at least two more years before it qualifies for replacement with the insurance company. But not with the pricier model."

"Even if it'd be better, help reduce risk of infection and additional surgeries." Man, it just ate her lunch. Watching Dad struggle with his prosthetic leg gave her a sinking feeling in her stomach. Every time. He'd had this one in particular for nearly five years. Three years was the max, usually.

She ducked back under the 4x4 and taped the hole in the reservoir. Must've caught on a branch or something in the mud. Though she could fix this with duct tape, she couldn't do anything for what her ineptitude had cost Dad. And he deserved the best. Which brought her right back around to that convo she needed to broach with him.

No time like the present. Delaney climbed out from under the Jeep and wiped the mud from her face. "Guess what? Surge and I are being sent on a mission to Singapore, and I'm buying you a new leg with the money. It's just extra pay." She pulled out a KONG and tossed it toward the trees. Surge sailed after it.

"A mission?" Dad balked. "You're a trainer, not a military handler."

"That's what I told Heath, but they need Surge, and he does best with me. Heath said he wouldn't send us if he didn't think we were ready. And that bonus is going to fix you right up with a new leg."

He blinked. Then hesitated. "Are you sure?"

About helping him with the leg? "Absolutely." About going off halfway around the world with a grumpy Bear? Not so much.

"Well," he said, "I trust you, Delaney, so if you think you can do this, then I'm proud of you. And I know where Heath lives if anything happens." He grinned. "Seriously—congratulations to you and Surge." Dad looked up at her. "So, I guess this means you got him past his nonreaction."

"I did." Mostly. She didn't want to talk about the whole middle school faux pas. She and Heath had dealt with that, anyway.

Dad pulled out a handkerchief and pretended it was good enough to wipe her mud off himself.

"Let's eat!" Delaney jogged to the back of the 4x4 and pulled out the bag of sub sandwiches and chips.

And dog food.

"I just saw that sticker on your Jeep," she said as she handed Dad the food.

"Oh, the Prosthetic Rated sticker?" He reached into the Wrangler for the cooler of soda they'd brought.

"Yeah." She poured Surge's kibble out in the high grass near the table, and he gladly went on a hide-and-seek game for it. Delaney slid onto the picnic bench across from Dad.

"How'd you afford to get it prosthetic rated when the insurance wouldn't pay for a new prosthetic?"

"It wasn't much money. Off-Road Sports and Repair only charged me the price of a fancy cup of coffee." He tapped his fingers on the table, then stood and got out the ball launcher from the Jeep.

He walked away and played with Surge. She sat at the table, looking at her sandwich. Drank her Dr. Pepper.

A couple minutes later, Surge sought the perfect spot to do his business, and Dad walked back over and sat back down with a huge sigh. "Why are you doing this mission for me, when I'm content?"

"I love you."

"Me, you too. But that doesn't answer why."

She pinched her lips. "I want to go on this mission to do this for you."

He shook his head hard. "The money is yours." He reached across the table for her hand. "The mission is yours too. Given to you by Heath. If you want it."

Her head dropped. No. She wasn't a droopy kinda gal. She lifted her head and looked into Dad's eyes.

He tilted his head. "Okay." He sipped his water. "How was the scent demonstration?"

Dad read her well.

She sighed. Surge quit chewing the KONG and sat up to reach her face and cover it with dog kisses. She massaged her buddy's muscular shoulders. "I froze."

Dad snorted. "What do you mean?"

"Surge refused to seek. We had to leave."

"You got stage fright? Or Surge did?"

She nearly spat out her sip of water around a laugh. "No. I froze, unable to pull him out of his nonresponse." Caused by the sneaky noise from sneaky Heath's phone.

He shook his head. "You don't freeze, Delaney."

"I did at the middle school." Just like when that creep had robbed the store.

"No. You don't freeze," he repeated. "Heath wouldn't have given you Singapore if you did."

"He does call me Maverick."

Dad squeezed her hand and let go. He patted his leg, and Surge put his front paws up on him and got a pet. "And this guy is the other reason Heath gave you the mission."

She pulled a KONG out of her muddy jacket pocket. "Ready, Surge?"

He jumped up to stand in front of her, eyes flicking between her and the KONG.

"If you could speak English, you'd be saying, 'Please with a cherry on top.'" She smiled as he stood in front of her, edging away, anticipating her throwing it. She raised her eyebrows. "Ahem, sir."

He sat, leaning forward, anxious for action. She tossed it into the trees, and he charged after it, then returned and plopped under the table, teeth squeaking over the rubber toy.

Dad smiled at the Mal, then her. "And here's the final thing. Learning—from Heath—"

Her face heated at the memory of doing community service at the ranch for her stupid graffiti back in high school. But it led to this passion, this career of her life.

Dad squeezed her hands again. "When he taught you about dog training, he trained *you* too. You are unafraid—a maverick, yes, but you're also wise enough to listen to those in authority over you. An independent thinker. Just like MWDs." He nodded. "You can handle this mission."

How'd she get this man for a father? *Thank You, God.*

Surge sat up and poked his snout into her hand, and she scratched behind his ears.

Dad pointed at her. "Singapore is your mission. If you want it. And I'm guessing you do. I don't think it has anything to do with the money or Surge or Heath. Maybe it does have all of those. But really, deep down inside, you want to be a hero." He looked at her. "The hero that you wanted to be back at our store."

Her eyes filled with tears. "Maybe."

He chuckled. "Just for the record, you're already a hero in my book." He put his helmet on and nodded to the Jeep. "Let's get home."

"Hey, my turn to drive."

Dad waggled his eyebrows. "If you want to drive without power steering."

She flexed her arms to show off her biceps.

He laughed and tossed the keys to her.

"Let's go," she called, and they all three climbed into the Jeep. She'd rather drive this thing without power steering across the country and back than go on this mission with the arrogant frogman. But she wanted that titanium leg for Dad.

And she wanted Heath to see his belief in her was deserved.

A BREED APART RANCH, HILL COUNTRY, TEXAS

Garrett studied Singapore and Southeast Asia on the wall map, tapping his foot under the conference table as he half listened to Caldwell and Zim chat. He'd been sort of listening to them for at least ten minutes since they arrived. Singapore was a ball of worry in his stomach. Caldwell was a tension headache. But his problem was Thompson. This briefing was her first chance to prove to him that she had what it took, and she was already late.

He looked at the boring schoolroom clock on the boring white wall. 1905 hours. So much for things being done his way and her showing up at nineteen hundred.

Maverick.

Rogues didn't belong on teams. They got people killed. "Caldwell." He waited for the guy to turn to him. "You said this dog was the only one with training, right?"

The spook's gaze narrowed. "Yes." His definitive answer warned not to go there.

The door swung open, and Daniels entered with Thompson, who had a wet braid hanging down her back. Surge trotted into the room and ran a perimeter check, his intensity raw and on full display. Daniels stood at the table, and Surge sat next to him, leaning in for a pet.

Garrett stood.

But Daniels sat down and nodded his head at Zim. "Delaney, you've already met Petty Officer Zimmerman, I understand."

Zim stood. "Hey, Thompson. Been a while," he said with a wink.

"Oh." Her smile wavered, then recognition seemed to hit her. "Yes—nice to see you again."

Why did he take so much pleasure in her not immediately recognizing Zim?

Daniels indicated to the spook. "That is Bryan Caldwell with the Central Intelligence Agency. His intel is driving the mission."

Delaney's eyes widened, but she smiled and shook his hand. "Mr. Caldwell."

"Just Caldwell," Spook said.

"Nice to meet you."

Garrett stiffened. The smug man with the graying hair and ski-slope nose was nice to meet? She'd regret those words by the end of the mission.

"And you met Walker." Daniels waved in Garrett's general direction.

Thompson gave him a nod. "Hello, Master Chief."

Huh. He'd been ready for a confrontation. "Thompson."

Daniels looked around at each of the group one by one, his gaze finally resting on Thompson. "Stay frosty." He strode out of the room.

Surge jumped on the empty seat and everyone laughed.

"Zim is a SEAL," Garrett said, "but he also has a couple of degrees in science—chemistry and biochemical."

"Right," Thompson said with a smile at the comms specialist. "You created the scent tin for the lipid to help train Tsunami and Surge."

"Exactly." His grin was unabashed. "Glad you remembered."

"Down boy," Garrett said. "We'll use his chemistry skills on the op. Caldwell will—"

"I'm sorry—chemistry for what?" Thompson asked, as though he hadn't been in the middle of a sentence.

Garrett swung his arm toward Zim. "Go ahead." He didn't need to actually lead the briefing, right?

Zim grinned and wrote the chemical symbols on the whiteboard. "We are looking for sulfamic acid and potassium cyanide. The terrorists we're after are processing them into vials."

Delaney's face puckered. "The specialized lipids . . ."

"Yeah. Without that special formula, he'd just find sulfamic acid and potassium cyanide, not the Sachaai's cache in particular. And we really need to stop these guys from using that chemical and killing more people."

"Well, I'm glad he's so smart and ready to work," Thompson said.

She seemed like she was trying to convince somebody . . . Herself? Or him?

Garrett cleared his throat. "Caldwell's CIA skills mean he'll be our overwatch, monitoring from the safe house."

Caldwell locked his hands behind his head and nodded to his laptop on the table. "Technology and terrorist chatter. My two skills. And they're what is sending us to Singapore after Sachaai."

"Sa . . .?" Thompson asked.

Garrett fought the urge to stifle her constant interruptions, but she did need to catch up on the info, and the team did need to gel.

"They're a terrorist group who have been doing some serious damage around the world," Caldwell responded. "Intel chatter says they want to use these specialized chemicals to attack America and keep us from interfering with their jihadist goals in Pakistan."

Thompson nodded at Caldwell. "Thanks."

Garrett waited for more questions from her, but when the silence gaped, he went on. "Okay then. The plan is for me to go undercover and meet one of the small-fry Sachaai to procure a sample of the capsulized chemicals. From there, Surge can lead us to their stash in Singapore. We'll send that intel to the CIA and they'll interdict." He rapped the table. "We'll hit the ground running, so sleep up on the C-130. We leave for Singapore at zero-five-hundred tomorrow."

"Why are we in such a hurry?"

"*They* are in a hurry," he corrected. "Per intel, the chems fly out of Southeast Asia on Wednesday. We don't know exactly from where or to where, but we do know their attack is planned around the six-month anniversary of the death of Hakim's father in Djibouti."

"Who's Hakim?"

Man, she had a thousand questions, but it just made him aware how little she really knew. He prayed it wasn't a mistake bringing her. "Hakim Ansari is the leader of the Sachaai terrorists. Their poisoned food will hit US streets next week if we don't stop them. Hundreds of thousands of dead Americans are what they want."

Her voice croaked. "Hundreds of thousands . . ."

"So, am I coming with you on this undercover?" Zim asked.

This team was full of questions. "Negative. You'll cover Thompson and wait with her and the dog out of sight around the corner." He pulled out his phone, and on the ABA screen, he threw up a picture of the Singapore corner where he'd meet the seller in front of the legal building. Another spot marked with an X where Zim would wait with Surge and Thompson.

Zim leaned back in his chair. "But if Hakim, for whatever reason, shows up at the meet, you need some backup, Boss."

Right, and get ghosted by Heath? "You know how this works, Zim. This is the plan. We're not making changes if we don't have to." He nodded to the spook. "Caldwell, there's a security cam in the area, right? You'll have overwatch."

Caldwell's computer keys went crazy for a minute. "Yep."

"Okay, next." Garrett pulled up the picture of Hakim, the Pakistani man in a black T-shirt and black jeans, with black eyes under angled eyebrows, perfectly tidy black beard and long hair. Full lips nearly in a smile. "Hakim Ansari despises America for corrupting Pakistan. And he blames us for killing Fahmi—his father."

Thompson frowned. "We killed his father?"

Garrett locked eyes with hers. "Fahmi died when he killed Sam and Tsunami."

Her hand settled on Surge, who sat at her side. "Djibouti."

He nodded. "Hakim is hellbent on vengeance."

"We have a truck for the chem stash once Surge leads us to it?" Zim asked.

He looked over at Caldwell, who nodded.

"Already set."

"Other questions?"

No one said anything.

"Okay then. Get home, get some rest. The C-130 is a red-eye."

Zim snickered and Caldwell rolled his eyes as everyone gathered their things.

60

But Garrett stopped Thompson. "Just a minute, please." If he was going to be her leader, she couldn't be a maverick. Okay. Rogue. She couldn't be a rogue. Time for that stiff chat.

"Sure." She took a step toward the entry table and grabbed a bottle of water, popped it open, then sat back down.

"I need to know that you're okay for this mission."

She hesitated. "Oookaaaaay." One eyebrow rose.

He scrolled through his mind about what to say. How to say it. But there was only one answer. "Maverick."

"Heath's nickname for me?"

"I mean you're a maverick," he growled. "Surge's nose for these lipids or not . . . I need someone who can work as part of a team."

She shrugged. "I need someone who knows how to lead a team. Sam told me about you, your anger."

He locked his hands behind his head—but that was a smug Caldwell posture. He lowered his hands to the table. "That was last year when he ignored the order to avoid exercise or activity to let his ankle heal."

She nodded. "You are an angry bear. Sam was just trying to be diligent about his SEAL service."

He bit his tongue for a long moment. "I called it idiocy. He needed me to get in his face when I caught him in the gym. He ended up with his ankle in that orthopedic boot. For six weeks. Six weeks we needed him. He learned about listening to the doc. And me."

Her jaw clenched, and she started to say something but instead gave a heavy sigh. "Six weeks? He should've listened to the doc." Her lips twisted. "And you."

He jutted his chin in agreement.

"And I need to listen to you." Her croaky voice again. "I didn't think through what terrorists—Sachaai—would do with this chemical if we don't find it." She exhaled heavily. "You're acerbic and rude, but you want to stop them. That's what I want, so . . . yeah, I'll comply."

"So you and I have the same goal in Singapore."

"Save Americans."

"Yes." He extended his hand. "Since we have the same goal, let's start fresh."

"But you hate me for being a woman."

"I don't hate you for being a woman. I just don't work with women."

She stared at him for a long second.

He studied his feet, then looked back up. "Let me try that again. I've never worked with female special operators—there aren't any in the SEALs. Especially ones without military training or experience. We do need Surge. I'm . . . open to working with you."

She chuckled. "Sounds like that hurt." She smiled. "Okay then, I'll work with you."

He extended his hand again. Maybe now was time for a fresh start. "Hello. I'm Garrett."

"Wow. First name, even." She smiled. "And I'm Delaney. Committed to this mission."

They shook hands.

Her head tilted. "Garrett, I do need you to understand that while Heath sent me, I am not ready to carry a gun and fight. But I am totally ready to deploy Surge."

"Without you qualifying, I wouldn't put one in your hand." He reached for his water bottle, took a long guzzle. "I'll give you some SEAL self-defense training before we go."

"Right now?"

No reason why not. "We'll start simple. Krav Maga—Israeli street fighting—will help and is practical."

"Sounds intimidating." She popped her hands together and stood. "Let's do it."

He moved the tables to the side.

She gave Surge a chew treat under the corner table, and he was obviously one extraordinarily happy dog.

"Is that a jerky stick?" Garrett asked.

"Sort of. It's a bully stick. They're great. He can chew on them at least a half hour." She stood opposite him, squared her shoulders. "So, how do we do this?"

"What do you do when I do this?" Garrett grabbed her shoulder.

She wrenched away and fell on her rear. She pushed herself to a stand. "What happened there?"

He chuckled. "Remember, I'm the bad guy. When I grab your shoulder, put that hand down on the crook of my elbow. Force my arm close to you. No hesitation."

She nodded.

He caught her shoulder. She put her hand in his elbow, drew him close. Her sweet-smelling shampoo swept over him. He jumped back, straightened his shirt. "You've got it. But no gentleness. Be assertive."

Garrett took her shoulder again. Her hand hit his elbow like a karate chop.

A huge smile lit her face. "Assertive, right?"

"Perfect." They high-fived.

She tossed the braid behind her back. "Okay, what's the next move?"

"We haven't finished this move." He took her hand, rubbed his index finger in the L of her thumb.

Her deep-brown eyes widened.

He let go. "That part of your hand? It's your weapon."

She looked at her hand like she'd never seen it before. "A weapon."

He put the L of her hand at his throat. "Ninety-degree angle. Clothesline the jerk like this." He eased her hand against his throat and stepped backward, dropped her hand.

She bounced on her toes. "My hand in your elbow pulls you close enough I can reach your throat with my other hand."

"That's it. Let's try it slow motion."

He reached for her shoulder but stepped back. "When a bad guy approaches, hold your hands up like you're innocent."

"I see what you mean. The innocent-hands move puts your hand in the right position if he grabs you."

"And do not lose his eyes. Maintain eye contact."

"Got it."

He caught her shoulder, and Delaney put up her hands, pushing down into the crook of his elbow. He stepped closer, and she put the L of her hand on his throat, breaking his hold.

"Good. Again." After the fifth try, he shot her a high five. "Way to go. Now, let's try it at street speed."

Her jaw dropped. "I don't want to hurt you."

Hurting him was her concern? "You won't."

"Are you sure?"

He snatched at her shoulder, and she karate-chopped his arm, pressed her hand against his throat. Surge jumped out from under the table with a warning growl.

Garrett looked at the MWD.

Delaney's other hand pushed against his chest and sent him backward. He fell on the floor against the wall. Surge jumped on him, his snout against Garrett's nose as he unleashed a preternatural growl.

Garrett curled his head down as much as he could with the MWD's weight on his shoulders.

"Surge, out!" She caught his collar and pulled him off. "Sorry. Let me secure him." She tethered the dog to one of the table legs. "Should've done that before we started."

"Just glad he didn't go for the jugular." Garrett chuckled, sat back against the wall. Apparently, touching her was not the thing to do with Surge anywhere nearby.

Delaney joined him, reached for the waters and handed him his. "I told you I didn't want to hurt you."

"When I grabbed your shoulders, you didn't worry, you just acted, right?"

She gave a slow nod. "Good thing for me to learn."

"Okay, just a prelim lesson on the choke-hold defense." And for the next twenty minutes, he showed her how to defend herself if she got in a choke hold from behind. He wiped sweat from his brow and nodded at her. "We have to work on some muscle memory, but that's what training is all about."

"With Surge in a kennel."

He grinned. "Please and thank you."

"And thanks in advance for the self-defense. I obviously need it."

"Heath threatened my life if I let anything happen to you or Surge. Trying to prevent that." He took a sip of water. Maybe he'd misjudged this woman.

She laughed. "Don't want you to get Ghosted."

The pun wasn't lost on him, considering Heath Daniels's callsign, Ghost. "But if something does happen to you, will I be able to get that Mal home safely?"

She frowned. "Thanks to Sam, you know how to be around an MWD."

"Mals are intense, though." He took a last drink of water.

A long, slow nod. "I'm not a SEAL, and you're not a dog trainer." She twisted her lips into a smile. "You train me in self-defense, and I train you to work with Surge."

That surprised him. "Agreed." He took her empty bottle and tossed both in the trash. When he started to move the tables back, Delaney helped him.

It just took a minute, then they headed toward the door.

He snatched her shoulder and in just a second found the L of her hand at his neck. With a smirk, he released her. "Okay. You're on our team."

She had a wide smile.

"But don't screw up."

4

CORE, SINGAPORE

GARRETT WALKED THROUGH THE FOGGY DOWNTOWN SINGAPORE
street market toward the circular skyscraper law building that
stood among tall gray buildings for his undercover meetup.
Made him think of a World War II spy—which was Delaney's
fault. She'd offered him a headset while she streamed
Casablanca on the C-130 flight over. He still hated the movie, but
the haze swarming around him this evening, the buzzing of
relentless traffic, reminded him of that "beginning of a beautiful
friendship" scene.

Get your head in the game. He stretched his neck and kept
moving. Caldwell had arranged for the Sachaai guy to meet him
nearby to sell Garrett a sample of the chem vials. So here he was,
walking past vendors selling wares in stands and shops. He eyed
a display of watches—for five Singapore dollars? But how long
would a cheap watch last? He took a second to inspect one of the
watches—or at least look like he was. The tension for the mission
had ratcheted with Tyson Chapel's warning from an hour ago
that, apparently, after working a deal with an African chem
supplier, Hakim was returning to Core. And the guy liked

66

hands-on control of Sachaai's movements within planned attacks. So it wouldn't be out of the question for Garrett to find himself facing him.

Garrett roughed his hair, slid into his undercover devil-may-care persona. Chems were the sole focus of this mission. Not him constantly fighting his instinct to eliminate the source of so many deaths and the anticipated Wednesday attack. But that was revenge. The attack was on Americans—innocent bystanders in this game.

So Garrett refocused. "Everybody there?" he subvocalized.

"Overwatch here. Where else would I be?" Caldwell said from the safe house computer room. "I've accessed street cams and local business security cams."

Sarcastic as usual. Caldwell had been frustrated his sources hadn't alerted him to Hakim's incoming return, that Damocles had preempted him.

"Eagle Three in position with Cerberus One and Two," Zim confirmed, indicating he was at the corner rendezvous site with Thompson and the mighty mutt.

"Approaching stand." He reached it and walked the perimeter of the busy eating area with shop vendors, trucks, stands, and a few tables and chairs. Garrett studied the signs on the side of the truck, made a show of eyeing the various pots sitting to the side, knowing the contact would likely be watching for him.

"Heads-up, Bear," Caldwell comm'd. "Andre incoming on your three."

"Copy." Garrett slid his gaze to his right and saw a twenty-something guy saunter from the law office's side door. Despite the darkness, his black hair and cheek mole were easily identifiable beneath the streetlights. He wore standard jeans and a hoodie. Just like the image Caldwell had found.

"I see him," Garrett said as he angled back around. No sign of Hakim, thank God.

Lord, let this work. No going sideways. Please.

Andre ambled up, passed the truck, his gaze sliding along the truck and hitting Garrett, then he stepped in line next to him.

Garrett scanned the pots and the menus plastered to the interior walls of the truck, the lone lighted sign casting a strange orange glow over him. "Would you pick chicken clay pot rice or Chinese sausage with rice?"

"Chicken," the guy responded, giving the prearranged answer.

Garrett eyed the twenty-something. "I'll take the sausage, I think."

Andre shrugged as they stepped to the counter.

"For your help, I'll pay." Garrett stood at the counter with the contact and pulled out five Singapore dollars. "One chicken, one sausage," he told the vendor.

At his left, Andre placed his hand on the counter, then removed it.

There lay a small baggie with the lipids—ten blue and ten yellow—which Garrett palmed. Tucked in his pocket.

Amid the sizzle of chicken and sausage being cooked, Andre spoke quietly. "Rashid will have your order by tomorrow."

Garrett kept his face blank. Give Surge a sniff of these, and he'd meet Rashid much sooner. Unlikely he'd get anything out of this punk, but he'd try. "Where did he get these?"

Andre shrugged. "He just told me to bring the sample."

The vendor piled two boxes of food on the counter and stared at them, waiting for them to leave so he could get to his next customers.

Garrett took his and banked away from the stand. "Package secured," he comm'd. Didn't matter what Andre didn't know. Surge's nose would know. He ducked into a side alley and pivoted back, eyeballing the punk as he returned to the law building. "Overwatch, we know anything about that building?"

"It's legit," Caldwell said. "No connection to Hakim or the chems that we can find."

"Watch the building," he stated and headed to rendezvous with Thompson and Surge.

"Already on it," the spook said, a little irritation in his words. "Contact just exited the front of the building."

"Cerberus One and Two, en route to your position."

"Copy that," Zim reported. "We have you in sight."

Streetlights glowed brighter here, where the street vendors and businesses didn't dampen their power. A dull ache in his shoulder reminded Garrett of sparring with Thompson. He'd never tell her, but that chop she'd delivered to his shoulder had left a little bruise. She was stronger than he'd expected. And she had worked with SEALs to help specialize their combat assault dogs. She might have a lot of attitude, but the girl clearly knew her stuff.

He slipped into the small alley. Steady panting drew him to the right, where he found the trio, blending well into the shadows.

"You have them?" Zim asked.

Garrett showed them the baggie and eyed Thompson. "Ready?"

"Yes." Nerves quavered in her answer, but her shoulders were squared, and she seemed to draw up her courage as she looked at Surge, who was on all fours. "We both are."

Garrett mentally patted the weapon holstered at his back and the one in his ankle holster. He eyed the bulge in the pocket of Delaney's green denim jacket. "Ninety degrees and you're wearing a jacket—it could stand out. But let me guess. KONG?"

"Of course."

Garrett passed the sample packet to her. "The vials." He swung around and aimed toward the street again. "He went back into the law building, so that's probably the best place to start. I'll let you take the lead and trail you, so we aren't obvious."

"As planned." She flashed him a nervous smile and another nod.

Surge's golden eyes went from eager to intense, his tail whipping the air. He sniffed the vials a couple seconds and lay down, ears forward, staring at them.

The tubes definitely had Sachaai lipids.

"Okay, handsome," she said and strode out of the alley. They made their way back to the street market and the truck vendor. Delaney took her time, like a pro, eyeing the shops, letting Surge do his thing.

The MWD stuck his nose in the air, turned a half circle, and paused. He loped the few feet to Garrett and lay down, his black ears pointed at him.

Delaney watched him for a moment, then her lips screwed up. "Garrett, you have any other chem tubes?"

"Nope. You have them."

"Right." She frowned, then drew Surge around to face the opposite direction. She guided him to the stoop the contact had entered through, then repeated the command. "Seek." They made a slow, steady circle around the alley.

Garrett paced the vendors, never more than twenty feet from the two. He skirted a small jewelry vendor when the Mal trotted back to him, sniffed him, then went into a down.

Ears forward, Surge stared at him.

Delaney huffed, apparently feeling the same frustration as Garrett, but she kept her voice light and firm. She drew him back to the alley entrance. "C'mon, Surge. Seek." More than once, she stepped toward the dog, then back.

At the end of the long leash, he went a little way down the street, and Garrett had hope this might actually work. But then the Malinois returned to him, throwing his front paws onto his shoulders, knocking him backward a step.

"Out!" Delaney ordered, and he sat looking at Garrett, ears pointed at him.

Frustration tightened Garrett's shoulders and jaw. "What's going on? Why's he coming back to me? We're going to give ourselves away."

"I don't know." Delaney pursed her lips, then considered him. "You held the baggie. I'm guessing you got more than a residue in your pocket."

Caldwell chimed in on the comms. "Hey, team. Got a problem. Need to clear out. In reviewing footage of the drop, I have positive ID on Rashid. Recommend you clear out in case he ID'd you and returns with backup."

Frustration morphing to irritation, Garrett clenched his jaw. "Rogue, try seeking from the building Andre went into, then we're out of here."

"Stay here," she said, her expression knotted. "Maybe if he doesn't keep thinking it's you, he'll catch the real trail."

"I'll hang back," Garrett said, understanding her concern, "but leaving you unprotected isn't happening."

"Fine, but Zim is with you."

She backtracked to the building. Circled and patrolled. She stroked Surge's head. "Nothing. No hits," Thompson said.

He strode to Delaney, ticked at himself for trusting a newb with no military experience on such an important op. This was on him. He should've known better. "Are you doing something wrong?"

Her jaw dropped. "Of course not!"

"Well, now we have to go through with the buy from Rashid. He's a—" Garrett paced into the alley's entrance, trying to find a word that wouldn't have his grandmother rolling over in her grave. "Rashid is extremely dangerous and ruthless. I told you we needed Surge to find the stash. Now the risk to life is elevated." He shook his head. "You told me you could do this—that he could."

She opened her mouth, then closed it.

He looked down at Surge. Tsunami wouldn't have missed the scent. Now that stakes were up, they had one last chance to fix this. But . . . facing Rashid—man, it scared him. More than it should. A trained SEAL, and he was afraid. For himself. His team. For Thompson. Even for the dog that had failed them.

He scrubbed his hands through his hair. Something nagged at him—Surge came from A Breed Apart. Ghost had vouched for him, so . . . what was wrong? "Back to the safe house. Let's go."

Delaney stepped into his path, locked her eyes on his. "Hey, there are off days for every MWD."

"I know, I know." Garrett looked at his feet, lifted his gaze back to hers. "But if things go south at the buy . . ." He waved his hand in the air.

Surge sat up, wagging his tail as though a ball game were about to start.

Delaney rubbed Surge's velvety black ears. "Garrett, this is going to work. We just need to figure out what's tripping him up."

He nodded. "Then work on it at the safe house. And once there, don't go out alone. There's a garden on the lower level for him to relieve himself."

They silently got in the SUV and headed back to the safe house, and Garrett vanished. Needing to work off her own frustration and nerves, Delaney headed into the kitchen and made a towering plateful of turkey sandwiches for the team while she thought over and over every moment of the meetup and Surge's fails. No idea what'd happened with Surge tonight. Too bad she hadn't had a camera on Surge to review and figure out what'd gone wrong.

She carried the sandwiches and a platter of veggies into the living room, set them on the coffee table next to a party-sized bag of chips.

Caldwell walked in from the Command room and plopped down on the couch. "Walker is used to bearing the burden of the team and mission success, so naturally he's not happy. Luckily we had the buy already set up for tomorrow. At least he didn't punch you. He did punch me when things went wrong on our Djibouti mission."

With a half laugh, half sigh, she sat in the office chair. "Garrett punched you? What happened?"

He shrugged. "My intel sucked."

"You had bad intel?"

His eyebrows gathered in a pained expression for a split second, but he focused on a random piece of soft purple plastic he was squeezing between his fingers.

Delaney started to repeat her question, but Zim walked in.

"Starving!" he announced.

She pointed at the plate on the coffee table. "I made turkey sandwiches."

"Thanks." He grabbed one and settled in the recliner. Surge jumped up to sit on his lap. The Malinois licked his chops. Zim took a huge bite, Surge leaning closer and closer with hope.

Delaney laughed. "Surge, let him eat. I've got food for you. Come here, boy."

Surge jumped off and sat in front of her, still licking his chops. She scratched behind Surge's ears. "Caldwell, is there a way to get footage from the search?"

"Sure. The law building even had security cams in the alley." He stuffed chips into his mouth. "Get it to you in a minute."

She nodded her thanks, piling her sandwich and some veggies on a plate. Surge followed her back to her room, eyeing the sandwich the whole way. She set the bowl on the side table, then headed to the food container stowed in the corner and filled the bowl. Goofy dog dug in as though she hadn't fed him that morning like usual.

"Hey," Caldwell said, rapping on the open door. "I sent you the files from the search. Should be in your inbox."

"Perfect. Thanks." She took a bite of her sandwich and grabbed her laptop. They'd secured it and set it up to work here with the secure satellite. Now . . . time to figure out what happened. She opened her email, and there was the video from

Caldwell. She owed the man some pizza when they got back to the States.

Delaney plugged in her earphones and hit play. She watched the whole search until Garrett walked away from the team. She plumped up the pillows to lean against, then started the video back at the beginning, crunching on some carrot sticks as she watched.

First one, Surge was standing there, watching her for a cue, then he suddenly turned and stared at Garrett on the other entry to the alley. But when she called his name, he jumped up and followed her seek cue.

Wait . . . that . . . wasn't a hit on Garrett.

Oh no . . .

She forwarded the video to the second hit. Surge was focused on Garrett, maybe because of the remnant from the vials he'd handled. Then she saw it—the moment she turned and looked at Garrett, Surge hit on him, ears pricked forward, staring at him. *Following my cue . . .*

It was the same at the third hit.

Why had she turned her head, looked at Garrett? Oh yeah, she'd thought she'd heard him say something. When she looked back, Surge went to the end of the long leash, practically knocked him to the ground.

Garrett had been right—she *had* done something wrong.

Inadvertent cues.

She had inadvertently given Surge cues on where to find the source. False leading. It was her fault. All because she'd been so worried about what Garrett thought, feeling his gaze tracking her every move, assessing her, judging her . . . finding her wanting.

Augh! For crying out loud, she was a professional. Not like she had some high school crush on a former SEAL. Even more than that, she cursed herself for pressing and urging Surge all through the search instead of trusting him to do what he did best.

Finished gobbling his dog food, Surge mouthed his KONG tug on the floor and dropped it at her feet, staring at the toy expectantly.

She picked it up and whispered, "Surge, we aren't targeting Garrett. Only tube vials that smell of Sachaai lipids. Okay?"

He barked.

Delaney laughed, and the game of tug began.

"Zim, is that thing some sort of outer space alien detector?" Caldwell's voice carried easily through the thin walls.

"No, Mr. Intelligence." Zim laughed. "It's a handheld FTIR, a Fourier-Transform Infrared spectrometer. I need to test the sample tubes Walker procured. Surge's nose is awesome, but courts want science."

Delaney tossed the rope on the bed and dove for the door. She jogged out to the cramped living room, Surge behind her. "Zim, you have an FTIR spectrometer?"

He lifted the device that looked like a camera with a trigger and a screen all attached to a plastic dumbbell. Surge went up on his hind legs and sniffed at it. Laughing, Zim hefted the device higher. "No nose prints, thank you very much."

Surge sat, looking at it.

Zim grinned at her. "Rogue, you've heard of these?"

Oh boy, the call sign was catching on, apparently. "Science has always been my hobby-passion since Mrs. Hayes in seventh grade." She squinted at the device. "I didn't know there were handheld FTIRs. This is so cool."

He waggled his brows. "You can help me test the chem vials, if you want."

"Of course I do!"

Bored now, Surge hopped up on the couch and lay down.

Zim pulled the baggie of tubes out of the equipment bag, and they walked over to the kitchen table.

"You point it at the vials and pull that trigger, right?"

"The lens has to touch them." He shrugged. "Otherwise, yep, basically the same as taking a picture."

She grinned and stretched her fingers in and out.

He opened its case and took out a different type of lens. "Damocles loaned this to me, and I am definitely nerding out." He took off the lens casing and switched lenses, then popped the casing back on. "Here you go."

She touched the spectrometer to them, pulled the trigger, and handed it back to Zim. Twenty seconds later, it beeped. He looked at the screen and tilted it so Delaney could see. "And there's our proof."

The screen read: LIPID 2304A.

"Scientific evidence to back up what Surge's nose detected— this is definitely Sachaai's lipid," Zim confirmed.

They whooped and slapped high fives.

Garrett walked in. He stood inside the door, staring at them, arms crossed.

She and Zim looked at each other like they'd been caught. Caught doing what, Delaney had no idea.

"FTIR spectrometer," Zim explained. "It identified Sachaai's lipids in your sample tubes. Success today."

"No success today." Garrett's voice was soft. "Surge failed, and despite having the buy tomorrow, I have no confidence he won't fail again tomorrow."

Her stomach fell, having an inkling where this was going.

"I think it best—"

"Garrett." She was not going home. "Could I talk to you, please?"

He lowered his head for a moment. "Fine."

"Wait here a second." She jogged to her bedroom and brought out her laptop, opened it up on the kitchen table. "I was trying to figure out what went wrong with Surge out there."

With a grunt, Garrett drew closer.

Stepping up behind them, Caldwell and Zim crowded the small kitchen. She'd known this would happen. But what was she going to do, hide this from the rest of the team to avoid being embarrassed?

Surge joined the crew, looked at the screen like he knew what he was looking at.

"I had Caldwell send me the video of the search this morning." She hit play.

They all stood there silently as the video ran.

It finished, and Garrett said, "I know what happened—I was there."

"This time watch what I do." She rewound and showed them the hits again, skipping the first one.

"Huh," Caldwell said. "You look at Garrett, and Surge hits on him."

"Yes," she said quietly. "An inadvertent cue—leading, as it were. Surge thought I was cuing him to hit on Walker. My fault. I own that."

Garrett's lips twisted in thought. "What about that first hit?"

"It's not a hit." She rewound to it and hit pause when Surge turned to stare at him. "He's on the other side of the alley, by me." She zoomed in. "He's caught sight of another dog. No behavior break, though. When I said his name, he immediately focused on me and went on the seek. Like I said, not a hit."

Zim started laughing. "A dog in the middle of an MWD detection."

Garrett's jaw jerked to the side. "Inadvertent cues were your fault, Delaney?"

"Yes. I own that."

He didn't respond. Just stared at the video, jaw muscle twitching. Hard.

Man . . . tough audience. Delaney gulped, thinking of going back to Heath as a failure and with no new titanium prosthetic leg for Dad. She was a disappointment to God. Again.

Zim shrugged. "Boss, we need Surge. Especially now. *Inadvertent* means inadvertent—unintentional."

"What it means is that she cost us time and possibly the chance to get this sorted and stop the Sachaai."

"C'mon," Zim said, his voice quieter. "She's here. Our only

chance to get Surge in the field. If Ghost sent her . . . maybe let her do her job. So she messed up. It happens. We all make mistakes. Let her try again."

Caldwell nodded. "Delaney keeps looking at you because she's worried that you're going to cut her. You lasered her the whole time during that search. You interfered, so if you want to blame someone—"

"I want the op to succeed," Garrett said.

"Then let her focus on what she's doing."

Obviously irritated, Garrett signaled Caldwell and Zim aside.

As usual, God wasn't letting her have a chance. Her stomach clenched.

Garrett's right cheek twitched, and he jerked his thumb at the screen. "These inadvertent cues are solvable, right?"

She straightened. "Absolutely. Now that I know what happened, I fix it."

Silence stretched between them for a long second. Then he exhaled heavily. "I'm not sending you home." He met her gaze. "You found your mistake. Owned it. And you paid attention to Surge this time."

This time? Oh, wow—he'd heard that dressing down from Heath? She bit her lip.

"Yeah. I heard Daniels call you out about that."

But he wasn't firing her? "You still sound unsure . . ."

"A lot is riding on you doing your job correctly. A lot of lives." He stood silently for a second. "Meet me downstairs in twenty." He pivoted and walked down the hall into his room.

He had something up his sleeve.

5

Never let it be said he hadn't given her a fair shake. But this was it—her last chance to prove to him she could handle the dog and get the job done. They didn't have time for games. He stepped back, eyeing the long room that served as the weight room. It had a walled-in garden with trellis, which gave the combat assault dog a place to take care of business. As close to a yard as one got in a city dominated by high-rises.

Arms folded, Garrett stood surveying the space.

"What happens if he doesn't find them?" Zim asked, returning to his side.

Garrett gave a cockeyed nod. "Ship her back and focus on what we have." He dragged a hand over his mouth. "Can't afford another fail like we had earlier."

"She said it wasn't a fail but inadver—"

"Did we track down the production site?"

Zim sighed. "No."

"Fail." He jutted his jaw. "Bring her in."

As Zim slipped out to find Thompson and Surge, Garrett thought about sending her back. Hanged if he knew why, but it

79

went crossways in his gut. Telling Daniels the dog and handler had failed wasn't a conversation he wanted to have. Somehow, Garrett would make the mission happen, find those lipids before they made it to American soil, but Thompson . . . her determination to get it done, and do it right, said something. Impressed him. He'd seen Surge find the tin in the training yard, even when the girl hadn't known about it. Remembered Daniels's words about Thompson having a way with the dog nobody else did

She'd failed to read the dog . . . *because she was reading me.*

What did that mean? Making sure the guys did the job was part of his responsibility as master chief. He took that responsibility seriously, to make sure things went well, the guys came home, and the mission accomplished its objective. And this one threatened home turf and lives. So yeah . . . maybe he had been breathing down her neck a lot.

When he heard the door open, he shifted back, retrieved his stainless steel tumbler of black coffee and waited. The dog team entered, Thompson's gaze flying to his. Surge had his black KONG snagged between his teeth. He spotted Garrett—and the KONG popped out. Surge lunged after it, and Thompson released him to retrieve it.

Not exactly a strong first impression.

Neck breathing, remember?

Thompson slid him a nervous glance.

Surge returned with his KONG and dropped it at Garrett's boots.

Thompson scoffed. "Traitor, again, doggo."

Garrett picked it up and tossed the KONG, wondering if the dog would catch the scent on his own.

Lightning fast, Surge secured the toy and returned, this time depositing it in front of Thompson.

"At least you haven't forgotten me just because Walker's here." She smoothed her caramel-brown hair behind her ear. "So, what's up?"

He adjusted his ballcap and narrowed his eyes at her. "You know no inadvertent cues, right?"

Her chagrin worked against the smile that flashed. "Like I said, I know the mistake and won't repeat it."

"Time to prove it." Garrett chucked Surge's snout. "We've hidden the vials in this weight training room. I want him to find them."

She swallowed and gave a hesitant nod.

He edged forward. "Look. We both know he can do it—I saw you two at the ranch. He found the chem scent tin. But what I need proof of is that in a strange environment, under stress and pressure, time constraints, amped energy, the two of you can do what needs to be done. We can't afford another fail—and that's what it was because we did not find where they're operating. So." Maybe a bit too heavy, but she needed to understand the risks. "American lives depend on you two gelling and getting this done. You said he's ready . . ."

She leaned in, pushed up her sleeves. "No doubt whatsoever."

Panting steadily, Surge looked up at her expectantly.

"Then prove it." He handed her the baggie with the remaining vials.

"Surge, ready to work?" When he jumped up, she held the baggie open for him. "Check."

He thrust his snout into the baggie, hauling in heavy scents. His whole body shivered with excitement.

"Surge, seek!"

He immediately diverted toward the nearest weight bench.

Garrett deliberately shifted his position, testing her. Seeing if he could pull her attention off the dog.

But her eyes did not leave Surge. The Malinois followed her hand when she signaled him to check the shelf piled with towels and weight belts. He stopped, going stock still halfway there, his nose sucking in air, then continued.

Tugging out his phone, Garrett eyed the two working the

training room that ran the entire length of the building. He hit the volume to full and played a hard rock song. Bounced his gaze to the duo as the screaming guitars rent the silence of the test. Surge stuck his snout along a rack of weights but never faltered. Thompson hesitated, her head angling toward him, but she never took her focus off working the room with Surge.

Surge finally moved on past the weight rack and drove toward the squat stations near the cable exercise area. At the anchor for the pull station, he circled in, his draughts of air deep and focused. Then he sat, ears pointed forward, staring at the base.

Delaney crouched and retrieved the dirty sock. Her brow rippled as she felt the toe and then grinned. "Good boy, Surge." Holding the sock, she pulled out the KONG and tossed it.

Okay, they'd done it. "Good job." With all his attempts at distraction, Garrett hadn't been able to distract them. Or her. Why did that bug him? Surge had found the tin with the chems. But in a controlled environment was one thing. Out there, risks were high . . .

Delaney turned to him and proffered the sock. "Yours?"

He smirked. "Thankfully, no." He took the baggie and sock back. "So . . . you satisfied?"

"Are *you*?" She squinted at him as he put the vials from the sock into the baggie.

Garrett shook his head. "I'm . . . not convinced."

Delaney sucked in a breath. "We met the exercise, Garrett."

"In a controlled environment. But out there . . . it didn't work." He rubbed the back of his neck. "We're too close to the deadline to find another dog team, or I would. I think it's best we develop a plan without a dog."

She froze in place. "I'm glad you've never failed."

He stabbed her with a glare.

"I mean, clearly you haven't, because you're here. What would that be like, to never—"

"Enough snark." He squared his shoulders, taking her point

quite sharply. "This isn't a game, Rogue. This is lives we're messing with. Lives we determine by our actions if they live or die."

Her brow rippled and she eased up. "Garrett, I'm well aware of that. My saying we can do it is not arrogance or me being cavalier. I know what's at stake. But I also know that he"—she stabbed her finger at Surge—"is the best chance of locating this stash and protecting the very lives you just mentioned."

He knew, as much as it grated, she was right. And he needed the dog . . . "Okay. I'll concede. We'll give it one last shot—but understand this: it truly is the last shot. And if things go south again, it's not just your ego and position here on the line. It's the lives of thousands of Americans. So out there, you have to do what I say, when I say it. I will not have time to explain why—it just needs to be done. Surge needs us both to be on the same team to make this happen."

"I hear you, but he can only have one trainer."

She was the trainer on the team. A good one too. He wouldn't let anything happen to Delaney or Surge . . . "True. But if something happens to you, I will need to be able to take control of him."

"Nothing's going to happen to me with this SEAL God sent with me." She scratched behind the Mal's ears. Then she tapped Garrett's chest. "Or this SEAL."

Her finger lingered. His heart skipped a beat. What a confident, determined woman.

Wait. Did he have feelings for her?

She lit up like a lightbulb. "I have an idea. Why don't you lead him to find the scent tins still out there?" She pulled out a birch scent tin from her hoodie pocket and handed it to him with the KONG. "He's a SEAL. You're a team leader. You've seen it done."

He tapped his finger on his chin. "Well, that will help Surge get used to following my lead."

She handed him a birch scent tin, stepped back. "Take it away."

He turned to the MWD. "Surge, ready to work?"

His black tail whipped through the air. Garrett opened the tin. "Check."

Surge sniffed eagerly. "Seek!"

He ran straight to the high grass and hit on one.

Garrett jogged after him and picked it up. "Good job, Surge. There's more." He waved his hand. "Seek!"

Surge came sprinting to Delaney and stood on his hind legs, paws on her shoulder. She hugged him, and he dropped down.

"See? The dog is not listening. Nonresponsive."

She laughed. "You waved toward me and commanded a seek. He thought you wanted him to find me."

"Oh. Yeah. My bad."

"Inadvertent," Delaney offered. "Now you know."

He bobbed his head. "Surge, come." The MWD jogged over, and Garrett held open the birch tin for him to sniff again. "Seek!"

And he did. Even when Delaney deliberately called the Mal, he glanced at her, but stayed focused tight on Garrett and the search. Four more times. Perfectly.

Garrett tossed the KONG for Surge, and the boy raced off. He captured it in the air and carried it around the grass in a victory lap. Then he screeched to a stop in front of Garrett, eyes on his pants pocket.

Delaney laughed. "You cheated! Surge stayed glued to you during the seek exercise because you stored liver treats in your pocket."

He turned his empty pockets inside out, grinned at her, pointed at her pockets.

She turned her pockets inside out to reveal two baggies of liver treats.

He threw his hands in the air in mock offense. "You sassy . . . you are the liver treat briber."

"Rewards, yes, never bribes. Now you know why dog

trainers smell like liver." She stuffed one into Surge's KONG and tossed it to him. He downed on the grass with a huff and grabbed it.

They laughed.

"But you had his full attention, the whole time," she said.

"It's good to know he's willing to pay attention to me." He grabbed his coffee and took a sip. "Rogue, where'd you get your attitude from? Daniels mentioned your dad . . ."

She tilted her head. "My sass is not *from* Dad. It's *for* Dad. He needs a new titanium prosthetic leg that insurance won't cover. I'm here to stop Sachaai's attack . . . and to earn the money for Dad's prosthetic."

He flinched. "I had no idea. What happened?"

Her jaw tightened. She gave him a long look, then blew out her breath. "Okay. I walked into our family store, and there was an armed man. He shot Dad. Hit him in the leg."

He hadn't meant . . . "Sorry."

She just nodded, stared out into the sunset.

New topic of conversation. "How'd you end up working with MWDs?"

A smile snuck onto her face. "Long story, but when I was a teen, a cop friend of ours . . . introduced me to Heath and the ranch. I never looked back."

"Is Surge your first dog?"

"Technically, he belongs to the ranch, but *my* first dog . . ." Her voice sounded thick. "Mega. A perfect German shepherd Heath let me adopt after I'd worked with him for a year. I lost her to cancer."

He'd done it again—stepped into tender territory—so he sought another topic.

"Dad told me, 'It's just a dog,'" she said, deepening her words and voice.

"Ouch."

"It took a long time before I realized he was just trying to help me with the grief. Even with all my years at the ranch and training dogs, it took a long time before I was ready to bring one home with me again." She smoothed her hands over Surge's back. "What about you? How'd you end up in the SEALs?"

"I defended my little brother against bullies. A lot." He twisted his mouth. "I got in trouble over it."

"Uh-oh."

"Yeah, it worked out okay. I was a defensive end on the high school football team, so I had a really good coach. He helped me see that protecting people, rescuing people—it's part of who I am." He shrugged. "I fought my way into the SEALs."

She simply nodded. "Protection. Rescue. Strength. Integrity. You are a SEAL kind of guy."

That sounded a lot like flirting. But that couldn't be. She was probably just saying it instead of the usual "Thank you for your service."

He drained his coffee. "We better get to bed. Another meetup tomorrow. I hope."

Five stinking a.m.

Surge's cold, wet nose had to wake her up at five a.m. He nudged her again.

Delaney rolled over and ran her hands through the thick hair on his neck. "Okay, boy. Let's go out."

She slipped out of her pajamas and into black jeans and an ABA hoodie, yanked her hair into a haphazard ponytail. When she grabbed the lead from the dresser, she heard Surge's tail whipping back and forth. She clipped it on.

They stepped out into the hall and headed to the kitchen and the lower level's walled-in garden. But her feet slowed as they reached Garrett's room, recalling his instruction not to go out alone. Had to admit, it gave her a giddy pleasure to wake him up so early to come with them.

She knocked lightly on the door and whispered, "Garrett? Surge has to go out. Want to provide escort?"

Garrett groaned. "Uh, yeah, sure. Just a sec."

Surge's toenails clicked as he came to stand with her at Garrett's door, whining.

She chuckled. "I suggest you hurry."

The door popped open, and he stood there in workout shorts, threading his arms through his black-ribbed shirt, which he pulled down.

She swallowed, taking note that he'd clearly used that weight room.

He stuffed his feet in his shoes. "Let's go."

His rough voice made her gulp again. She rolled her shoulders, looked away. "C'mon, Surge."

They walked down the hall and turned into the kitchen. Early morning sunlight brightened the soft yellow room. She wondered how Damocles had scored this nice downtown condo. Caldwell had said the team had it to themselves until the remodel was done.

"Just a minute." Garrett stopped by the coffeepot on the counter by the door to the walled-in garden, reached for the coffee pod.

Surge paced back and forth between her and the door as if telling her how to get outside.

And the coffee was ready. Garrett handed her a cup.

"Oh." She tried to act natural, not surprised. "Thanks."

"Let's get him outside before he does his job here." He punched open the back door.

The heat hadn't yet hit the nineties but sure was racing toward it. The city haze hadn't started yet. She stood silently next to Garrett in the walled-in area, the smell of the city and concrete mildew assaulting her. She took a sip from her mug.

Too bad it wasn't Choca Cantika, but coffee was coffee when you needed it. Especially when made by a handsome operator.

Garrett opened his mouth as if to say something, but Zim and Caldwell came jogging out into the long, narrow space.

"Hey, Boss," Zim called. "Good news!"

Caldwell nodded. "Message came through—Andre sent us the details on the meetup. So it's still on."

Delaney felt her heart jam into her throat. Things were getting real. She'd vouched for Surge, and now she'd without a doubt have the chance to make good on that promise.

Garrett's gaze hit hers, and she knew not to falter. She gave him a nod of assurance. Or maybe that was her subconscious trying to convince her things would be fine.

He returned his attention to the guys. "Hakim?"

"Intel reported the plane transporting him had engine trouble, so they diverted, delaying him. But the big guy is en route."

Garrett rubbed his chin. "You already hacked into the street cams in the area?"

"Have been since we got here." Caldwell's phone pinged. He pulled it out of his pocket and poked at it for a moment. "This is huge," he said, sliding a glance at Zim. "Intel suggests Tariq Sayyid will likely be in on the meetup."

"Tariq?" Zim gaped at him. "He's already here? The genius chemist who came up with Sachaai's lipid? Man, wish I knew how he did that! He's a stinking mad scientist. I mean, his use of science to kill and maim . . ."

"Yeah, not real sure why he's here, though. The formula is already in play. No need to have such a high-value asset here." Caldwell huffed. "Taking him out of the game would be doing everyone a favor." His jaw clenched. "Stakes are ramping up."

"When's Hakim due?" Garrett asked.

"Unknown. Damocles is feeding me intel as fast as it's coming in, but for now, we only have the time and place for the meetup with Rashid."

Again, Garrett's gaze found Delaney's, and he studied her for a long moment.

"We're ready," Delaney said, her pulse hammering, trying not to be overzealous but oddly desperate for him to believe in her—them. "Whatever you need, we can do it."

He looked to the others. "Okay. The meetup plan stays the same. Except, while I'm talking to Rashid to acquire the chems, Zim will try to make good with Tariq. Get some usable info on neutralizing it, if you can. Caldwell, get us a full background on this Tariq." He eyed Delaney. "Thompson, you and this combat assault dog"—he stroked the head of the Mal leaning against his leg—"will wait in the alley, a block from the meetup outside that law building."

Relief smeared a smile into her mood and face. "Understood."

She really was a maverick, something he was coming to like about her.

But his heart skipped a beat. He wouldn't let anything happen to her. Or Surge.

It was about Heath's warning to protect them, right? Their status on his team, right?

He adjusted his ball cap. "On my signal, you two approach from the corner. We'll pretend to be a couple meeting for a date in case the Sachaai guys return."

Her eyes widened, but she nodded.

"We leave in half an hour."

Zim swallowed back a grin. "I'll bring the FTIR for this chem search."

"Good," Garrett said, and the team hurried into the safe house and got ready.

Fifty minutes later, Garrett was in the perfectly clean, brightly sunny Singaporean street with Zim, behind the circular law office skyscraper. At least it wasn't Casablanca-foggy like last time.

He and Zim were ready—with Caldwell overwatching at the safe house. Delaney was in the alley he'd ordered her to stay in. He tapped the Sig in his tactical pants, keyed the comms. "Good to go, Rogue?"

"At my station, Surge eager to work."

He wished he had eyes on her. "Caldwell, have eyes out?"

"Eight street cameras are still feeding into my computer. I see all three of you."

Garrett rolled back his tense shoulders and leaned against the concrete blocks of the law building, settling into his chill undercover personality.

Zim stood next to him, tossing a smiley-face stress ball between his hands. Garrett shook his head with a chuckle. Zim smiled, tossed it high in the air, caught it behind his back.

"Your six, Bear," Caldwell said. "Coming out of the law building. Rashid appears to be armed. Bald, trim beard. Cream shirt. Black pants. Tariq behind him. Red collared shirt. Wire-rimmed glasses. Slick black hair."

"Got it." *God, help me focus.*

The two Sachaai approached.

Garrett met them. "Rashid?"

The tall man nodded, his gaze sweeping the area, likely making sure they were safe, with Tariq staying directly behind his boss. "You're the clay pot food guy. Andre told me you said the sample was 'the real thing.'"

"I did. I'm pleased. Ready for the product."

Acting casual, Zim moved to Tariq, held out his hand. "Who's this?"

Tariq just stood there.

Zim dropped his hand. "You make the chem vials?"

Tariq's black eyes lasered in on Zim, whose face was a mask of stone as he took another step forward.

Man wasn't going to talk.

And thankfully, Zim got the hint and backed off, leaning against the wall.

Clearly not pleased with that interaction, Rashid shifted closer. Extended his hand, and when Garrett took it, the guy yanked him forward. "Before we make this deal, understand that I have gunmen in place."

He and Zim had weapons too.

"I see three, Bear," Caldwell comm'd.

"I wouldn't expect any less," Garrett said, totally chill.

"I like to know who I'm doing business with."

Garrett shrugged. "Like you said, I'm Clay Pot. Anonymity helps keep me under radars."

Rashid scoffed. "I am not afraid of being caught."

"You must be. You showed up with gunmen. And Hakim is a coward too, sending you to do his business."

The metallic *shink* of a weapon chambering a round drew Garrett's gaze to Tariq, who now held a Glock to the side. Fourth gunman.

"Bear, I think he's testing you," Caldwell said.

Like Garrett needed the spook to tell him that. But the idea of Rogue a block away shot to the front of his mind. "What's the problem?"

"*You* need to know who *you're* dealing with—someone strong, willing to do the dirty job."

Garrett held the guy's gaze, knowing he was vetting him. "I'm here for the goods, not you. We can deal and I'm out of here." Besides, the man in front of him was not the man his sights were set on. "If Hakim were so strong, he'd come do this deal himself."

Rashid's lips twitched. "I can show you how strong we are."

The deal was high dollar and solid. No way the guy would walk. "Enough," Garrett said. "I'm walking away." He strode away, feeling Zim fall in behind him.

"Stay put, Rogue!" Caldwell bit out. "Don't move."

At the mention of Delaney, Garrett slid his gaze in her direction—but stopped halfway when he spotted her at the back door entry of the building next to the law building. Holy—how had she gotten that close? Worry smeared her pretty face. He gave her a silent, subtle shake of his head.

"You want the chemicals, don't you?" Rashid called.

At the callback, he winged up an eyebrow at Delaney, who withdrew into the shadows with Surge.

"Told you it was a test," Caldwell said, relief coloring his voice. "Rogue. Stay."

Garrett turned his attention on Rashid. "You done vetting me?"

A broad smile filled Rashid's face as he laughed. "We're like those American convenience stores, checking ID of people purchasing alcohol." He hefted a briefcase onto the hood of a vehicle. "Real thing. Exact amount you ordered."

To the side, Garrett said, "Zim, check it."

The petty officer strode over and took a look, then backed up and nodded.

So far so good. Garrett drew out the envelope of money, handed it to Rashid, and took the briefcase.

Rashid flipped through the cash. "Good. Next time we won't vet you, Clay Pot."

He walked away with Tariq even as Garrett started backing up toward their exit.

"He's gone," Caldwell said two minutes later.

"Rogue, you still at the law building?"

"Yes—I moved into the—" A gasp severed her words.

Garrett's heart jammed. "Rogue. What's wrong?"

Nothing.

"I don't have eyes on her," Caldwell stated.

"Rogue!"

"I'm here," came her hushed, frantic words. "Rashid just walked right past me. He's here!" she hissed.

"On my way!" Garrett shouted and moved fast, avoiding a full-out run in case they still had eyes on the area.

"No! Wait." Her breaths came heavy through the comms. "He's gone. I turned my back to him, petting Surge like he's my pet. Didn't even notice us. Turned left a block down from me."

"He's not on my cameras," Caldwell said, clicking away on his keyboard. "Gunmen are gone too. Okay, got him—three blocks east, getting into a black sedan. Muddy license plate. Can't read it."

Garrett grunted. "Let's get after the chemicals, then. Join us, Rogue. Now."

As planned, when she got to Garrett on the street, they held hands, chatting about the weather as he petted Surge.

A few minutes later, he squeezed her hand and opened the briefcase.

"Surge, time to work," Delaney said as the Malinois's sleek black tail thwapped Garrett's leg. She pointed to the briefcase. "Check."

Surge sniffed from one end of the case to the other, his snout digging into the vial packets for a long draught.

"Good boy," she said. "Now, seek-seek."

The Malinois swiveled around and homed in on Garrett, who held his breath—another fail?—but the MWD lifted his nose in the air for a moment, then dropped to all fours and started out of the alley. He zigzagged down the street, narrowing the scent cone past more skyscrapers . . . gratefully in the direction Caldwell said Rashid had climbed into the car. Surge stopped at the corner, sniffed, and headed right.

"This is where Rashid turned left," Rogue admitted. "But he's certain."

"Hope he's right. Maybe they deliberately headed away from the stash," Garrett mumbled.

She nodded, and they followed the dog as he worked the scent. On the long leash ahead of them, Surge turned down a short set of concrete stairs that led into the basement of a building and scratched at the door at the bottom.

"Hold up, boy," Rogue said, following him. "Boss, he wants in. What do you want to do?"

Garrett saw a small engraved sign above the door. "Caldwell, can you translate for me?" He read aloud the Malay sign, spelled it while the spook entered it into his computer.

"Shoemakers Extraordinaire," Caldwell reported.

Shoes? Huh. "Thanks." He walked down to the door and tested the doorknob. Locked.

"I got it." Zim worked a lockpick and the door swung open.

Garrett pulled out his Sig and did a quick look-see into the long hall lit by the occasional light. "Send the dog."

Surge spurted inside, making quick work of reaching the end with no diversions right or left. No windows. Garrett advanced behind the dog team, verifying the area was clear.

Surge stopped and sniffed at a door room labeled "Janitorial," then continued on to the next door . . . but nothing.

"Has he lost it?" Zim asked from behind.

"No," Rogue said quietly, "he just hasn't found it yet."

Garrett worked his jaw.

Surge trotted down the hall, then skidded to a stop and circled back. He scratched at a door. Whimpered and downed, ears and eyes trained on the door.

After visually tracing the jamb for sign of explosives or trip wires, Garrett tested the door. Locked. "Zim."

"On it." The guy worked his magic, then backed up, bringing his weapon to the ready.

Garrett flicked open the door and verified no unfriendlies in sight. "Send him," he instructed Delaney, who moved into the room with her four-legged partner.

Trailing them with Zim, Garrett eyed the boxes for labels.

Surge began barking.

A crash sounded amid a shout.

He doubled back and found Zim on the floor, grappling against a blond man for control of a handgun. Garrett kicked the man's arm, and the gun spun across the floor. The man scrambled for the gun.

Garrett snapped his weapon at him. "Sto—"

A blow pummeled his shoulders. Felt like steel or something. The impact thrust him forward, but he staggered up and around just in time to see a bald Asian man coming at him again with a pipe.

The blond smashed Zim up against the wall.

Crack!

The report of the weapon startled Garrett, and he wondered who'd shot. The blond tipped into Zim, going limp.

Baldie swung at Garrett, yanking him back to his own life-or-death fight. He dodged the pipe, coming up with a hard knife hand—but Baldie tackled him. Garrett's head bounced, giving his attacker the split second necessary to get him in a choke hold. The grip proved lethal, and Garrett struggled to free himself.

A blur of black sailed at him. He felt the brush of fur even as a vicious snarl-snap sounded from Surge, who nailed the guy.

Garrett seized the distraction and freed himself. Whipped around with his weapon. Aimed at the guy and fired. Once, twice. As he watched the last breath wheeze from the guy, he spotted an S-shaped tattoo on his neck. He eyed Zim's attacker and saw the same thing.

"Surge, out!" Rogue commanded, catching the dog's collar and drawing him back.

Gaining his feet, Garrett eyed Zim to be sure he was okay, then walked the perimeter of the room, circling back to the team.

"You okay?" Delaney asked.

"Yes, thanks to Surge." He exhaled, studying the force multiplier who'd interdicted just in time. "He saved my life."

Surge wandered to one of the upturned boxes, sniffing.

"I wish I could say I gave him the order to do that, but he ripped away from me without hesitation," Delaney admitted.

"Good. This time, I'm glad." He smirked, watching as the Malinois focused on a particular box.

Surge took in long draughts, started to sit, then moved to another box. Same thing.

"He looks confused."

RONIE KENDIG & VONI HARRIS

"I . . . don't think that's it."

Surge finally downed in the middle of the room, ears pointed to the boxes.

"Wait," she gasped, her face alight. "You don't think . . ."

"Mother lode," Garrett murmured. "Just don't understand why there isn't more security."

"Overconfidence," Zim suggested.

"Way to go, Surge," Rogue exclaimed.

Then the Mal rushed out into the hall and into another open door. Garrett and Zim flew past Rogue, found him sitting at the edge of the empty room, alerting on a long workbench. But he moved to a line of sewing machines, same. And a pile of leather in one corner.

Shoeboxes filled another corner.

Garrett signaled Rogue into the room. "Saw you coming out of the alley during the meetup."

She cringed and wrinkled her nose. "I got worried . . ." She patted her leg, and Surge rushed in to sit next to her.

"Point is, you stayed, though you wanted to go rogue and do your own thing. That would've compromised all of us. You did good." He nodded around the room. "Especially here. Thanks."

Surprise rippled through her face, and she seemed to soften. "You're welcome."

They cleared the rest of the building with little effort and no further contact. Which just didn't sit right. Too easy.

While waiting for Caldwell's people to come inventory the warehouse of shoes, Surge whined.

Delaney thumbed over her shoulder. "There's a small park with grass just past the front gate. I'd like to let him take care of business."

Garrett pointed out the window at a park in front of the building. "Okay. He deserves a break. You both do."

Her eyes blinked fast.

Which surprised him. He wasn't always a cranky bear. Was

he? "Be back in fifteen. We don't have much left but stay close. They could return, and it won't be friendly if they do."

She smiled. "Will do, Boss."

As she headed out, Garrett took the briefcase into the other room where Zim was photographing the Sachaai-labeled boxes, which Caldwell's people were loading into a vehicle to take back to the safe house.

This was a significant stash of Sachaai chemicals. But it still grated. Why wasn't there more security? He eyed the warehouse, wondering what they'd missed. Maybe he should do another search . . .

6

CORE, SINGAPORE

SO MUCH FOR THAT. STANDING ACROSS FROM THE PARK GARRETT had green-lighted, Delaney shifted Surge's lead from one hand to the other. A small traffic jam had built up behind a black-and-gold beer truck that had a spill, split-open cases and broken glass littering the street. No way could she take him through that.

Two Pakistanis in fluorescent brewery T-shirts moved to the back of the semi and pulled shovels out. They joined a couple of law enforcement officers, who were already scraping the asphalt to collect the muddle and throw the glass into a nearby dumpster. Drivers waited outside their vehicles, playing with phones.

Delaney and Surge walked up the street, passing the line of traffic, the silver semi stuck right behind the beer truck and the culprit truck itself. They crossed the street in front of the mess and headed to the park.

Surge sniffed every stick, rock, pole, and bench that existed before finally hiking a leg to take care of business. She spied a small area hemmed in by shrub and thought it a great place to let him chase his KONG. He seemed to read her body language as

98

much as she read his, because he spun a circle around her, tail going a hundred miles an hour. He had his priorities.

She led him to the area, relieved to find a chain-link fence closed in on three sides. She dug into her hoodie pocket for the rope KONG and sent it sailing through the air.

Surge darted after it and snagged it off the ground. He trotted around, then slowed, the KONG dangling from his mouth, his attention locked on the men cleaning up the mess.

"Bring it, Surge," she said, keeping her voice calm and steady, doing her best to keep emotion out of it and draw him back to her before he bolted away.

He sidestepped toward her, his eyes not leaving the men.

She took the KONG and bounced it between her hands, but his attention had locked on the men again. In full alert, he wasn't deterred.

What was Surge seeing?

She knew better than to let him focus on that. "Let's play, Surge," she said, twirling the KONG.

Except the Mal wasn't breaking focus. He'd been trained not to let any distraction divert him when he detected something. She clipped the lead to him before he bolted off to investigate for himself. Time to head back to the warehouse. Garrett had warned her not to go far and to be back in fifteen minutes. She headed back that route, but it unfortunately took them right past the accident again.

They passed the car behind the silver semi, and one of the two men stopped working to wipe his brow.

"Hurry up," the other said in English with a heavy Pakistani Urdu accent. "Hakim's waiting for us."

Hakim!

Delaney's heart charged into her throat. "Surge, with me," she said softly and led him behind the car. She peeked around the car at the guy in the cream shirt and black jeans.

Oh no. That was Rashid—the bald guy with the trim beard who'd passed behind her after the meetup. Her gaze shifted to the guy with the wire-rimmed glasses, who fit Caldwell's description of Tariq, the Sachaai chemist—red shirt, slicked-back hair. He frowned at Rashid but went to work with his shovel. Why on earth would these two be doing cleanup?

That didn't matter—what did was that they were here.

She had to tell Garrett. She hustled Surge quietly down the street, staying behind cars in the traffic jam. Touched her comms piece. "Eagle One, this is Cerberus One."

Nothing. She frowned and pressed it again—this time felt a small spark sizzle against her ear. She tugged it out and drew the coiled cord so she could see it. Wiped it. Tried it again, only this time, there was a distinct emptiness to the communication channel.

Of course! Augh! What was she going to do now?

The SAT phone. She snatched it out and went for the power button. But Garrett had ordered them to keep the phones powered off during the mission. Unless it was an emergency. Which this definitely was, right?

Scraping of the shovels fell silent, creating a gaping, ominous void in the noisy city.

Delaney spun around and eyed the crew—they were done, tossing shovels in the back.

What on earth? She caught a glimpse of the interior—silver containers with purple stylish S emblems, crammed full. Given those box labels, they were certainly full of chem vials like the boxes in the warehouse. Were the glass bottles they'd been cleaning up just cover? Either way, it was clear this was more boxes from the warehouse. The team hadn't found all of them.

Rashid and Tariq closed the back doors with a clang. Dark eyes looked straight at her.

Delaney sucked in a breath and ducked behind a car, praying he hadn't seen her.

When she braved a look, she found them climbing into the cab.

Frantic, she fumbled with the phone, trying fast to get Garrett.

Shoot. The truck engine revved to life.

She had no idea where they were going, and she couldn't alert Garrett in time.

"With me, Surge." With him at her side, she crouched behind another car.

The semi axle groaned and squeaked as it lurched away.

Surge whined.

"I know. They're leaving!" she whispered.

Americans would die if these silver half-containers made it to the US. Given those box labels, they were certainly full of chem vials with Sachaai lipids, like the boxes in the warehouse.

No time for prayer.

Her eyes caught a taxi stand half a block down. "C'mon, Surge." They took off running. This was her chance.

She stopped at the cab, opened the back door, and climbed in the back. She patted the seat next to her and Surge jumped in. "Follow that silver semi. Quick. Please."

The man with thick blue glasses and a stubby nose turned in his seat. "Not with that big black monster dog. Get out of my cab."

"But—"

"No! Out! Get that mutt out of my cab."

"He won't hurt anything."

"*Out!*"

She bit the inside of her cheek to avoid what she wanted to say. "Let's go, Surge." He jumped out, and she joined him on the sidewalk.

The cab left, practically squealing his tires.

Surge nosed her hand. *Yeah, now what?*

A young twenty-something with a man bun jogged up to her. "You need a ride? I was waiting for the traffic to clear when I saw that guy throw you out. If you need a ride, I'm a Grab driver. I'll take you and your beautiful dog. My car's right there." He pointed at a metallic blue Hyundai. It boasted a Grab logo sticker, like an American Uber sticker. But that Hyundai was rather rusty.

What choice was there? Garrett would kill her either way, but at least she might be able to help make sure thousands of Americans wouldn't die. "Thanks. I need to follow that silver semi, please." The traffic was easing up. The semi was just under three blocks down the road and had a left turn signal on.

He gazed at her, one eye closed.

C'mon, kid. I need Rashid. She didn't say it; she put on a smile. Her brain dug for a good reason, then she patted her pocket. "My boyfriend is driving that semi," she said, hating the lie. "He left his phone behind."

He grinned. "No wonder you don't just text the driver. I got ya." He jogged to his car, and she and Surge piled into the back, barely closing the door before the kid zipped around cars and turned left where the silver semi had.

There it was, a couple blocks ahead. *Thanks, dude.*

She needed to text Garrett.

DELANEY

> In a Grab rideshare. With Surge. Following a semi full of boxes with the Sachaai logo. Follow his tracker. Please.

The kid was—thankfully—driving like crazy trying to catch up with the semi, which was headed for Hakim.

She clutched the grab handle with her right hand, and with her other, she rubbed between Surge's shoulders, where his tracker was inserted.

Her breath hitched as her phone blinked.

> Network issue. Text message not delivered.

She hit send again.

The same network issue message came down.

God, please get Garrett to us. Fast. And don't let him kill me.

No "if" or "make him come" to her prayer, because she didn't *hope* that Garrett would follow—she *trusted* he already was.

"Two floors of shoe production," Garrett commented to Zim as they stood at the stairwell, looking back at the pallets of shoeboxes lining the walls and rows of sewing machines in the center that they'd already swept.

"One more floor. Let's see more empty shoe factory," Zim said.

He lifted his Sig and climbed the stairs, his thoughts bouncing to the MWD team. Had it been fifteen mikes yet?

Zim whistled low when they reached the third level. "We got a chem lab to sweep, Boss."

Garrett took a left as they stole around the room, meeting in the middle. Clear, thank God. "Confirm." If they'd found someone in this stainless steel chemistry wonderland, it would've gotten complicated.

As he looked at the microscopes, Bunsen burners, deep metal sinks, three tall tables and stools, computers, refrigeration, Zim practically drooled.

This lab was a few levels up from his high school chemistry class. A lot of levels up. He keyed his comms. "Cerberus One, return to base."

No answer.

"Eagle Actual to Cerberus One. Come in."

"Boss. You need to see this."

Nerves tight, Garrett joined Zim at the fridge with the glass door. His eyes blinked fast. Dangerous was an understatement. Then he caught sight of the pile of folders on the desk next to the fridge. Thumbed through them. "Big names here. And this is one high-end computer."

Zim joined him. "No kidding. Fahmi Ansari—Hakim's dad."

"We definitely need to take a look at these and the computer. They'll lead us to them."

"We're only stopping the chemical weapon. Not the Sachaai people."

Garrett's jaw jerked. He longed for justice for Samwise. But without official support from the government and local authorities, their hands were tied. They had to stay within the scope of this op.

He closed his eyes, then opened them again. He knew what his mission was. The people the chemicals were meant to poison. "Take the computer. We'll get it back to Caldwell to do his thing on it." His shoulders wanted to rise up by his ears, but he kept them down. "Still haven't heard from Delaney."

Zim play-punched him in the arm. "Maybe she's already on her way up."

He stepped over to the table in front of the window and looked down into the park across the street from this lab, shoe factory, warehouse place.

His phone buzzed. He glanced at the message and his curse seared the air.

Eyes wide, Zim glanced up.

"She's in a rideshare tracking a truck she spotted. Said it's Sachaai." He started for the door. "Grab the computer. Let's go!"

They sprinted down to the SUV loaded with evidence and climbed in. "Eagle Three," he said to Caldwell, "get me tied into Surge's tracker."

"Already on it."

Garrett whipped out, wanting to reach through the comms and make it happen.

"Here we go," Caldwell said. "Fastest route is second right, then west for a klick."

Garrett gunned it, heart racing.

A few moments later, Caldwell came back on the comms. "Okay, I've researched the Grab—she's in a—whoa, left turn ahead. Seventy meters, bank right onto Tanglin Road and head south for two klicks."

"Copy!" Garrett gritted his teeth. "I'm going to kill her."

Zim side-eyed him.

"Well, she did give you the way to find her, and if she hadn't tracked them—"

"Intel, Caldwell. I don't need your therapy sessions."

"Apparently you do." The spook snickered, then cleared his throat. "Grab shows this rideshare is a metallic blue Hyundai sedan. Annnd from what I can tell from the satellite relay I'm hijacking—shh, don't tell—she does look to be following a semi a couple blocks ahead."

"Semi info," Garrett demanded.

"Unlabeled. No plates, but when you hit Alexandra Road and head east, you won't be far behind them."

What was Rogue doing? "Find her! Facial recognition on the driver."

"You're less than a klick from her. Traveling east now. Fast."

Garrett scowled. "You're overwatch—how did you miss that she left the site?"

"Same as you, I guess," Caldwell threw back.

He zipped around a gray sedan. "I'm not seeing her."

But then a burst of blue in the array of drab vehicles caught his attention.

Delaney was in over her head.

7

CORE, SINGAPORE

The Hyundai's tires squealed around a corner, following the silver semi.

Holding tight as the car careened into traffic, Delaney thanked God the metal box shipping containers bearing the Sachaai S weren't volatile unless mixed. But also—*let's not mix them.* She slid into the car door, and Surge nearly ended up in her lap. She put her arm around him to keep him steady. A keen awareness hit her—they were heading away from downtown and the shoe factory. Farther from Garrett.

"Where are they going?" the Grab driver asked, gaze bouncing to the mirror.

"Not sure."

"You don't know where your boyfriend's going?"

"I . . ." She eyed him, then saw beyond him as the semi was turning, grateful she wouldn't have to answer his question. "They're turning!"

"Chen Street. Got it. I'll catch up to them." He hit the gas hard. "I'm Torrence."

"Hi, Torrence. Delaney." Surge whined a little as he laid his head in her lap.

She didn't blame him. Those chemicals were destined for her country. She chucked his chin. "We're behind them, boy. I promise."

"Delaney?" Torrence's voice sounded tight. "I hate to ask, but we're not doing this ride Grab-official, since you are in a hurry. You do have cash, don't you?"

"Y—" The answer died in her throat. Oh no. She'd left her wallet at the safe house for operational security. But Garrett was tracking them.

Absolutely.

She hoped. With cash.

"Yeah. I do." Her voice pitched high.

Delaney looked down at the SAT phone she'd pretended belonged to a "boyfriend."

This was undercover, not lying, right?

He made a halfway stop at the light, then took a hard left. She snagged the grab handle again. Torrence obviously had taken her mission on as his own. He negotiated around a parked truck on the side, veered hard left to avoid a blue sedan.

Don't let him get in an accident. Please, God.

Where was Garrett? She drew out her SAT phone and eyed it. No reply. She hoped the messages were getting through.

"I can still see the semi up there," Torrence said, "but traffic is getting bad."

She looked up as the light changed and a large group stepped away from a crowded gelato shop into the street.

Torrence ground down on the brakes.

The phone sailed out of Delaney's hand onto the seat next to Surge. She grabbed for it before it ended up on the floor. Swallowing hard at how close they'd come to hitting the people, to running a red light, Delaney tensed. Saw the large truck turn out of sight. "We're losing them!"

Torrence veered around a motorcycle, pitching her toward Surge.

"Shoot!" he exclaimed. "I lost them! Did you see them turn?"

She tossed the phone back in her pocket. "Sorry. Keep driving, and I'll look down the cross streets for them."

"Okay. This is your boyfriend, lady."

Rashid her boyfriend. The thought nauseated her. At the third cross street, she spotted the truck sailing past a UPS truck. "Left here!"

"Can't. I'll take the next one." He lurched to the right around the car in front of them, rumble strips sending vibrations through the car. He cut into the left lane and swerved left at the next intersection, then gunned it back toward the street where she'd seen the semi.

She kept her eyes peeled and scanned the vehicles ahead of them. Buildings, cars, street vendors all vied for what little space stretched between skyscrapers. Past a row of food trucks, she saw the silver bullet glide by.

"There! I saw it," she called. "Turned right at that building that looks like it's made of children's blocks, but concrete."

He laughed. "Shang Tower. That's Stratus Street." He ground to a halt at a red light, impatiently tapping his fingers on the steering wheel.

God, don't let police catch this kid speeding. But please help us catch up to that semi.

And do what?

She'd figure that out.

The light changed, and he took off.

She gasped as he turned right . . . in front of a line of cars. Then blew out the breath she was holding. He was supposed to do that. This was Singapore—left-lane driving.

"I don't see them," he said.

She shook it off and strained to look out the window. A digital billboard about Singapore Grand Prix, yes. The silver semi, no. "Man! I don't see it either."

"Sorry," he said, the car easing back to the speed limit.

She kept looking up and down the cross streets. Saw nothing but businesses, mothers with strollers, workers speed-walking into buildings. "No apology needed. You really tried for me."

"I guess he'll have to travel without his phone. That stinks."

Delaney sighed. She'd have to tell Garrett what'd happened. And that it'd failed. And that she didn't have cash to pay Torrence. "Thanks so much. Please just take me back to—"

"Hold on." His eyes met hers in the rearview mirror. "I might know where your boyfriend is headed." He pointed ahead to a sign that read SE Asia Container Action Corp with an arrow to the right. "He's driving a semi." Torrence shrugged. "We can at least check it out."

Her stomach clenched at the airport sign beside the first sign. Those chemicals could be headed anywhere from the airport. Anytime.

"Let's do it." She lifted the phone to try and call Garrett. Let him know—

The Hyundai dove around a corner.

Pitched left, she struggled to hold on to both the phone and Surge, whose nails were digging into her leg. So she ditched the phone again. Trusted Garrett—like she'd said she did—that he was tracking her via Surge's chip locator.

Torrence hung a right and sped around sedans and SUVs. She snagged the grab handle above her, put her other arm around Surge, hoping Garrett wouldn't be too ticked with her, that this would pay off and he'd agree she had no choice but to follow. Granted, they'd located a huge Sachaai chem stash at the shoe factory, but this was Rashid and Tariq—and they'd said Hakim was waiting. This had to be important. Well aware she wasn't trained, she again prayed Garrett and Zim weren't far behind.

"This is it," Torrence said as he eased along the curb. He scanned the area and frowned at her in the rearview.

She eyed the six-foot chain-link fence that barricaded the

front of the property, a gate locked and preventing entrance to Container Action. She could see the silver semi sitting in front of an office. Tariq and Rashid stood next to it, talking with a third man, his back to her. She was too far away to confirm, but she had a strong hunch that was Hakim!

Where was Garrett?

"You sure about this?" Torrence asked. "It feels . . . off."

So has my last week.

"I know. I think I see him"—which was true and should buy her time—"but let me make sure that's him. Please wait—"

"I . . . I don't know. I'm illegally parked—"

"Just two minutes. Please." She climbed out before he could argue further, trusting how nice he'd been to rescue her in the first place. Hopefully, he wouldn't abandon her.

Was there another way in? An entrance farther on? She moved a few feet down, crouched to stay in the shadows of a tall building as she crept out to see better.

A featherlight touch against her leg startled her—even as her brain registered Surge trotting ahead, sniffing around a building and stoop. "No! Surge, heel," she hissed.

She darted her gaze to the container yard and saw Hakim's gaze swivel in her direction. She ducked and eyed Surge. "Surge, come. Heel."

He hiked up his leg and relieved himself on the corner of a wall.

Of course you have to do that now.

"Hey." A hissed voice came from behind. "I'm leaving."

She shifted in her crouched position and looked back. Saw the driver slinking closer. "No, please—"

"This is sketch. I don't think . . . I'm out of here."

She straightened. "No. Please!" Her own words bounced to her, and she feared she'd given herself away to the three men in the yard. She eyed them, saw Rashid looking this way now too. They couldn't see her, but she couldn't afford for the driver to abandon her here.

God! Help Hakim not see us. Send Garrett! Fast!

"Get down," she urged the driver.

"Sorry, I'm not dying for you!"

"Please. Wai—" Her breath backed into her throat as she saw a large shape blur at the driver.

Garrett threw himself at the guy going after Rogue. They went to ground, and he flipped the guy and drew back his fist.

"Garrett, no!"

"Hey!" the kid yelped.

Fury stayed, Garrett considered the two. "What're you doing?"

"He's my *driver*," came Delaney's whispered cry.

Garrett thought to punch the punk anyway for bringing her to this place—begging for danger. Standing out in the open with trouble across the road.

"He's my Grab driver," Delaney snapped as she trotted over and crouched with Surge.

Garrett hauled the guy upright, then pitched him aside.

"Forget the pay. I'm outta here." Man Bun sprang into his car and pulled out of the parking lot.

Garrett turned to Delaney, trying not to yell at her. "Behind the SUV," Garrett ordered, pulling out his gun and following her into the SUV's shadows. "What were you thinking? Why'd you leave the shoe factory?"

She clenched her fists around Surge's leash. "Hakim, Rashid, and Tariq are over there in that storage yard."

He eyed the yard, then thumbed her toward the SUV. "Let's get out of view." In the SUV, he used his binoculars and found the three men, just as she'd said. He swallowed. Man . . . Hakim.

Zim snatched his camera out of his backpack, screwed on a zoom lens. "Confirm eyes on Rashid, Tariq, and that's Hakim."

He snapped pictures of the men standing under the streetlights in the growing dark.

Garrett clenched his jaw, all his preconceived verbal lashings falling to his feet like wet noodles. She'd done it. Yeah, he'd been ticked that she'd taken off from the factory, left them, compromised the op, them, herself—but she'd done it. What intel had failed to do. She'd found Hakim.

"Look, I know what I did wasn't ideal, but when I saw Hakim, then Torrence threatened to leave me here . . . I didn't feel I had a choice." She sighed heavily from the back seat. "But I'm glad you're here—that you came."

Garrett didn't trust himself to answer that, wasn't sure what it meant that she was glad to see him. He eyed the yard again through the nocs. "How did you know to follow them?"

"There was an accident—beer spilled over the road from a truck"—she nodded toward the semi parked in front of the office—"and I caught a glimpse of the boxes inside one of them. They had the Sachaai S, exactly like the boxes in the factory. The containers both did too."

"Describe them. Please."

"Silver cubes with triangular cutouts on the bottom. I've seen semis putting two or three of them on their beds instead of a regular-sized shipping container. Not sure what they're called. Square pods?"

Garrett used his phone and pulled up images of the LD3 containers and turned the phone to her. "Containers like this?"

"That's it." She waved at the fenced container yard. "I only saw the semi come in here, but I would guess they're all in here somewhere."

Garrett again used his nocs and surveyed the container yard.

"There are a ton of silver containers in there, of all sizes," Zim said, still peering through his zoom camera.

"And security cameras." Garrett comm'd Caldwell to hack into them, take a look around the container yard.

Zim clicked his camera. "I got a pic. Five-six-four."

"What's that?"

"The last digits of a silver container ID number. Can't read the rest. This one looks like it was just put in place, even though I can't see a Sachaai S." He glanced at Delaney. "I don't see a second."

Delaney's brow furrowed. "I definitely saw two."

"Maybe they already loaded one. Caldwell's accessing Agency channels to run the numbers," Garrett said. "Zim, find a way into the container yard."

"On it." Zim took off, jogging around the fence.

"This has got to be bigger than we thought," Delaney said.

"Agreed. Or Hakim wouldn't be here." Garrett closed his eyes for a moment. Their path forward depended on Caldwell's intel. In the past, that had compromised ops and cost lives.

Zim came sprinting up to them. "Boss, move! Tariq incoming!"

Garrett looked to the yard.

"Black Land Rover."

As if his words had brought it to life, the vehicle bounced around the corner. Tires screeched as headlamps swung toward them.

"Go!" Garrett shouted, urging Zim into the SUV.

Zim slammed the door shut and sped away.

Bullets pinged off the vehicle. Garrett prayed none hit them as they ripped through traffic until they lost the Sachaai.

Zim finally slowed to the speed limit. "I think we're good."

Garrett's heart rate slowed to the speed limit too. "Eagle Three, we are returning to the warehouse. Rendezvous there." When Surge's nose nudged his arm, he reached back to chuck the Mal's chin. Eyed Thompson. "I'm going to let it go that you did not stay close. At least now we have a location to give the Agency. Second, while you were defying my orders, Zim and I unearthed a lab on the third level of the shoe factory."

Her eyebrows lifted. "When we get back, I can have Surge check it."

"Exactly why I'm telling you."

Zim finally pulled up behind the factory.

Caldwell emerged from a door and hustled toward them.

"What's he doing?" Zim asked, slowing the SUV.

"No idea." Garrett eyed the door that opened, and the spook climbing in. "What's—"

"*Go*, move!"

Zim faltered for a second, then hit the gas. "Why am I doing this?"

After winking at Delaney, Caldwell buckled himself in. "I accessed that computer Zim pulled. Found messages about a meetup here. Sachaai will be here soon. Get me back to the safe house and I can finish dissecting the computer. I have a team monitoring the container yard. We can go through that to find them."

Zim pulled into traffic.

"Where are those shipping containers, Spook?" Garrett demanded.

Caldwell sneered. "Unknown at this time. They had a pretty advanced system. I took the motherboard." He patted a satchel he had.

Great. Fine. Garrett's phone pinged, and he looked at it. He took a deep breath. The pressure was on now. "Damocles is watching the factory, and when it's clear, they'll work with local law enforcement to raid it. And Chapel's hunting down a semi to transport the chems once we find them."

As Zim stopped at a traffic light, Garrett's stomach growled. Loudly.

Surge woofed.

Garrett looked at his watch. "Almost twenty hundred. Let's grab some takeout, then get back and get to work."

"We get to have something besides turkey sandwiches?" Zim quipped.

"Hey," Delaney laughed. "A lot of blood, sweat, and tears went into those sandwiches."

"Tasted like it too," Zim teased back.

They pulled up in front of a food truck, and ten minutes later they had chicken satays. The deep, rich spices filled the SUV. Back at the safe house, Caldwell dropped the order on the kitchen table while Zim pulled down plates and sodas from the fridge.

Garrett was starving and wanted to enjoy his satays instead of his anger. "Delaney."

She looked over.

He tipped his head toward the living room. "We need to talk."

She nodded, grabbed a Dr. Pepper from the table, and went into the living room ahead of him.

Zim put a hand on his shoulder and jerked his head to the living room. "You like her, Boss?"

Garrett squared his shoulders. "No. Teammates."

"Why? Yeah, a team player, tons of dog skills. But she's a looker, and you two talk a lot. And she's so—"

"Fearless?"

Zim grinned. "See? Perfect for you, Master Chief."

Garrett narrowed his eyes. "Mission focus, Petty Officer." He headed out of the kitchen and joined Delaney on the couch. But they sat there like strangers in an elevator.

She toyed with her watch. "Guess this is 'later.' About following the semi—I wasn't trying to go rogue—I just didn't see how we wouldn't lose the trucks if I didn't. I was going to come back in when I heard them mention Hakim, then start to leave. I couldn't waste time."

Good start. He raised an eyebrow. "Why didn't you let me know on comms?"

"I tried but the piece was damaged. So I sent a text—but I wasn't sure that went through. Which I guess worked well, since Rashid and Tariq would've recognized you too easily, so I just rode it out. Figured it was best to—"

"Communication is vital. That was my decision to make—

you're not an operator with the full breadth of intel at your disposal."

She swallowed. "You're right."

Her concession startled him. "Bet that hurt."

Her lips quirked. "More than you'll ever know." She shrugged. "Look, it all happened so fast and I just reacted. Did the best with the limited skills I had."

"I hear you. Makes sense."

Again her lips quirked. "Bet that hurt."

He wanted to scowl, but a smile hit his face instead. She was so . . . bold. Yeah, bold. Not many women were like that.

Trust her.

He sat next to her on the couch. "I was angry that you left the team. Worried for your safety. But you didn't let that stash just vanish. Now we know what we're looking for and we have a starting point—the container yard. Good job, Delaney." He gave her a small smile. If the guys hadn't been right there in the kitchen, he'd probably have hugged her.

Smiling back, she tilted her head up at him, her ponytail swishing against his arm. Their gazes locked. Holy guacamole. He was having feelings.

Surge jumped onto the couch and jammed himself between them. His tongue withdrew into his snout, and those knowing eyes hit Garrett, as if to say, "I got eyes on you, slick."

He'd almost kissed her!

Laughing, Delaney shook her head. "Off, Surge."

The Mal jumped over to her, lay down, his eyes not leaving Garrett.

Time to eat satays and talk LD3 containers.

Surge was on to him.

8

CORE, SINGAPORE

Even after brushing her teeth post-shower, Delaney could still taste the curry from the gently spicy chicken satay. It had been good to shower away the tension of tracking those terrorists and two—*two!*—containers full of chem vials.

She grinned. Garrett had rewarded Surge with one of his chicken satay skewers. Human food was extremely rare for him, but she'd allowed the treat. That sleek jet-black Mal had proven himself.

Proven her.

She'd even earned a "good job" from Garrett. She was more than an outsider to play nice with, at last. Warmth stirred through her, remembering how Garrett had tackled the rideshare driver, fear and protectiveness in his face . . .

That man was real flesh and blood, not some fairy-tale prince.

A couple of days ago, when he'd sat on the couch with her, her hair brushed up against his biceps. His bright amber eyes gazed into hers. Ribbons had swirled through her belly. He'd been stargazing?

Oh, yeah . . . she'd gazed right back.

They had been stargazing.

It was best to stop that right now. She didn't have any brain space for it. She looked at her watch. It was time for her to rejoin the team discussion.

She unwrapped the towel around her wet hair—

"Surge! What did you do?" Garrett yelled.

Delaney took off running into the living room.

Surge sat on a pile of men's underwear in the center of the room, a pair of boxers hanging from his mouth.

Garrett's sea bag unzipped in the corner.

Zim waved Surge's KONG in the air. Caldwell held out a bully stick. Garrett squatted with a liver treat, tapping his legs. All three called, "Surge, come!"

Surge just looked from man to man, acting like a king on his spot on the yellow-and-white geometric throw rug.

Oh men of little Surge skill. Delaney couldn't hold back a chuckle, but she was smart enough not to pull out her phone to take a picture. Barely.

"Surge, leave it. Come," she commanded.

He huffed, dropped the underwear, and came over to her.

Walker strode over to stuff the pile into his duffel. "Just got these out of the dryer," he groaned. "Your dog's a hot mess."

"He didn't destroy your . . . stuff," she pointed out.

Zim plopped in the black leather armchair, nearly cracking his knee on the coffee table. This was one tight living room. Laughing, he proclaimed, "Surge wants to knock you down a peg, take over as team leader."

Garrett gave him a fake death glare. "Better him than you, Zim!"

She snorted a laugh. Zim and Caldwell were alternately laughing and snorting.

Garrett laughed, held up a hand. "Time to reel it in, get back to it. I'll put these in the washer. Back in a mike." He jogged off to the super-tiny laundry room.

Caldwell, of course, sat on the couch—small enough to fit in the cramped living room—with his laptop and papers spread over the coffee table. He and Zim talked quietly over whatever was on the computer.

She took a step toward them to join that conversation.

Garrett returned. "Okay, so what do you have over there?" He took the other black leather armchair.

The straight-backed chair, the only thing in the room not either gentle green or soft yellow, was her option: upholstered with flowers. No wonder the men had taken the armchairs. Surge followed her over to it and sat on the floor beside her as though joining the convo. She stroked the thick hair around his neck. He sighed happily and downed.

Zim cleared his throat. "Caldwell hasn't been able to find the one container I noticed in the container yard."

"It's not on me," Caldwell objected. "Zim thinks he gave me three of the container ID numbers, so I quickly ran a search to identify the container. The last number is only partially readable. A three, a two, an eight, who knows? I'm still running searches, but it's a long shot."

Zim scowled, crossed one leg over the other. "Yeah, right, it's on me. Like I should've worked for a different angle to see the whole number. Like I could have once those Sachaai saw us."

"Let it go, Zim," Garrett warned.

The petty officer didn't take his eyes off Caldwell.

For crying out loud. What was with these men? "Nobody can find a container from a partial number," Delaney said. "I mean, right? Add to that the fact it's not crystal clear if Zim found the same containers Rashid and Tariq took to Hakim at the container yard. Or where the second one is."

They all turned and stared at her like she was a purple elephant.

She sat back in her chair. Truth was what it was.

Garrett rubbed his chin as he appraised Zim and Caldwell. "She's on point."

Whoa. She hadn't expected Garrett to back her up. She reached down to pet Surge, fast asleep, spread out like a bearskin rug.

"Besides," he continued, "we needed to focus on finding the container with chem tubes. Plain and simple."

Zim pursed his lips. "I need better footage of the container yard to find those containers, or even if we can find images or footage from last night to see if I can work angles to get the full number."

"Caldwell, I saw cameras onsite. What'd you find?"

"Sadly," Caldwell said, "they were fakes—designed as deterrents, but they weren't live that I could tell. Not even in that office. All I found was a traffic cam a mile away showing the cab turning toward that street. Blurry. Useless."

Garrett narrowed his eyes at Caldwell, his nose twitching like the man was a bad smell.

Caldwell and Garrett were both wound tighter than guitar strings about to snap. As a strained quiet stole into the room, Caldwell fidgeted with that piece of purple plastic while Garrett leaned back in his chair, hands laced behind his head, contemplating. Zim produced his smiley-face stress ball from his pocket and tossed it from hand to hand.

Delaney tilted her head. Maybe what she'd read as tension between Caldwell and Garrett was actually stress, since they'd lost the chems.

Garrett walked to the window to gaze out for a long moment, then finally turned around, making eye contact with each of them. "Sachaai wants to kill hundreds of thousands of Americans. Your mom, your cousin. Grandma, Grandpa."

Delaney thought of Dad. Heath. A Breed Apart.

"We need to chase down that stash of chemicals." He smacked his hands together. "Let's work the problem."

Before her eyes, they drew silent, intent. Hunters.

Elbow on the armrest, she tapped her chin.

Caldwell was still tossing that weird piece of plastic between his hands. Was it the same plastic he'd been messing with the other day? He pitched it into his ruck, sitting in the corner. "I haven't finished digging into that shoe factory computer motherboard. I'll get on that." He took his computer off the coffee table.

Zim reached for his camera on the side table next to him. "I'm going to look back through the pics I took at the container yard, see if I missed anything."

Garrett nodded.

Surge shifted onto his side and began snoring.

Wait. She and Surge were not bumps on a log. It was an easy solution. "Why don't we sneak into Container Action, let Surge search?"

They all stared at her. Garrett raised an eyebrow.

Sachaai were probably hanging out around the container yard. But she'd follow Walker. It was a good idea.

"We could do that," Zim said. "The safe house has some conduit with their leftover remodel supplies in the entryway. We'd easily get past that electric fence."

"Possibility," Garrett agreed.

Caldwell winced as he pounded away on his keyboard. "No cameras in the yard. I won't be able to monitor the perimeter."

"Hmmm. True. Okay. Let me think this through a minute." Garrett looked up as if reading words written on the ceiling.

Caldwell's computer pinged. His head bounced forward, his eyes bulging. "Wow. It wasn't in the factory's main shipping documents. I found it in a sub-sub-sub-document file."

"Found what?" Garrett asked.

Caldwell's eyes sparked. "The real shipping document with"—he cocked his head with a grin—"our full container number, as well as a number for a second."

Zim pumped his arm in the air. "Then where are they in the container yard?"

Scuffing his hands through his hair, Caldwell groaned.

"They're gone. On a plane to Jakarta, Indonesia, as of an hour ago."

"Indonesia?" Zim threw his hands in the air. "What the—"

"Why Indonesia?" Delaney asked.

"Likely waystation." Garrett jutted his jaw at Caldwell. "Where in the city?"

"Uh . . ." Caldwell scrolled through the document on his computer. "Not listed. But we can work with this—they're aboard a combi passenger-cargo flight, chartered by Sachaai." He tucked a pen in his mouth and typed rapidly, scrolled, clicked. "Okay, they filed a flight manifest. Shows nine passengers aboard."

"We need to get there."

Nodding, Caldwell spat the pen out and grabbed his SAT phone. "This likely means Sachaai terrorists are traveling with the product. I'll loop in Damocles and see if they can't get us a plane to Jakarta."

"Think that's a good idea? Aren't they tied up?"

Caldwell snatched up the pen, tapping it on the table as he hesitated with the call. "I do." He tapped the screen. "The combi has four other Southeast Asia stops before Jakarta. We can beat them there so you can get aboard before they unload. You're SEALs. Nine possible terrorists versus you, Zim, and the dog? Yeah, I think it's a good shot."

Garrett didn't look convinced.

Tension wound through the room, and Delaney tried to temper her rogue tendencies, but with Surge—

"Once they land," Caldwell said, "if we aren't there, those chemicals are in the wind."

Zim nodded "Hakim too."

"Exactly why we need to get aboard that plane," Delaney said, heart thumping as she spoke up. "We don't want those chem vials in Hakim's hands," she contended. "This is why we have Surge. He can read smells a thousand times faster than we can read container numbers. Ship, plane, container yard, wherever. But on the plane, this Mal will make short work of it. On the plane, the containers are contained."

Eyeing her, Garrett nodded. Rolled his shoulders forward and back. But it was those strong arms that had been around her during their self-defense training that she had to force her eyes away from.

"Okay. Another good point, Delaney."

Exultation spiraled through her, making her a bit giddy.

He nodded to Caldwell. "Make the call." Then he pulled out his phone. "Let me know when you have them—I'd like to talk to Chapel and the cargo building management. We're getting on that plane when it lands. Gear up. We're headed to Jakarta."

Zim grinned at Delaney. "Rogue, we should keep you around. I think you're a stabilizing force to the team."

Though Garrett hesitated, his gaze found hers. And he locked it for a long second. Simply nodded.

She stopped breathing a moment, captivated by the smile crinkles around his eyes—Garrett's light side.

His Adam's apple bounced as he broke the connection and focused on his phone. He walked down the hall.

Holy moly, what was happening here?

"All right then. Getting my bag ready." Zim gave her a fist bump on the way out of the room.

Laptop in hand, Caldwell headed into the kitchen and sat down at the table. His low voice rumbled as he talked with Damocles about needing a fast jet from Singapore to Jakarta.

A little bewildered and in awe of how things were changing, Delaney just sat in that straight-backed chair, absently petting Surge with her foot. She'd never been to Indonesia. Hakim, Tariq, Rashid . . . she knew what could lie ahead of them.

There was another thought she couldn't get rid of: two times in the same meeting, Garrett had listened to her.

She could be an asset to him. As long as her stupid heart didn't get in the way.

Because it was dangerously close to getting in the way.

9

JAKARTA, INDONESIA

"Still can't believe they slipped out from under our noses." Garrett slouched with his team in their green SUV, parked outside Cargo Building T63, which bore a red clay roof that matched the one on the Soekarno-Hatta/Jakarta International Airport and every building on the property.

Since there'd been no time to intercept the Combi 777, they'd done the next best thing and hired a faster jet to get them to the scheduled destination first.

Early morning sun shone strong, giving them a clear view into the wide-open building. And a view of the Combi 777 jet parked inside. Per intel's triple-check of the flight manifest, the nine passengers in the front third of the plane were simply shipping executives not affiliated with Sachaai. But the two Sachaai containers packed with chemicals were aboard.

Garrett adjusted his ball cap. They needed to access the cargo section and get those chems. Now. People began deboarding. "I count nine leaving the passenger section."

"Same," Zim answered, his toe tapping as he used his long-distance camera lens to stare at T63. "You'd think they'd take their eyes off their phones long enough to deplane."

Garrett lifted a shoulder. "The more they're focused on their phones, the less attention they'll pay us. But yeah, we need to get in there."

Behind them, Surge stuck his nose between them, woofed.

Garrett shifted in his seat and scratched Surge's ears. "You're ready to go, aren't you, boy? Me too." He wanted the passengers cleared out, preferably off the entire Soekarno-Hatta property.

Delaney leaned forward, her green jacket brushing his shoulder. "Who are the people that just deplaned?"

Garrett monitored the passengers heading into the cargo building. "Executives from one of the companies shipping things from Singapore to Jakarta. Now we wait for the pilots to leave too."

Zim indicated toward the plane. "And here they come. Crew is unloading the shipping containers into the building." He looked back at Delaney with a grin. "They won't be going in the wind."

They high-fived. "Like I said."

Conversing with one another, the pilots followed the rest of the group toward the long cargo building with large bay doors.

The building manager, no more than five feet tall, stood at the bottom of the stairs of the plane and waved at them. "Everyone's off. Unload crew is already finished with the combi. You've got about an hour before the plane will be moved to the runway."

Without another word, he caught up with the pilots on their way into the building.

"We're clear." Garrett flexed his hands, blew out a breath. He needed this mission to succeed so he could get his team out safely. With the chem vials.

"Stay here a minute," he reminded Delaney in the back.

Surge woofed.

Garrett chuckled. "Yeah, you too, you underwear-stealing mutt."

He and Zim shoved out of the SUV and bounded into the building to find neat stacks of shipping containers, some full size, some LD3 size that were sixty by thirty. He circled a finger in the air, and Zim nodded, jogged off to search the building.

Keying his comms, Garrett hoofed it in the opposite direction. "Eagle Three, what do you have?"

The spook was set up for oversight at their Jakarta safe house. "I've got eyes on the exterior of the building and access to local security feeds. Execs are outside on the other side of the building, waiting for rides. Pilots have already left."

That meeting he'd led last night had apparently focused the team. Garrett had to admit things were changing, maybe for the better. Caldwell wasn't even close to caustic at the moment, and Delaney was working *with* him, not against him. His mind ricocheted back to the safe house, that moment on the couch when their faces had been inches apart . . .

Shoot, he was starting to like her. That was dangerous.

Mind on the mission, Walker.

He and Zim met halfway around the cargo building. "Find anything?"

"Nothing."

"Me either." He signaled to the front, and they worked their way toward it as he called Caldwell. "Eagle Three, what's the twenty on the building manager?"

"Upstairs, in his office."

"Come on in, Rogue," Garrett comm'd. Maybe Surge's nose would find the chems.

He and Zim reached the front just as Delaney and Surge jogged into the building. When she gave him that little smile of hers, he couldn't help returning the smile. Then cleared his throat. "Ready?"

"We are."

She took the baggie of vials from her pocket. When she opened it, she smiled at Surge, whose tail started wagging. She let him sniff it, and the wag grew sharper, more focused. Ears alert. Body alert.

Garrett eased back from the entry to give Surge the room to work.

After returning the baggie to her pocket, Delaney nodded to the sleek black Malinois. "Seek-seek-seek!"

The fur-missile roved through the cargo building, sniffing the air, the containers as Delaney trailed him, doing her best not to influence his search with guiding.

But he didn't hit on anything.

Garrett stood in the doorway, hands on hips, surveying the room. Neither had he nor Zim. No boxes marked with the Sachaai S mark. What was going on?

On the long leash, Surge trotted past him, loped up the ramp into the belly of the cargo plane, sniffed in the air, reared on his hind legs, then lowered himself and plunked down on the ramp.

"Good job, Surge." Delaney looked up into the cave-like darkness of the entry to the plane, then back at Garrett. "I thought the cargo was all unloaded."

Having recognized the signal for a hit, he stalked up past them. "So did we."

Zim scratched his head. "Did they have time to drop a load somewhere else before landing here? Is the manifest wrong? Or maybe the building manager is?"

On his rear, Surge scooted closer to the plane's open bay door and gave a bark, his ears pointed straight into the plane.

Delaney tilted her head, frowned. "He's serious about this."

"Eagle Three, where are the passengers?"

"Uh, last one left about a minute ago."

"And the manager?"

"Still in his office."

"Copy that." He pivoted to the working dog team and nodded to Delaney. "Take him in."

"C'mon, boy. Seek!" she said and hurried up the rest of the ramp.

Surge plowed into the plane.

With Zim on his six, Garrett followed them.

The Mal stopped about a third of the way in, sniffing the air, looking around, ears pricked. But didn't zero in on anything.

But the manager had lied. Maybe a dozen sixty-by-thirty containers remained aboard, scattered like a kid's block collection. The hairs on Garrett's neck stood on end.

Surge suddenly took off toward the back, pulling Delaney, but screeched to a stop, circled back. He sniffed hard and long, going on his hind legs again as he traced the upper portion of the container, then back down. Alerting on it, he sat and stared at the large pot.

Delaney glanced at Garrett. "He's hitting on that container marked as Box United Corp."

"That's a well-established company," Garrett answered, watching Delaney, who was monitoring her dog.

Zim pulled out his camera to take pictures. "It is." He clicked more pictures, then tapped the container. "Sachaai S logo in the corner."

Garrett eyed the curvy S with an extra curve shooting out of both the top and bottom of the S. "Just like the tats on those thugs in the shoe factory." He scanned the container again. "This is definitely the jackpot."

"Same there." Zim pointed at the container beside it.

"Talk about a mother lode." Garrett gave a low whistle. "Let's verify what's inside." No way was he going to notify the spook until they had eyes on the vials themselves. "Cut the lock."

Zim reached to the top of the LD3. Grabbing the rim, he swung his legs up and came to a stand.

Surge whined, his gaze on the back of the plane. But he whipped his attention back to the container. His muscles quivered as he again glanced to the back.

Garrett took a couple steps to see what had Surge's interest. Nothing but metal.

Behind him, Delaney yelped. Surge lunged, barked, echoing through the hold.

Garrett spun in time to see Surge leap at a man screaming Urdu, his S-tattooed arm hooked around Delaney's neck.

Weapon snapped up, Garrett aimed it at the Pakistani Sachaai. "Let her go!"

The Mal used every bit of his nearly two hundred pounds of bite pressure on the man's arm.

With a feral scream, the man released Delaney, pitching her forward.

She fell, and keeping his weapon trained on the guy, Garrett hustled toward her.

The Pakistani tried to shake Surge from his arm, but Surge's jaw was clamped on like an alligator seizing prey.

Delaney caught the long lead and scrambled back to her feet. She eyed Garrett with his weapon, then drew down on the lead until she had the collar in hand. She drew straight up. "Surge, out."

Screaming, the man now had tears running down his face.

"Out!" Delaney yelled.

With a keening, excited whimper, Surge unhooked his jaws, using his paws as he gave one last tug. Came free.

Delaney hauled him clear of her attacker. He quivered, straining to get at the Pakistani. She dragged him behind the big metal box.

That man wasn't leaving the plane. Garrett aimed and fired, neutralizing him. He shifted—

A fist crashed against his face even as force knocked his weapon from his hand.

Garrett staggered back with a bloody nose, straining to hear where his Sig went, but the slugger—a second Pakistani— lunged at him.

Not today. He slid in with a right hook. Knocked the guy backward, the impact ricocheting through his fist. He drove his heel into Two's chest. The man hit the side of the plane. Garrett rolled to his shoulders and arched to his feet.

Two punched at him again, but Garrett ducked. He grabbed Two's shoulders and slammed him up against a shipping container.

Two swung up between Garrett's arms, forcing them apart.

Garrett lost balance, grunted as he hit the ground. Hooked his legs around Two's, flipped himself on top, bashed his fist into the Pakistani's cheek.

The man's head slammed into the ground.

Garrett clouted him again.

Two slumped, unconscious.

Straightening, Garrett scanned for more unfriendlies, relieved Delaney and Surge had hidden. He scrambled for his weapon, searching the deck of the cargo plane. Shadows had swallowed it. On his feet, he moved toward the first, now dead, attacker. Felt more than saw movement.

A black blur streaked from behind the LD3 in front of Garrett. Surge charged toward him. He braced himself . . . but the black fur-missile sprinted past. Leaped at Pakistani Three—who'd been headed for Garrett!

Surge's jaw sank into Three's arm, eliciting a feral scream. Three shook his arm hard, slamming the black maligator into the nearest container. Surge fell but jumped back up, chasing the man as he ran for the access ramp. Garrett joined the chase.

Delaney stepped out. "Surge, out! Heel!"

The Mal skidded to a stop on the loading ramp. As Three bolted down the ramp just like One had, Surge returned to her side, blood at the edges of his jowls.

Delaney caught his lead and drew him around. Pointed past Garrett to the others. "Surge, attack! Get 'em!"

Surge hurtled past them, down the hold.

What was Surge after? And *where* was his gun? Garrett spun and couldn't believe his eyes. Atop one of the containers, with barely enough clearance to stand, Zim was fighting off three more Pakistanis. How'd they get up there?

Garrett sprinted after the Mal, who sailed through the air and landed atop the container. Bounded and latched onto the nearest Pakistani, shook him like a rat. Screams filled the hold.

The Pakistani wrestling Zim was startled by his buddy's agonized howls, giving Zim an opening. The wiry guy threw a hard right into the terrorist's jaw. The man stumbled backward and fell off the container.

He lay there in obvious pain, his ankle at an awkward angle. Broken.

Not willing to give the guy time to get up, Garrett landed on him. Yanked out a zip tie and restrained him even as a second Pakistani thudded to the deck next to him, Zim twisting in midair so the terrorist cushioned his fall.

"Dropping like flies," Garrett muttered, sliding in to help secure the second.

With a grunt, Zim flew upward. Collided with the third, who had high-ground advantage this time and pitched the tech nerd backward. He thudded to the ground. "Augh!" Grimacing, he grabbed his left wrist even as Surge barreled into Third. The two careened off the container.

Garrett tossed the flex tie to Zim, who caught it with his right hand and flex-cuffed the Pakistani with one hand. He reached up to the rim of the container, swung himself onto the LD3.

Surge was relentless, snarling and using that powerful Malinois neck to do serious damage to the fourth terrorist, who shrieked and writhed on the ground, his arm tearing to shreds.

"Surge, out!" Delaney ordered from below.

The intense force multiplier complied. Panting, he sat, laser-focused on the Pakistani.

Garrett grabbed Four's arms and flex-cuffed him. He sucked in a breath through his teeth as he saw the man's ink—that S tattoo. Sachaai. "Eagle Three, we have four unfriendlies in need of escort." His gaze then hit on a dark spot—his weapon! It was somehow wedged beneath one of the container corners. He retrieved his Sig, checked the chamber, and holstered it.

"Already on it, Bear. Local assets en route to retrieve them."

Garrett took Four by the elbow, forced him to the edge of the container. "Let yourself down," he ordered.

Shredded Arm sneered at him. With a grunt, he sat at the edge of the LD3 container, and Garrett lowered him down.

One-handed, Zim pushed him into a sit against the hull, next to his buddy.

Garrett jumped down, walked over to Delaney. He pulled her into a hug. "You did good," he whispered in her ear, then stepped back.

Zim's jaw hung open. Oops. Then he grinned, deliberately turned and started taking pics of the Pakistanis.

Garrett awkwardly put his hands on Delaney's shoulders and looked her over head to toe. "You're okay. Right?"

Tilting her head, she looked deep in his eyes, bit her bottom lip. Nodded.

Surge jumped down from the LD3 like a superhero—which he was—and stood next to Delaney, glaring at the two Pakistanis closest to them.

Garrett returned Delaney's nod and walked over to the man he'd just zip-tied. He grabbed the collar of his shirt. "What's going on here, Sachaai?" he demanded.

The guy spat onto the deck.

Garrett pressed his leg onto the guy's legs and pulled out another zip tie, secured his ankles.

Zim lifted the unconscious man's wrist as he flex-tied him.

Shaking his head, Garrett eyed the S tattoos all around. "Pics of their tatts, Zim."

"You got it. But first, here's Broken Ankle's phone. Guy's face got me into it." He handed it over, then reached for his camera and began to snap photos. "The last text convo was four minutes ago. With Hakim."

Garrett read the message.

HAKIM

Americans coming. Don't let them live. On
my way.

This team was ready for Hakim.

Except Zim's wrist was clearly dicey. The extent of Delaney's training was a couple short self-defense sessions with him. He looked at his watch. They couldn't secure two LD3s to the semi, much less figure out the semi, in one minute.

"Enough photos. Let's cut out of here."

They raced to the nose of the plane, down the stairs.

Of course, Surge beat them to the SUV. Delaney jumped in the back with him and shut the door.

Outside the SUV, Garrett paused. "Zim?"

Zim slid his camera back into the pocket of his tactical pants. "Yes, Boss?"

Once the guy looked up, Garrett held his gaze, pointed at the wrist he was rubbing. "I'm driving."

A defeated Zim huffed and tossed him the keys, then climbed in.

Behind the wheel, Garrett was more than ready to get out of here. He nailed the gas, tires squealing as they pulled onto the street.

Caldwell keyed the comms, sounding breathless. "Bear, that building manager? Just spotted the same Sachaai S tattoo as those guards in the shoe factory."

"That explains everything. What a bunch of—" Garrett bit back a curse, slammed the heel of his hand against the dash. "That building manager straight up lied to my face when he told me the unload crew was finished with the plane!"

Sometimes a leader failed. Sometimes a leader just plain got lied to.

Sometimes full intel—like Sachaai hiding on the plane, like cargo still on the plane—got held back from a leader.

The spook was good at that.

Another slam of his hand against the dash. *Can't believe You did this to me, God!*

His breath stopped for a long moment.

He'd just yelled at God.

Again. *Sorry, God.*

"Bear, what happened in the cargo plane?" the spook asked, snagging his attention back to the mission.

All his anger wasn't at his dad. It was at the intel-hoarding spook. And at God.

He didn't have time to deal with it right now.

"Not now. En route to you. Ten mikes out."

10

JAKARTA, INDONESIA

TWO SIXTY-BY-THIRTY CONTAINERS FILLED WITH CHEMICALS! Garrett's head ached just thinking about the scope this mission had taken. He had to figure it out.

The team sat silent in the SUV on the way to the Jakarta safe house, everyone caught in their thoughts after the cargo plane fight.

He had fought off a Pakistani. With Surge.

Zim had faced three Pakistanis at once. With Surge, thanks to Delaney.

That woman had surprised him. She was a warrior.

His whole team had absolutely shown what they were made of.

And while he still wouldn't let himself trust Caldwell after Samwise's death, the man had done okay. Except why had it taken him so long to identify the manager as connected to the Sachaai? Would've been a nice heads-up to know information from the manager couldn't be trusted.

He ran his hands through his hair and decided to deal with

that later. Except he did know tech was not instantaneous. And to be honest, it was that Sachaai man with his arms around Delaney's neck that his brain wouldn't let go of.

When Garrett had finally gotten Delaney free, he'd pulled her into his arms, relieved she was safe. And she'd tilted her head at him, leaning into the embrace. He couldn't let go of that either.

But he needed to in order to remain mission focused.

Zim reached from the passenger seat and clapped Garrett's shoulder. "Sometimes success is getting the heck out of there."

Zim was no Samwise. But he was solid.

"Adjust the plan," Garrett said, "and get back on mission."

"That's it, Boss. That's it."

He eyed Rogue in the rearview mirror. "Good job, Delaney."

Surge nudged his elbow, as if saying not to forget about him. He chuckled. "You too, you mutt."

Delaney chuckled. "You know better than to use that word about Surge."

"Excuse me, Surge L724."

She laughed.

He pulled onto the street of the safe house, a suburban neighborhood packed tight with houses, and full of weeping fig trees and kids riding bikes. Garrett thought through what he would need to do when they got to their ironwood-and-bamboo house. First, deal with Caldwell. Second, debrief the team. Third, adjust the plan.

"You sure this is the right place?" Zim joked. "We hardly saw it when we dropped off our stuff earlier this morning, left Caldwell and his tech."

Guiding the SUV along the bustling nightlife of Core, Garrett angled into the private underground parking garage of the safe house.

"At least we know how those Pakistanis got the drop on us since Caldwell saw the manager's Sachaai tattoo," Zim said.

Garrett sneered. "Would've been nice to know before." He clicked his tongue. "Not sure how he missed that." He swung the SUV into a spot and parked. After gathering his gear from the back, he stalked into the house. He'd lost it with Caldwell once. He wouldn't do it again, but . . . "Caldwell!" he shouted as he hit the living room painted in shades of gray.

Zim and Delaney froze in the entryway.

Caldwell came down the hall with his laptop. "Hey, Bear. What happened—"

He stepped up to Caldwell, gestured into the kitchen. "We need to talk."

Caldwell didn't move, eyeing him, then the team.

Garrett bet the vein in his neck was visibly throbbing. *Just like Dad's.* He needed to deal with his anger at Dad and God. But Caldwell did deserve a dressing-down for bad intel again. The team had barely gotten out of there.

His eyes pinned Caldwell like a bug in a science project. "There were more than nine passengers."

Caldwell shrugged. "Intel said nine. Cargo company's manifest too."

Garrett took another step closer to Caldwell. "I don't believe you."

"That's how many people came off the plane."

"Yeah, but you didn't tell us about the six terrorists in the cargo hold or that the manager was Sachaai."

"What?" Caldwell frowned, his eyes whipping to Delaney and Zim, back to the boss. "Everyone okay?"

"We made it," Garrett bit out. "How'd you miss that tattoo?"

Caldwell faltered, frowning. "I was working a lot of intel streaming in. I barely had time to set up and hack into the top-grade building security before your meeting. Guy wore long sleeves, and it was impossible to see until this one shot on the feed." Pinching his mouth closed, Caldwell set his laptop on the smooth gray wood dining table. "Take a look."

Garrett joined him on the black benches at the table, Zim next to him.

Caldwell pulled up a video with the Quest Cargo Corp logo,

hit play. On the screen, the five-foot manager walked in, stepped up to the computer, stretched out his arms, reached for the keyboard. Caldwell hit pause, poked his finger at the tattoo peeking out from under the manager's long sleeve. He thrust his finger at the time stamp.

Garrett expelled a long breath, rolled his shoulders. "Sorry."

"You love to pin everything on me, don't you, Bear?" Caldwell hissed.

"That's because you're so often to blame." He looked down and saw his fists tight with white knuckles. No. He was not going to turn into his father. He forced open his hands. "We need to go through the inventory from the containers."

"That's what I was working on." Caldwell grabbed his laptop, stomped over to the couch, and dove into the internet.

Garrett dropped next to him into the armchair with gray-and-black triangle fabric.

Zim came over and took the matching one, and Surge jumped up into the last chair like he was part of the meeting. Garrett chuckled. Couldn't help it.

Delaney walked in from the kitchen and stopped in front of Surge. She pointed to the floor. "Excuse me, young man."

Surge jumped off, and she sat down. "How's your wrist, Zim?"

He flexed his hand and rotated it. "Stiff, but the swelling's gone down."

"You could take ibuprofen or aspirin. Maybe an icepack." She gave a sheepish shrug. "That's what they've done for some dogs at the ranch."

"You saying I'm a dog?" Zim teased.

"Well . . ." she teased back. "I'll see if there's something we can use as an icepack in the freezer." When she stood, Delaney noticed Garrett eyeing them.

Smirking, he looked from Zim to her. "You two done?"

"You jealous she's paying attention to me now, Boss?"

Delaney nearly laughed, but the glower from Garrett silenced them both, and she headed into the kitchen.

"Okay," Caldwell said and cleared his throat. "Since I only had overwatch, brief me on what you saw so I can—"

"We had some leftover sandwiches." Delaney put a tray of sandwiches—turkey, of course—in the middle of the coffee table with a bag of chips.

As they dug into the sandwiches—they hadn't had breakfast, after all—they gave Caldwell a rundown of the incident at the airport.

Caldwell tossed aside his sandwich and grunted. Looked at the SAT. "Somebody must have told Sachaai you were coming."

"Yeah," Garrett bit out. "The building manager."

Bouncing his head, Caldwell tightened his jaw. "Obviously. But who told him?" He stared at his laptop screen, squinting as he worked. "I'm looking for the manager's connection to Sachaai. I wonder . . ." He did a few more clicks and scrolls, then a smirk slid onto his face. "And here we go—his cousin is Tariq."

Zim scowled. "For real? The chemist?"

Garrett shook his head slowly, absorbing. "What about the LD3 containers?"

"No joy yet. My search program is looking in the container yard for the ID numbers you confirmed, but they've apparently done something to hide the LD3s on the official paperwork."

Delaney groaned. "That's going to take a while."

Garrett stuffed the last of his sandwich in his mouth. She was right, considering the stacks of hundreds and hundreds of multicolored containers he'd seen while on the plane into Jakarta. Reminded him of his nephew's Lego collection. "We'll head back to the yard tonight, unless intel comes in to change that plan. Regardless, we know that Hakim, Rashid, and Tariq are in Jakarta. We'll leave Delaney and Surge here."

Her hand hung in the air above the bag of chips. She dropped it to her lap, her face like ice. "I'm not a member of the team—again?"

"Of course you are. But you're untrained. Sachaai is like playing with fire." Why wouldn't she understand that?

Her eyes flashed. "I know I'm not an operative. Surge is. Why waste precious search time? You need his nose. After everything the past two days, I would think that you'd know you could trust me."

"Trust you? To what, run after a terrorist?"

"Yeah, without my 'running away'"—she used her fingers to create air quotes—"we wouldn't know where he is. But now we do, and he's here—"

"And his goons nearly got you killed today! And I need you!"

The room fell silent, and Garrett found himself on his feet, Delaney staring at him. He roughed his hand through his hair. He hadn't faced an attack since Djibouti. Didn't want to see his team hurt. His eyes snapped up to Delaney. He lowered his voice. "I mean the team needs you. Surge—they need Surge. Which means you."

Caldwell coughed on a handful of chips, and Zim suddenly studied the ceiling.

His eyes bored into those two men. "You two look into the parents of Tariq and his building-manager cousin. Might be something there that will clue us in to Sachaai's purpose for the chems, give us an idea where they are headed."

Zim chuckled and moved his chair closer to Caldwell, who began pecking at the laptop.

Garrett jerked his head toward Delaney's backpack. "Pick yourself a room." He looked at his watch. "For me, it's almost time for a call from Chapel."

Delaney grabbed her pack and headed down the hall with Surge. Their room choice wasn't a debate at all. She chose the room with a creamy, barefoot-worthy carpet and a window that overlooked a grassy area enclosed by a chain-link fence. She guessed you could call it a yard, even if it was barely bigger than a fake grass dog potty station.

She dumped her pack next to the bed, sat down, and Surge jumped up to gaze out the window. She ran her hands over him, looking for any damage from the fight. Twice.

She had to be sure. She started back at Surge's head.

Surge shifted and licked her face, his eyes saying, "Stop running your hands all over me."

He was right. He was fine and didn't need a fourth head-to-tail—to foot—check. "Sorry, Buddy." She chucked his chin, and he rested his head on her lap. She roughed his hair.

She could still feel that Sachaai's arms around her neck. Surge had saved her.

Her sudden deep breath surprised her. She hadn't realized how tightly she'd been holding her breath. He sat up and nuzzled her ear.

While she'd seen Surge in training, experiencing him in real action had jolted her.

He'd attacked the other Sachaai before the guy'd even gotten to Walker.

He stinking leapt onto the top of the stinking sixty-four-inch LD3 container to fight three stinking terrorists beside Zim.

This Malinois was not a comfort pet. But the shaking in her hands was dying down, buried in his thick neck fur.

He twisted and looked out the window, then woofed in her face.

She laughed. "You want to go out?"

Another woof.

She grabbed his KONG tug. "Let's go."

His toenails clicked behind her through the hallway. Then they stopped. Where'd Surge go? She went back down the hallway a bit.

There he was, in the living room under Caldwell's chair, sniffing intently at his ruck.

Caldwell was intent on his computer work and didn't even notice Surge.

She patted her leg so the Mal would come to her instead of unzipping and emptying the ruck.

His gleaming brown eyes were so focused on it that she had to pat her leg again. He scooted backward out from under the chair. Slowly. She gave a low whistle to get his eyes on her, and he finally came.

Neither of the men noticed.

"With me, Surge," she whispered, and they jogged down the hallway to the kitchen and out to the tiny backyard accessorized with a bamboo sofa.

Outside, the sun high in the sky gave the Jakarta buildings a gleam, God the creator showcasing himself to the people who lived in this suburban Jakarta neighborhood. The hum of traffic was a sound that felt like home. The grassy area—like the other yards in the neighborhood—was well manicured, perfectly cut.

And it was stinky. Her nose wrinkled—chemicals and trash and mold all together. She looked across the street. There was the source of the stench—the river. The houses on the other side of the street were built right up to the serpentine brown river. There was just enough space between the houses that she could catch a glimpse of a multicolored walking bridge.

Delaney gazed at the houses around them. Some kids were playing out in their tiny yard. A couple walked down the street, carrying groceries. A crew painted the house across the street.

She didn't have a choice about this stinky yard. Surge needed time outside. But this was only for a few days. She didn't live here like the neighbors did. What would that even be like?

Done with his business, Surge trotted over and dropped the rope KONG at her feet. She didn't want to accidentally send a black Mal streaking into the river or onto a neighbor's lawn, so tug it was today. But her mind was only half on the game.

"Hey, Surge," she said.

He stopped and looked up at her, his ears flicking, listening as he held the KONG end of the tug in his mouth.

"You heard Garrett. Those goons who almost killed me scared him. I'm just a team member cause he needs you?" Scared? Not what she knew of Garrett. She sucked in a deep breath. "Surge, was he being personal?"

Surge gave a huff, then jerked the KONG back and forth so hard it nearly wrenched her shoulder. She laughed and pulled back but let him have it after a minute. The river's heavy stink was starting her in on a headache. She rolled her shoulders. If she ignored it, it wouldn't come.

Garrett came up behind them. "That dog pull your arm out of its socket?"

Had he heard her talking to Surge? She chose to wave like he'd just arrived. "Fortunately, he never has."

He laughed. "Sure, sure. This is a Mal."

Taking advantage of her distraction, Surge pulled the end of the KONG tug out of her hand and dropped it at Garrett's feet. The traitor.

Garrett scooped it up and tugged harder with Surge than she ever could. Surge practically had a giant grin on his face.

Delaney realized it wasn't the game that had her attention— she was staring at the bulge of Garrett's arms. Her eyes shifted to his hands that had been on her shoulders after that attack on the combi plane. "You don't have to stay out here in this river stink. Surge needs to play, but we'll come in in a bit."

Garrett let go of the KONG, which led Surge to parading around the yard with it. She warmed under the intensity of Garrett's bright amber eyes. The full attention of this man rocked her to her core, just like it had after the fight in the plane.

"Delaney, I know we debriefed while we ate those sandwiches, but I wanted to check how you're doing after the incident at the airport."

"Just a bit of a headache, that's all."

He pointed at her as she massaged the back of her neck. "Tell me."

"This stinky river is giving me a headache."

He crossed his arms.

What was she, a wuss? "The river is encouraging a headache, that's all. Yeah, I wanted you to see my capability on this mission. It's been a nice chance to prove myself—"

He pushed himself toward her, looked in her face. "I didn't want you in any fighting on this mission, but you were. You literally jumped out of hiding this morning! Delaney, you're not a maverick. You're a part of this team. Trustworthy. You did prove yourself."

She shifted from foot to foot. "I didn't think I—"

"You did!" Then his voice softened. "You don't see that?"

Words wanted to come, but they wouldn't.

"Delaney, it's my job to know my team."

She didn't want to talk about her failings. Except it was Garrett who asked it of her. She'd learned to trust him. She took a steeling breath. "One day after school, I went into our family store. A man was holding a gun on Dad. The guy reeked of this horrible cologne. Worse than this river, even." She dropped her hands from the back of her neck. "Anyway, I hid in the next aisle, behind the dog food. The jerk shot Dad and ran out with a bunch of money. Dad lost his leg. And our business."

"That's why the new prosthetic."

"Yeah." She tapped her foot on the concrete. "I should've distracted that robber. Shoved the endcap on him. Run to call the police." Her voice faded to a whisper. "Anything other than freeze in a store aisle when Dad was in danger. I just hate that my dad might see me as incompetent."

His touch against her shoulder was warm, gentle. "How old were you?"

"Eight."

"You were a little girl!"

She bit her lip. "But I froze and my dad got hurt."

"Delaney, by hiding, you probably saved his life, your own life. That wasn't incompetence."

She stared at him like he was nuts.

Chuckling, he held up his hands. "Do you and your dad get along?"

She smiled. "We've always been close. He keeps me grounded."

"Does your dad think you're incapable or incompetent—or do you?"

That bookshelf full of dog training books Dad had bought for her when she took the ABA job . . . Had he been worried about her ability? Or had he been showing support? That thought took her breath, and she could barely whisper it. She slouched against the wall next to Garrett. "You're right. Dad doesn't think I'm incapable. I disappointed God."

"Huh. So Christ didn't put MWDs in your DNA? Make you ready for this mission? For such a time as this?"

She huffed a laugh, elbowed him. "I know, I know. But it's also true I go rogue."

"You go rogue to test whether He believes in you?"

Her eyes blinked fast. "My maverick stuff in high school *did* lead me to A Breed Apart. And yeah, I wouldn't be here if He didn't believe in me. Maybe? I'm going to have to think about that."

She tipped back her head, closed her eyes. Silence grew between them. Peace.

"I still want to get Dad a new prosthetic," she said after a couple minutes. "Not to prove myself, though. Because I love him."

Garrett nodded. "It's cool that you get along. I wish my dad was like yours. Mine is, let's say, full of rage."

She winced. "I'm sorry."

"When I was ten, I got detention because of a fight with the bullies hurting my brother. I got home late, so my chores weren't done when Dad got home."

"Rage."

He held up his left arm. "Broken arm that time. Told the doc I fell down the stairs." He pinched his lips together. "I won't be like him."

Her heart broke. But you didn't hug a SEAL, right? She gently laid her hand on his left arm—couldn't help it.

He flinched but didn't move away.

Beneath her hand, she felt his muscles relax. But her blood sped up.

Delaney let go and pushed her hair behind her ear. "You like to always be in control. Like your dad wasn't."

He turned his head, looking through the neighborhood. "Sort of. I learned to be in control to avoid making Dad angry." His voice dropped so low she could barely hear him. "But I can't always maintain it."

She swallowed hard. Garrett lumped his dad and God into the same category. No wonder he walked through life on eggshells. He was sure he'd be punished and unloved if he ever messed up. "God doesn't expect you to be perfect, Garrett."

His lips set in a hard line.

"Garrett, I saw you fight in the combi plane. I saw you undercover, procuring the chem vials. Thanks to you and Heath." She whooshed out a breath. "Thanks to God, I see your leadership of this team every day. Yeah, you're called Bear. But you are fiercely protective, not a bear on a rampage. Nothing like what you said about your dad."

He didn't respond, just shoved his hands into the pockets of his tactical pants.

This man was frustrating. She gazed out at the multicolor bridge across the stinky brown river, then looked back in his face. "You talked about Christ and my DNA. I-I thought you believed."

He shrugged. "I do."

A motorcycle throttled past the house, making some dog a couple houses down bark.

"Okay then," she said. "Just remember, you're not like your dad. And God is nothing like your dad either."

Garrett gave her a brief nod. A leisurely breeze rustled her hair, and clouds lazed across the sky. He suddenly pushed away from the wall, turned to her. "I'm not like Dad?"

Her throat thickened, and she couldn't answer. She nodded, their eyes locking as they had on the couch.

His voice was a husky whisper. "Thank you." He stepped toward her.

She bit her lip. He was going to kiss her. Like he was a magnet, she stepped closer to him.

"Bear!" Caldwell and Zim stormed out the door.

He and Delaney backpedaled fast as the men appeared in the doorway.

Garrett's Adam's apple bounced. He turned toward them, and they all returned to the living room. "What's up?"

Zim's eyes sparked. "New intel! The building manager's parents are joint owners of the Container Port of Indonesia. The containers are there—Warehouse 79B. Restricted access."

"It narrows the search down to about two hundred containers," Caldwell said.

Raking a hand through his hair, Garrett nodded. "Not bad." His gaze hit Delaney's. "Especially with an MWD."

That warmed Delaney again, her thoughts lingering heavily on the near-kiss the guys had interrupted. But she appreciated this more—being included.

"I'll mess with 79B security cameras so they can't see you," Caldwell said. "Also, the container port hires roaming security guards."

Garrett's lips flattened as he scrutinized Caldwell. He dipped his head. "All right. We roll out in ten minutes. All black."

Zim and Caldwell sped off to get gear packed and loop in Damocles.

But Garrett hung back . . . and Delaney did too, busying herself with Surge, who was at his water bowl. She finally braved Garrett's gaze and felt the intensity of his eyes down to her toes.

The lines around his eyes softened. "Promise not to get killed."

"Back at you."

11

CONTAINER PORT OF INDONESIA

DELANEY WOULDN'T SAY A WORD, BUT THE NEW BLISTER WAS KILLING her. It seemed like they'd stolen from stack to stack of containers for miles in the dark nighttime maze of the container port to get to the right warehouse.

Garrett lifted a fist, and she and Zim stopped behind him. Following his lead, they backed up against a container, crouching to melt into its shadow cast by the light pole. She drew Surge to herself, but he remained on alert, head on a swivel.

A tactical mission like this was way beyond a search exercise.

Two of the roaming guards Caldwell had warned them about walked past. The snub-nosed one flashed his light as he chatted up his taller, skinnier counterpart.

Garrett signaled her and Zim to stay in the shadows of the container stack, and he sneaked off after the guards. Gentle ocean waves brought fresh salt air into her nose. And the sound of seagulls.

"What's he doing?" she whispered to Zim.

He shrugged. "Dunno."

Garrett returned a couple minutes later, and they followed him shadow to shadow, taking the next available turn to slip down the passage parallel to the one the guards were taking.

The heavy crunch of the guards' footsteps on the next aisle sent shivers down her spine. They were close—as close as the shooter in Dad's store had been from her hiding place in the dog food aisle.

These guards also had guns, also were ready to shoot. Would they shoot Garrett? Surge? Sweat beaded on her neck.

She'd never thought that simply telling Garrett about the shooting would bring up the memories like this.

She drew in a silent breath.

Thing was, issues or not, Garrett was right. Christ had put dog skills in her DNA, brought her here. A drop of sweat on her neck slid all the way down her spine.

Well, today, she wouldn't freeze. *Please, God.* She rubbed Surge's ear, focused her attention on Garrett.

He came to a sudden stop under a light pole, fist up, and she nearly smacked into him. Shifting back, she realized they were in front of a huge metal shed labeled "Warehouse 79B" and "Restricted Access" in English and Indonesian. The door had an electronic keypad. How were they going to get in?

Garrett pulled a keycard with a picture of the snub-nosed guard out of his pocket. No wonder he'd gone after the guards. He swung open the warehouse door, and they entered the dark space. He waited as Zim pulled the door closed behind them. "Eagle Three," he comm'd, "we are in Warehouse 79B. You take care of the cams?"

"I have their system looping nothing but container stacks, as planned," Caldwell reported back. "You're good to go. Looking like there's a couple hundred containers in there with you."

"Copy that." Garrett powered on his SureFire and let its beam trace the interior. With Zim's light added, the space was well lit, revealing that they stood in the middle of a wide aisle. On either side, rows of various-sized containers, including LD3s, filled the cavernous space held up by metal support beams. Forklifts hunched in the corner to their left.

Delaney let Surge do his thing, sniffing around to feel comfortable in here.

"Delaney, you and Surge ready to find the chems?" Garrett's low voice echoed off the high ceiling.

She nodded and turned to her sleek, powerful boy. "Time to work, buddy."

Surge started wagging his tail, but it slowed to a stop as he thrust his snout in the air. He angled toward a vertical support beam, trailing that knowing nose up and down it. Then he sat, ears pricked on a small piece of fabric caught on a nail sticking out of a support column.

"Um . . . good boy," Delaney said, scratching his ear. She was confident in Surge's nose, but that wasn't an LD3 container.

"What on earth?" Zim pulled it off the nail.

Surge barked.

The support beam behind them pinged, and Zim slammed into her, knocked her and Surge to the ground, pinning her under his weight. Heart in her throat, Delaney shoved aside the squall of panic, gripped Surge's lead tight but didn't dare move.

A *pop-pop* erupted from Garrett's direction, and a thud came about halfway down the middle aisle.

Still pinned, Delaney shifted her eyes down the concrete aisle to . . . a body.

"Stay to the side with Surge," Zim hissed. He rose, gun at the ready.

Weapon trained on the body, Garrett advanced, signaled left to Zim, and he went right.

Delaney signaled Surge to come and crawled behind the container. Surge crawled in next to her. She shoved herself to a sit, her hand over her mouth as she gasped for air. Surge stood in front of her, his muscles rippling as he leaned forward, watching for bad guys. She might not be trained, but he was.

"Clear," called Zim.

"Clear." Garrett—in one piece, *Thank You, God*—banked around a corner and motioned her toward him. Even as she emerged and nodded, he keyed his comms. "Three, how'd you miss active unfriendlies in here?"

No answer in the comms.

Delaney took one last deep breath. Emotions travel down lead, and she did not need to set Surge off with her newbie reactions. She and Surge joined the men.

Garrett looked her up and down, his forehead creasing. "You okay?"

She drew in a shaky breath and released it, appreciating his raw intensity, that he was on her side. She'd never want to be on the receiving end of that. "All good. You?"

His face smoothed. "Obviously fine, Rogue." He jerked his thumb toward the body. "That fabric Surge hit on? It's from his shirt."

"Let me guess, he had a Sachaai tattoo," she said.

Garrett nodded. "Probably handled the chem vials."

Zim held up a phone. "Thanks for the use of your dead face, Mr. Bukhari." He rubbed his nose. "Check out this last text on his phone. Half hour ago. From Hakim."

HAKIM

Americans headed to container yard. Kill them.

Garrett roughed his hand through his hair. "They knew . . ." His shoulders drew back. "Like they did with the cargo plane." He closed his eyes for a long moment, then he gazed at each of them in turn. "Let's find those chemicals before Hakim realizes his goon didn't make it and sends more goons."

"Or shows up himself." Zim shoved his gun in his holster and the phone in his tac pants pocket. "Lead us to it, Surge."

Delaney pulled out the baggie of tubes and extended it to him. "Check."

The Mal sniffed and his eyes shimmered with anticipation.

She loved his constant readiness when his nose work was needed. "Surge, seek!"

The maligator swiftly fell into working the scent cone, his pace fast, determined. He raced down the aisle, straining at the end of the long lead. Then he twisted to the left, another left. He skidded to a stop, hauling long draughts as his ears pricked on an LD3 container, then the one next to it. Both had the Sachaai S. He sat between the two, staring as if he had Superman's laser vision and could see the stash inside.

"Good boy," Delaney exclaimed, drawing him to the side for Garrett and Zim to step in and do their thing. "Can you imagine how long we would've had to search for these without this nose?"

"No kidding." Zim grinned.

Garrett slid back the two sliding bolts on the container door and opened the hatch.

Empty.

Surge jumped in, his ears pointing everywhere, but then he downed in the middle of the container.

"Is he overwhelmed?" Garrett asked.

"Overwhelmed by *what*?" she asked, still watching Surge, confused about his behavior since the container was empty and there wasn't a blaring or annoying sound. Yes, Surge had alerted in the center of the container. His nose kept sniffing the air, but he wasn't confused or panting a thousand miles an hour—he was relaxed. Chill. "This isn't overwhelm."

A flicker spirited through Garrett's face, as if he wasn't sure. Or maybe he was just as confused as Delaney.

She shifted her gaze to Zim. "You have that FTIR with you?" If he could check for Sachaai lipid readings to prove the chem vials had been here . . .

"I do." He set down his ruck, pulled out the FTIR, and stepped into the container as he quickly scanned all over the walls and the floor.

Metallic clanks sounded from outside, and Delaney guessed

that was Garrett inspecting the other Sachaai S container. His low curse told her it was empty too.

"Like we thought," he snarled. "Someone knew we were coming."

It was an entire waste of time and assets.

"Eagle Three, exiting Building 1." Garrett swiveled his head, watching for the roaming guards as they left the metal warehouse building. He could hear Surge panting, feel the heat of Delaney close behind him, sense Zim bringing up the rear, watching their six. Why wasn't Caldwell communicating? Either way, Garrett would do his job, even if this op—maybe the dog—had failed.

"You okay?" Delaney said, her voice soft.

"Not even a little," he said under his breath, not looking back.

He'd been blindsided again. Had a guess who was responsible. He slowed as they approached the office, but the Mal surged forward on the long lead, stopping right in front of him. He plopped his rear on the ground and pricked his ears, staring at the ground on the other side of the road.

"What's he doing?" he asked quietly.

Delaney studied her working dog. "He's alerting, but to what, I don't know."

Garrett jerked his head toward the spot Surge was staring at.

She and Surge walked over, and he sat again. Delaney bent and retrieved something from the ground. They returned, and she handed it to him.

"A glove," he grunted. A random, ratty glove. He held his sigh.

The Mal seemed off today. Delaney had worked through his whole overwhelm thing, but Surge kept hitting in strange places. An empty container. A glove out here . . .

Clearly it wasn't just the Mal that was off today.

He slid the glove into his pocket and signaled them onward.

A security guard emerged from the office, flipping off the inside lights and shining a flashlight around the area.

Garrett slid for cover, sensing Zim and Delaney diving behind the container with him.

Hunkered down, Delaney slid her hands around Surge's tac harness.

When the guard walked past on the other side of the container, Garrett prayed the guy didn't detect the team. If Surge started panting . . .

But the guy kept walking that direction, deeper among the containers, farther from the office.

An idea sparked in Garrett's brain—if the Sachaai had loaded the chem vials into another shipping container, where was it headed? There was definitely a mole . . . and he wanted to see if it was Caldwell.

But he had no proof . . . yet.

He shifted and slid over to Zim. "I'm going to slip into the office and find the cargo manifest. Take a picture."

"I can do it—that's what I'm here for."

"This is on me." His phone would take pictures well enough, and he was done trusting others to get the job done and having it backfire. "Give me four mikes, max."

He sneaked around and up to the door of the office, jimmied it open, and crept into the room. After verifying there were no cameras, he slid his back against the wall and straightened. Scanned the space. A single table held a paper tray loaded with perfectly straightened paperwork. He picked up the top packet of papers and used his torch to illuminate the text. Riffled through the pages, bills of lading, invoices, and . . . "Here we go." A cargo manifest with today's date. Hakim's name.

Bingo.

Garrett drew out his phone and snapped a picture. He put the manifest back upside down on top of the paper tray as it had been. Then he dropped the roaming guard's ID on the floor, shut the door, and slipped out. He was nearly across the street when he saw the security guard returning.

Hitting the ground, he rolled himself into the shadow of the container stack. He lay still, barely allowing himself to breathe as he eyed the guard booking up the stairs as his phone trilled. The guard answered, strolling right past Garrett.

Once the office door clicked shut, Garrett checked the area, saw the guard settle in, then hustled and crept to the container stack the team was behind. At his signal, they fell in behind him, and he led them out of the cargo yard and to the SUV.

Caldwell met them at the door when they arrived at the safe house.

Garrett had four words for him. "We need to talk."

Caldwell rolled his eyes. "Now what?"

Garrett jerked his head toward Zim and Delaney, who'd followed him into the kitchen. He held out the pic of the shipping manifest on his phone as Delaney and Zim flanked him.

Bemused, Caldwell scanned it, lifted his hands in the air.

Garrett seethed. His voice croaked. He pointed the phone at Caldwell. "You went silent on comms."

"I had technical difficulties. Signal went—"

"Not only did you withhold the fact that unfriendlies were waiting in the combi plane yesterday, today you bailed on us and forced us to operate without up-to-date intel, *and* you withheld info from this shipping manifest."

Caldwell's jaw dropped. "I already told you the signal dropped. The building manager's Sachaai tattoo, the Sachaai waiting to attack—I didn't know."

"It's all about you not sharing full intel. Djibouti. Burma. Now here."

The spook jabbed a finger in his face. "Those situations weren't me."

Garrett's heart pounded in his ears. Sure, Caldwell's bosses had cleared his name. But somehow, in some way, every shortfall of intel on their past few missions was associated with this man. And now—Garrett lunged. Caught Caldwell's collar. "I'm sick of you putting me and my team in danger!"

Face cherry red, Caldwell clawed at his hand, but Garrett tightened his hold. "I'm done with you. Done trusting you. Done—"

"Bear." The whisper of a cool breeze preceded Delaney's hand landing gently on his arm. Her voice was barely audible. "Don't do this."

Garrett looked down at the spook . . . who was gasping for air. *What am I doing?* Choking the man? He released the guy, stepped back. *Too far, Walker.* The spook deserved to be called on the carpet, but not this. He forced himself to turn back to Caldwell. "Sorry."

Looking like he'd chewed on a lemon, Caldwell straightened his collar. "Fine. Fine as frog hair."

Garrett pointed at the floor. "Stay," he ordered. He strode toward the front yard.

Delaney stood. "I'll come with—"

Garrett spun, stabbed a finger at her, the floor. He didn't need her to lecture him. Delaney sat down, innocent hands in the air.

Surge jumped between them, eyes lasered on him, his growl thrumming deep in his throat.

He yanked his hand back. Great. He'd deserve to lose his hand. The shiny black Mal was dead right. He needed to get himself under control. To do that, he needed some breathing space, so he stormed into the postage-stamp yard.

12

JAKARTA, INDONESIA

THEY'D BEEN BETRAYED, AND THAT LEAK WAS TRYING TO SPLIT THEIR team in two. Sitting at the kitchen table, Delaney kept thinking about the argument last night.

This was a gray table in a shades-of-gray kitchen. The safe house here was nicer than the one in Singapore. More space but no color. Garrett walked in with his huge stainless steel coffee tumbler and aimed straight for the pot. Which he emptied into his mug.

She eyed his freshly showered wet hair and his tight black tactical shirt.

Delaney looked away, the heat in her cheeks telling her they were probably pink. She forced her attention to her plate and picked up her toast as he started a new pot of coffee.

"Sorry to interrupt your breakfast," he said, "but it's time to recalibrate our mission. Living room." He strode under the arched entry between the rooms and claimed one of the armchairs, and Surge followed him in.

She shoved in the last bite of her scrambled eggs and pushed away from the table. Whatever he had in mind for this mission recalibration, she would make sure Surge's nose was part of it after Garrett's whole "overwhelm" comment last night.

She walked in behind Zim as he wiped peanut butter off his mouth with his hand. She pushed him from behind, and he grinned back at her, wiped his face with his hand again.

Caldwell already sat on the couch with his laptop, feet on the coffee table, frowning at his screen. He pushed his laptop to the table, then scowled at his phone, poking it. He shook his head.

Delaney slid off her shoes and socks and headed for the rocker. Surge sprawled on the floor beside her . . . eagle-eyeing Garrett. She knew Garrett was mad at Caldwell, not her. But Surge obviously still remembered he'd laid into her last night.

He'd hugged her in the container yard too. And he'd protected her—his team—in the warehouse. She took a breath. This took up way too much time in her brain.

Oh. He was watching her watch him. Yeah, anything between them would only be a distraction—for both of them. She tore her eyes away.

Garrett cleared his throat. "Let's start. At the container yard, I got a picture of the cargo manifest. I've sent images to your phones. It lists shoes as the goods on the LD3s. No surprise, considering where we found the first stash. But yesterday, the containers were empty. Where'd they go? Any ideas, Caldwell?"

The CIA operative sighed and chucked his phone onto the couch. "I've been hunting for them, but no joy yet."

"Those plastic tubes can't magically disappear out of the containers."

Caldwell leaned forward. "Yet," Caldwell repeated. "No joy on the intel . . . yet." He snatched up his phone and glared at Garrett, his face pinched like a rotten apple. "Like intel magically appears. I'm working on it."

There was something about this man that made it hard for Delaney to figure out if she liked him or not. On one hand, he seemed skilled. But on the other . . . he took no small pleasure from annoying Garrett, to the point of acting like a victim about it.

Garrett's jaw worked. He looked at his phone. "Be right back." He put it to his ear and stalked toward the front of the house and out the door.

Had he gotten a call? She hadn't seen his screen light up . . .

Phone in hand, she started looking at some photos.

"Garrett's being a bear because he expects immediate and perfect intel." Caldwell pulled his laptop to himself, peered at the screen. "But I've got seven different search engines looking for this freaking mother lode. Nothing. I tried to contact my HUMINT. Haven't heard back. Garrett's asking for the impossible." He tossed his phone back on the couch. "Right, Delaney?"

Oh no. Delaney was not going down that conversation path with him. "You might call him Bear, but you weren't there yesterday. You didn't see that moment when we realized the container was empty. So yeah, he's a little grumpy, but he's on a mission—we all are. And I, for one, feel a little bearish about these guys getting away with the LD3 containers. And we all know, Garrett included, that *accurate* intel is the right intel."

Caldwell glared, but again picked up his phone and poked away at it.

Guess the meeting was over, and she wasn't going to get a chance to bring up the power of Surge's nose for the team. At least, not yet.

It had been a couple days since she'd worked with him on the desensitization of that triggering tone. She wanted to keep working it every so often, so she reached down to wake Surge up. But he wasn't there. He'd gone off to explore the safe house again. Nah. Bet he'd sneaked outside with Garrett.

She heard a whine in the other room.

"Surge?"

Another whine.

Working dogs didn't just randomly whine. She followed the

sound down the hallway and into the laundry room, where he was sniffing Caldwell's duffel in the corner under the stainless steel utility sink.

He saw her and planted his rump on the floor, ears pointed at it. He nudged it with his nose, eyes lasered on the duffel.

Heart jamming in her throat, she gaped. This wasn't obsession with dirty socks. This was a *hit*.

"Good boy," she whispered, stock still, listening for what was going on in the living room. Caldwell and Zim were intent on a conversation. She quietly closed the laundry room door, pulled the duffel to herself, and unzipped the front pocket. Looked over her shoulder again.

Deep breath. She opened the pocket and peeked in. Nothing. Wait. Something was stuck in the corner. She pulled it out.

The random purple plastic trash she'd seen Caldwell fidgeting with the other day. What was it doing here? There had to be something in Caldwell's duffel that'd rubbed off on it.

Delaney unzipped the main part of the bag. "Check it, Surge."

He sniffed it, then he nosed her hand holding the plastic and downed, his ears pointed at it. His tail twitched, and he woofed as he belly-crawled even closer to the piece of purple plastic. "It's this, Delaney. Are you stupid?" he seemed to say.

"Good boy." She chucked his chin, then stood and studied the translucent, glittery plastic that gave beneath her fingers. Silicone.

Surge was homed in on this thing. Whatever it was, it must've been exposed to Sachaai's chemical encapsulation lipid. She had to talk with Garrett.

Zim and Caldwell were up and moving in the living room.

She shoved the silicone in her pocket. "With me," she signaled. They left the room and headed down the hall to the front door. She stuffed on her socks and shoes.

What was Caldwell even doing with this silicone . . . thing? Maybe Garrett was right about the CIA operative.

"You're sure?"

"I don't bull people, Walker."

At Chapel's terse response, Garrett nodded. "Thanks. Appreciate it." Call ended, he rammed his cell into his pocket, paced the safe house's tiny yard that reeked of the river. According to Chapel, he had vetted Caldwell before even recommending him to ABA.

So . . . Caldwell was Caldwell. He didn't care if the man liked or trusted him.

But Zim . . . Samwise was no longer here, but Zim, he had become more than a friend to him. A battle buddy. Iron sharpening iron.

Garrett's stomach twisted, knowing he'd done a fine job of making the whole team not trust him, including Delaney. Shoot, even Surge.

Frankly, he was starting to doubt himself.

He hopped up, grabbed the handrail of the deck above him, and began chin-ups. He had to recalibrate *himself* first. Then the mission. Hopefully convince the team.

"Garrett?"

At the soft, warm voice, Garrett dropped to the ground, a strange something spiraling through his chest as he faced her. "Hey, Delaney."

"Hey." She entered the yard with Surge, then paused and glanced back to the house. "I need to talk to you."

"Sure. But first, I owe you an apology for laying into you last night."

She smiled. "We're good. And I—"

"I've lost the trust of the team." He couldn't stop talking. "It's my fault we don't have the chems now."

"How?" Delaney asked.

"I led us to empty LD3s." He shook his head. "I had Chapel's backing, but I doubt that will ever happen again."

"But you're team leader for a reason—and you're a good one."

That strange warmth simmered, but he squelched it, his own anger too fresh in his mind. Anger at the team, at everyone else. Now at himself. He rubbed his arm as memories of Dad's rage flooded in.

Her voice was just loud enough to hear. "God corrects mistakes. No more, no less."

"I royally reamed Caldwell after the fight on the combi plane." Garrett slumped against the railing of the deck. "Then he proved that he didn't even know the building manager was Sachaai and that no Sachaai were linked to the plane's passengers. He couldn't have known about the hidden men waiting to attack us."

He paced out to the fence and leaned against it with both hands. He was half tempted to jump it and take a long run. "I should've left picture-taking to Zim. Nearly unreadable pictures of the manifest were all I got. I should've waited for Caldwell to get accurate intel instead of racing the team into the container yard. An unnecessary risk. An unnecessary waste of time."

He stopped and leaned against the fence again. "And I hammered you."

"That wasn't a hammer. And your team is still with you." She laid her hand on his arm, where she had last night. "You're not your dad."

"If I don't get control, this team will fall apart. We will fail the mission. Americans will die. That will be on me."

"Leadership is not control."

Oh, her head tilt.

"My dad taught me that, and he was right. But some wise guy named Heath showed it to me. You are not leading a dog if you're yanking him around on a lead." She waggled her eyebrows. "Surge, come!"

The Malinois sniffed along the fence and shot toward her.

"Crawl!"

Surge dropped to the ground and squirmed the rest of the way.

Ugh. Control again. Garrett knew better.

Where was Lieutenant Commander Taylor? He needed his Navy boss to slap him on the back of his head. Hard. Order him to do push-ups. Five hundred of them.

He deserved it.

Surge and Delaney trusted each other.

Instead of controlling his team, he had to work with and trust each of them. They needed everyone's skills, working together. That was the only way they could stop Sachaai's chemical attack.

He bowed his head. *Forgive me, God.*

He lifted his head and couldn't help but smile to see Delaney on her knees ruffling Surge's neck fur. "We call that combat crawl."

"Makes sense." She gave him a smile, but then her face turned dead serious. "Boss, I'm sorry I intervened between you and Caldwell last night."

He frowned. "It could've ended badly. So you deserve a thank-you."

Her lips flattened. "Well, I have to tell you, something is off with Caldwell."

Feeling a bit of whiplash hearing that, Garrett struggled to know how to respond. Hadn't he just asked God to forgive him? But for Delaney to say that . . . he wanted to kick open the safe-house door and take down Caldwell. Instead, he leaned against the fence with his hip. "Why do you say that?"

She held out a strange piece of translucent purple plastic.

He took it and turned it around, trying to get a bead on it. Nothing. "What is it?"

"No clue. But Surge straight-out hit on it in Caldwell's duffel. I'm 99.9 percent sure this is the plastic he was fidgeting with in Singapore. I thought it was trash, but he stuck it in his duffel." She puffed out her cheeks and blew out the air. She lifted her palms up with a shrug. "Surge was obsessed with his duffel again yesterday. I thought it was his weird, uh, you know . . . clothing thing." She blushed, shook her head. "But today he hit on this. So I brought it straight to you."

He held it up to the sun and studied it. "Weird. There's kind of a gap—a pocket—on either side. What even is this thing?"

Delaney lifted one shoulder, checked behind her, then inched nearer. "Garrett, I don't want to imply anything, but what is Caldwell doing with a piece of plastic that Surge recognizes as Sachaai lipids?"

Staring into her eyes, he felt his heart jar at the verbal connection between this and the lipids. "I need to think about this."

Surge sat in front of Delaney and pawed at the pocket of the olive green jacket she was wearing. "Okay, buddy." She pulled out the KONG and tossed it into the yard.

Bolting after it, Surge seized it in midair. Took turns which one of them he brought it back to as Garrett and Delaney threw it for him. Not a dumb dog, for sure. She finally reached into her magical pocket, and out came a bully stick. Her constant hoodies and jackets with pockets of dog stuff made him laugh. Surge dropped the KONG and sat politely in front of her, his tail wagging. She handed it to him, and he sank to the ground with a contented sigh.

Garrett leaned against the safe house. "What do you mean, something's off with Caldwell?"

"The plastic, most of all. But there's also living on tech twenty-four seven." She looked him straight in the eyes. "And you punched him on another mission."

"What does that have to do with this?"

"I thought it was just a piece of history, but now . . ." She waved her hand at the plastic he was holding. "I think your instincts might be spot-on."

Yeah. He didn't trust Caldwell, for sure now. He stuck the plastic in his pocket.

"So, what is it between the two of you, Garrett? You're not a hate 'em, punch 'em kinda guy."

He looked at her. "I punched Caldwell in Djibouti, over Sam and Tsunami."

She nodded slowly and leaned against the safe house with him. "I get that." Another captivating head tilt. "What happened?"

He'd told her about his dad's rage. Yet she was still here. Willing to listen.

He cleared his throat. "We didn't know Fahmi was in Djibouti. That bit of missing intel is what killed Sam—and Tsunami. So I punched Caldwell. With our history in Burma, I lost it."

"Burma?"

He didn't talk about this, especially after the call from his CO. But the gentleness in her eyes . . . he sucked in air. "My team was tasked with locating a missing American missionary woman there to help the people standing against the military junta. I found her, but bad intel made things go south. Sam and Tsunami had to rush in and pull us out of there."

Her eyebrows rose. "Thank God for Sam and Tsunami. But you found her. You got her out of there. Of course Caldwell thought of you when he thought of undercover and leadership for this mission." She crossed her arms with a sniff. "But bad intel. Both times. From Caldwell. Both times. No wonder you distrust him."

"There's more."

Her hands fell to her sides. "Okay."

"I did not re-up after Djibouti. I walked away from the Navy SEALS. But my CO called me a few days later. Grieved about Sam, he'd checked into the incident. Turns out Caldwell's HUMINT contact in Djibouti was simply wrong. Then my CO checked into what'd happened in Burma. Turns out that contact was simply a liar. So technically, it wasn't on Caldwell."

"And still you don't trust him."

"Caldwell has a strong CIA operator record, or else Damocles wouldn't have sent him out with this team. Wouldn't even have allowed him to build a team for this mission."

"Heath wouldn't have sent me with Caldwell."

He nodded. "He checked into it himself, before I even showed up at A Breed Apart."

"Sounds like Heath." She laughed. "He wanted to be certain I could trust you as leader. And at the same time, leadership means trusting the team."

What, was she reading his mind? "Yeah. Not controlling them. God's teaching me that."

She chuckled. "God has a way of teaching us things, doesn't He?"

"Yeah. I'm learning. Except truth is, I keep my eyes on Caldwell twenty-four seven."

Her hand on his chest spread a warmth through him. "But after the cargo plane fight, you let Caldwell explain how he couldn't have known about them. That's leadership." She screwed her face in thought. "Leadership doesn't mean perfect, Garrett. God is perfect, not you or me."

He nodded, lips pursed. "Caldwell probably doesn't trust me any more than I trust him."

She quirked an eyebrow. "Probably not, given yesterday's fight."

"Right." He had to think about this thing. If they were going to trust him, that meant—Caldwell or not—apologies. Starting with Rogue.

Surge decided he was done with his bully stick, stood up, and dropped his KONG at Garrett's feet, begging for a game. Garrett gave in, tossing it across the postage-stamp yard. He scampered after it, then skidded to a stop in front of them when he dashed back.

"Delaney, while I'm at it, sorry I questioned you last night at the port."

Her grin at Surge's skid faded. She picked up the KONG,

shook it at him. "I've seen his overwhelm with that sound trigger. In the empty LD3s, that was not it. The whole empty area smelled of lipids that used to be there." She spun the black rubber toy out to the corner of the grassy area. "I know dogs. I know Surge."

"I know. And I'm sorry." Nothing more or better to say to a fearless dog trainer.

Surge paraded the KONG around the yard. "You didn't lose your faith in Surge's nose?" Her deep-brown eyes lasered him. "Or in me as a teammate?"

"I trust you." He swallowed hard. He hadn't meant to let his personal thoughts out. "You and Surge."

"You trust me?"

Yes. And more, maybe. Probably. He offered a smile and nodded.

She grinned. "Okay then."

Surge returned, picked up his bully stick, and plopped down between them.

Garrett pulled the plastic out of his pocket, tossed it back and forth between his hands. His subconscious decided not to be *sub* anymore. "Surge hit on this piece of silicone we know nothing about." He held it in his right hand and just stood there. "And he hit on cartons all over the shoe factory in Singapore. Then empty LD3s that the manifest says were loaded with shoes."

Delaney bit her lip. "Surge hit on this plastic and on shoes, but that plastic doesn't look like it has anything to do with shoes. So what's the connection?"

He nodded slowly. With a final toss of the unknown thing, he stuck it back in his pocket. "That's what I want to know." He pulled out his phone. "Zim, meet us in the living room with your FTIR. We're on the way in."

Surge trotted backward with them, proudly carrying the bully stick in his mouth.

They walked through the kitchen into the living room as Zim barreled down the hallway, bearing the infrared spectroscope and a smile as wide as his face. "What do you need me to take a chemical fingerprint of?"

Garrett laughed. "Easy. This." He lobbed the silicone to him.

Surge sniffed at it in Zim's hand, then walked over to his mat beside Delaney's rocking chair and plopped down for a nap. Delaney took off her shoes and sat in the rocker.

Caldwell walked in and saw Zim holding the purple plastic. Paused. "Where'd you get that?" he asked, his voice low.

Zim was focused on the plastic. "Bear gave it to me."

Watching him, feeling uneasy and uncertain, Delaney said nothing.

Caldwell spun toward him. "Bear?"

"Delaney found—"

He spun toward her. "You were in my duffel bag, Thompson?"

She cringed, then squared her shoulders. "Surge—"

The spook grabbed for the plastic, but Zim stared him down, then calmly walked to the dining room table, got the FTIR ready.

Caldwell whirled back to Delaney, his ears bright red. "Your dog got in my private duffel like he got into Bear's? Thought he was trained."

Surge sprang to her side and went on alert, eyeing Caldwell and very ready to address any aggression.

Delaney settled her hand on his head, met Caldwell's stare. "He smells what he smells. He is a working dog trained to sniff out chemicals—Sachaai's lipid in particular."

Garrett knew she didn't need him to defend her, but he was the team leader, so he simply took her six.

Caldwell stepped closer. "You dug into my duffel to see what he was sniffing."

"I did." She jutted her jaw. "We are on mission. When Surge hits on Sachaai lipids, it's my job to check it out, turn it over to Garrett. This was his second hit on your duffel."

Caldwell stared at them, shook his head. "That's insane."

"What is the plastic?" Garrett asked as Zim aimed the FTIR at it.

Caldwell watched. "I have no clue. My Singapore asset gave it to me. I've been trying to puzzle it out ever since." He shrugged. "Maybe it had nothing to do with Sachaai. I simply don't know."

Garrett stepped into his space. "We need to know why Surge hit on it." And he needed to make a choice—choose to believe the spook or ditch him now. The latter seemed a stretch. So, believe it was.

A shrill beep sounded, and Zim scrolled through the report on the screen. "Positive for Sachaai lipids."

"It is?" Caldwell balked, his face slack.

Garrett pulled over his laptop on the coffee table. "Plastic, silicone, Sachaai," he murmured as he pounded the words into the search engine. He read his screen, pounded some more. "What's the connection? It's not . . . Work your sources."

As everyone went to work, Garrett rubbed his chin. Maybe "shoes" was the terrorists' code, their front, whatever. No. That just didn't feel right. He strode to the window, squinted out at the river for a long minute, running through all they'd seen on the mission, starting at the shoe factory.

Then it hit him. Garrett sucked in a hard breath. The puzzle pieces suddenly fit. "Zim! They actually made shoes at the Singapore factory-slash-chem lab. Agree?"

"Don't think they'd fill up the place with shoeboxes and leather and twenty-four sewing machines if they didn't."

Garrett sat back down, pulled out his phone, and clicked away on the search engine until—he popped out of his seat. "Caldwell, what about this?" He held his phone to the spook. "Shoemakers Extraordinaire is connected to Shoe Luxe on the web. They're based in Jakarta." He nodded. "Look at this listing."

"Wow. The biggest shoe retailer in the States," Delaney said, pointing down at the leather boots she was wearing.

"Unbelievable. I could have found that in a second." Caldwell reached for his laptop.

Garrett snagged the computer. And Caldwell's phone next to it. "No you don't. No way are you going to leak this."

Caldwell lifted his hands in innocence. "You can't seriously believe I'm behind this or to blame."

"You don't leave my sight until the mission is complete." He spun his index finger in the air. "Everyone load up. We're heading to the Shoe Luxe warehouse."

13

OF COURSE THE SHOE LUXE WAREHOUSE WAS EMPTY.

Exhausted and more than a little frustrated, Delaney rubbed her tight shoulder as they trudged back into the safe house after their nighttime sneak-and-peek.

Garrett dropped his pack in the entryway, moved into the kitchen, and pulled a soda out of the fridge. He slid onto the black bench at the gray kitchen table and opened it. He shoved over Caldwell's laptop and smartphone, which hadn't come with them. "Caldwell was obviously not the leak. Do you think I got it wrong, connecting Sachaai to Shoe Luxe?"

"I don't think so." Delaney let out a huge breath as she joined him in the kitchen. "Surge downed and gazed around the same way he did in the empty LD3s, so there must've been Sachaai vials in there, even if we found all shoes, no chems." She filled Surge's food and water bowls and signaled him to come for his dinner. Then she grabbed a bottle of juice from the fridge and sat across from Garrett.

"She's absolutely right." Zim slid in next to Delaney and sipped his energy drink. "We're not Sachaai, so we didn't get the

172

memo about loading the chems onto a semi." He frowned. "Or a boat. Or a train. Or a plane . . . How on earth are we going to find out where it went?"

"Don't know." At the table, Caldwell confiscated his laptop and phone with a scowl, then opened it up. He did some clicking and scrolling before shaking his head. "No street cams in the area to feed me intel." He eyed Garrett. "Sometimes the best plans don't work out, Bear."

Garrett did a double take. "Umm, thank you."

"You know I've been there before where things don't work out. 'Bout time you got to see how these things sometimes happen."

Sensing the quick tightening of tension—especially with the way Garrett's lips pinched into a line, Delaney wanted to explain the spook was joking. "I—"

"Absolutely." Garrett smiled. "It happens. So, readjust, get back in."

To her amazement, the two fist-bumped. Huh. Maybe they could get along for more than two seconds.

Garrett scratched his head, gazing at Caldwell for a moment, then, "Okay, team. Is there more to discover on the connection between Shoemakers Extraordinaire and Shoe Luxe, or do any of you have another idea? Caldwell, we could use your HUMINT ASAP."

Zim started coughing. "Oh, that's bad!" he croaked.

Caldwell fanned the air in front of his face. "Whoa! Who did that?"

The nasty smell reached her, and Delaney wrinkled her nose. "Sorry. Surge has room-clearing flatulence some days." She felt herself gagging. "C'mon, dude—outside."

The Mal was a black blur sprinting to the front door, and she followed.

"Always blame the dog, right, Rogue?" Zim teased.

She turned and glared at him. "Ha, ha, ha! Y'all must be fifth graders."

The men started laughing. With a grin, she opened the door and went out with Surge.

Garrett came out into the grassy area as Surge took care of business and stank up the yard.

"That smell is worse than the river!" He grinned and lobbed the KONG to her. "Thought you might need this."

"Aw, thanks. Definitely."

Surge pounced in front of her, tail whipping through the air as he stared at his toy.

She tossed it, and he sprinted for it, then came back and dropped it in front of Garrett. She shook her head. "Y'all have really gotten to be friends."

He cocked his head. "Friends? Caldwell and me?"

She laughed and choked at the same time. "You and Surge."

He thrust out his chin and winked. "True, this dog and I are friends now. And that's thanks to your training sessions."

Somehow that warmed her, and she hoped it wasn't showing as a blush since the Jakarta evening was starting to darken the grassy area.

Surge brought the KONG and dropped it in front of her, and she focused on him. "We're taking turns, huh?" She lobbed it over by the fence, and Surge dashed after it.

"Remember when you made me play hide-and-seek with Surge so we'd get used to responding to each other?"

She smiled. "I tried not to laugh as you squeezed under the porch. Neither of you needed to learn the commands. You just needed time working together."

Surge dropped the KONG at his feet, but Garrett ignored it and raised his arms. The Malinois leaped into them, tail wagging.

Garrett's eyes widened. "He does trust me."

Staring at them, Delaney smiled. "He doesn't jump into Dad's arms. Or Heath's," she said, her voice cracking.

"He doesn't?" Garrett let him jump down, tossed the black rubber toy into the corner. Surge chased it down.

"Nope." She grinned. "Time built trust."

He whooshed out a breath. "Sure did."

Delaney faced him. "What are you thinking about?"

When Surge came running back on Garrett's second toss, he called, "Crawl!" and Surge dropped the toy, came crawling to him on his belly.

He scratched behind Surge's ears. "Do I trust God like Surge trusts you? I do . . . I want to."

"But your dad . . ."

"Yeah. Dad. It's a struggle. Even though I know who God really is."

"Let me put it this way. You asked if God put dog training into my DNA. I needed that question. He did. Thus I'm here. Didn't He install SEALs into your DNA?"

One corner of his mouth rose. "True."

Surge brought her the KONG this time, and she offered a game of tug to the beautiful black dog she was somehow on a mission with. "You know, most men don't make it into SEALs," she said in grunts as Surge jerked the dog toy. "But you jumped in a hundred ten percent. I think that's a hundred ten percent of trust in God right there."

"Same one hundred ten percent trust in Him as when you jumped one hundred ten percent onto the mission team."

She threw her head back with a grin. "Once I finally did."

"True." He smiled at her and reached for the KONG. She let him take it so Surge could kill his shoulders instead of hers.

With one giant pull, the Mal yanked it out of his hands.

She snickered as he shook out his arm.

He snorted. "All right, Kongmeister, no more tug with you till I hit the gym back home. Bring it here, buddy." When Surge complied, Garrett tossed it over by the house.

A woman and a preschool-age girl were approaching outside the fence. The adorable little girl duck-walked, slapping her feet on the sidewalk, laughing and pointing at her shoes. Bright brown eyes lit on Surge, and she raced to the fence, rambling in

her native language. The source of her excitement was obvious—
Surge.

Delaney smiled.

But then Surge veered off, planted himself in the corner, ears
pointed at the preschooler. He just sat there, staring at her. Hard.

The girl frowned and let go of the fence, stepped behind her
mama.

What was going on?

"That's a hit, right?" Garrett asked softly, looking to her.

"It is," Delaney said quietly.

Realizing Surge was scaring the little one, Delaney jogged
over and heard Garrett coming too. "Good boy," she said to her
four-legged hero as she gripped his collar and drew him back,
but his gaze remained locked on the pair. Wondering what had
set him off, she angled for a better view and scanned the woman.
She wasn't carrying anything. Morning light caught on
something and glinted. Sparkling—

Delaney drew in a breath. "The shoes." Her voice and
realization mingled with Garrett's, and she looked at him.

He nodded at her as he lowered his phone. "Got a pic."

She smiled. While it was a nice, connecting moment between
them, Delaney was more excited about the connection to the
shoes. They were adorable Mary Jane–style jelly sandals with
glittery 3D plastic butterflies fastened to the toe. A tag dangled
from the side—likely just purchased from the nearby market.
"Purple," she mumbled, her brain linking the plastic Caldwell
had in his ruck.

Garrett tapped his thigh, eyes on the pair as the mama picked
up her daughter. "Caldwell's plastic . . ."

"I know," she whispered.

He pulled it out of his pocket, turned it over in his fingers,
looking between it and the little girl's shoes as the pair
continued down the sidewalk, past the safe house fence.

That's when Delaney realized. "That tag! They're new—that's
why she's so proud."

Eyes wide, Garrett pivoted. "I've got an idea. Inside."

"Surge, with me." Delaney snagged the KONG, and the three of them jogged into the dining room.

"Living room," Garrett called.

Caldwell and Zim each came wandering down the hallway, and they all took seats.

"Got a heads-up from my contact," Caldwell said. "He still knows nothing about the plastic."

"Understood," Garrett said with a nod. "Outside just now, Surge hit on a preschooler walking past the safe house, or rather he hit on the shoes she was wearing—they had glittery butterflies on the top." He held up Caldwell's plastic. "The butterfly was made of silicone that looked just like this."

Zim frowned, rubbed his chin. "Hmm. They could have been just exposed in the shoe factory-slash-chem lab. I'd like to test them."

"They looked brand new—the price tag was still on the strap, probably too hard for the mom to break off," Delaney said.

Garrett stilled, eyeing her. "Exactly. I'm guessing they just came from the market down the street." He pointed at her. "Thompson, how do you feel about going into the neighborhood marketplace and pretending you're trying to find some cute shoes for your niece. Buy a pair for Zim's FTIR."

Oh. The plan centered on her. Her eyebrows rose into her hair. "I . . . I'm not an operator, but I'll do what I can. What if I don't find the shoes?" A worse thought hit her and tied her tummy in knots. "What if Hakim is here, in the market, and he sees me?"

He tapped his finger on his chin, then nodded. "You're not an operator, but you are fearless and bold. And two gruff operators going in looking at sparkly shoes would draw attention."

"Fearless?" That word almost took her breath. "But you're right . . . it would look odd for you two to go in." She cocked her head, then circled back to one particular thought that still had her heart jammed in her throat. "You really think I'm fearless?"

177

"Wouldn't have said it if I didn't." He quirked an eyebrow. "You said I was a good leader."

She had meant it too. "I did."

His eyes held hers.

Fearless. Bold. That's how Garrett saw her? Not frozen, incapable?

Zim snickered.

Oh yeah, Zim and Caldwell were standing right there.

Delaney lowered her eyes, biting her lip, halfway grinning. What had this turned into between her and Garrett?

"So, you good to do this?" Garrett asked.

She looked around at the team. "I am." She drew in a steadying breath. "So, do I say, 'I'm looking for chemical weapons—where are the shoes?'"

Caldwell snorted, rolled his eyes.

Garrett chuckled. "You probably wouldn't get very far with that, Rogue," he teased back.

Flashing him a smile, she nodded. "Okay, so I'll find a friendly booth owner—"

"Who speaks English," Garrett added.

"That'd be helpful." Her nerves were playing havoc with her. "And I say, 'My niece is infatuated with shoes. Is there a booth selling any little girls' shoes here?'"

"Something like that. Keep it simple. Buy a trinket from the booth."

Caldwell nodded. "If anyone asks why you're in Jakarta, say you're visiting Southeast Asia with friends. Best lies are the ones based in truth, and they're easier to remember later."

"Good point. I'm definitely not good at lying." She twisted her lips to the side. "I am actually in Southeast Asia with friends"—she stole a peek at Garrett, and she felt the heat of his gaze to her toes—"so that's not a real lie."

"We'll be near and on comms, so you won't be alone," Garrett said. "Nice and easy. No worries."

Yeah, despite her feelings for him, they were friends. And that was enough. "No worries." They high-fived.

Caldwell walked over to the corner and reached into the durable plastic bin where he kept his tech, pulled out comms pieces for everyone. His eyes were tight as he handed her one.

"Sorry about getting into your duffel," she said. Not that she'd done anything wrong, but they were teammates. Making peace was right.

Caldwell shrugged. "It served its purpose—if you hadn't, you and Bear wouldn't have recognized the plastic outside. Violation of property forgiven." He pointed at his laptop on the coffee table. "I'll have oversight from her and will have eyes on you at all times. Comms are short range, but you should be fine at the market. Check the map and get familiar with the location." He pulled up the map on his phone and showed it to her.

"Thank you." And she stuck the earpiece in her ear.

Garrett picked up his SAT phone from the table next to him, held it out. "Of course, there's Surge's tracking device." He stuck it in his pocket. "We've got your six, Thompson."

Feeling a tremor in her hands—nerves—Delaney glanced away from the men. She wasn't going to freeze. Just wasn't going to. Good thing she happened to have put on her olive green jacket and her soft black jeans this morning—the clothes she'd had on when Heath had made her an official trainer at ABA.

She threw out a prayer. *Don't let me freeze up, God. Fearlessness, please?*

She centered her attention back on the team. "Okay, anything else?"

Garrett gave a slight shake of his head, but there seemed something more in his expression. Like . . . worry.

No. He was confident, the plan-maker. The team leader.

"Okay, then . . ."

"Just get in, get out." He squeezed her shoulder. "You'll do great. Just another walk in the city with your dog, okay?"

"Right." She took Surge's lead and clipped it on. She hoofed it out of the safe house, working hard to feel the boldness Garrett saw in her. She was with Surge anyway. They would find the shoes and confirm them positive for Sachaai lipids. Call in the team. Just do it. Get in and out.

It was only a half mile from the safe house to the marketplace, and she stopped shy of it, awareness springing through her that she was alone. *Not alone. I have Surge. And the guys in comms.* "I'm at the marketplace," she whispered.

"Copy that—we can see you," came Garrett's calm, smooth reply. "Remember, get in and out. You've got this, Rogue."

Firming her grip, she smiled at how much his confidence in her fueled her own. Nudged her into action. Garrett wouldn't have trusted her with this at the beginning of this mission. But he did now.

No hiding in a store aisle. No freezing in fear. Not today.

"Okay, Surge," she said to her gorgeous Malinois as they strode past the first stall. "Let's make Garrett proud."

A voice cleared in her comms.

Mortified she'd forgotten the others could hear every word, she cringed.

"Make yourself proud, Rogue."

Man, the guy knew what to say, didn't he?

Drawing up her courage, she kept moving. Smiled at Surge, who hauled in big draughts as they navigated around a vendor with meat and rice. More than once, he diverted toward some of the trash lining the narrow street that housed the marketplace, but she didn't let him stop to linger.

A lady bumped into her as a motorcycle weaving around the throng of people jostled her. "*Saya minta maaf,*" she said, pressing her hand to her heart.

Delaney didn't know Indonesian, but she could see the apology.

"She's just saying sorry." Caldwell's voice came through the comms.

With a smile, Delaney accepted the woman's apology and watched as she disappeared into the crowd. And that's when she spotted tables lining the street market with everything from chilies to T-shirts and sarongs. Just what she could see from the entry.

This is your chance.

"I think I found where they probably got the shoes." Bending to pet Surge—and to hide her update with the team—she rubbed the thick fur around his neck.

"Doing good, Rogue. Slow and steady wins the race."

Having him in her ear was an anchor in the chaos. She felt Surge nudge her hip, as if telling her to get moving. "Okay, okay. Let's go shopping."

They entered and wound their way among the crowd in the narrow street lined with booth after booth. It felt like forever, and she had nothing, no sign of the shoes. Feeling a bit demoralized, she decided to ask around like they'd planned.

She slowed at a table that offered fresh cut-up mango coated with chili powder, cayenne, and sugar. The vendor joked with customers in broken English. She got at the end of his long line. Ten minutes later, she and Surge reached the front. He sniffed around the corner of the table, then sat, body in full alert as he stared at something.

Oh no. Not now . . .

But then she spotted a cute preschooler playing with a doll behind the table—and she wore glittery jelly shoes, a purple butterfly on each. Of course.

"Out," she whispered to Surge. He huffed, but sniffed around the other side of the booth at the end of his lead as she looked over the menu board.

The owner wore a bright yellow shirt reading Mangga Berbumbu, the name of his booth. The owner waved. "You American, yes?"

"I am. How are you today?" She forced her nerves back

down and firmed her grip on Surge's lead, more a reflexive act than any concern he would do something.

"A good day. Sorry my English not good, but talk to tourists like you make good practice."

She laughed. "You speak English well."

"Thank you." He pointed to his shirt "You want spiced mango?"

"Absolutely. That's what I'm in line for, please."

"Popular today," he said, and spun around to fill a baggie with mango, then the spice mix. He shook it up and handed it to her.

She withdrew the cash Garrett had given her and handed the owner a bill. While he got her change, she took a bite. The spice heated her mouth, and the mango sweetened it. "This is remarkable!" He handed her the change, and Delaney stuffed the entire amount into his tip jar.

His smile was huge.

"Oh," she said, putting syrup in her words, "is she your daughter?"

"Yes, yes."

"I love her cute, glittery shoes," Delaney said, trying to act natural. "I think my niece would love them! Can you tell me where you got them? Was it here?"

"Yes-yes—today. There, where we came in." He pointed down the avenue, away from the marketplace entrance.

"Yay, thanks! Let's go, Surge."

This was undercover, but Delaney wanted to pump her arm in victory. She hadn't lied. Nothing bad had happened. She'd scored directions to the shoe vendor.

"That was epic," Garrett said.

Reveling in his praise, Delaney couldn't keep the smile from her face. "I'm headed to the shoe vendor now. It's on the opposite side of the market from the entry."

"Copy that," Garrett said. "We're coming around the perimeter. It'll take us a few. Meet you there."

She'd done it—though she was no operator nor operative. Exultant still, she did have to actually find the shoes. Locate the vendor. Sobered that this wasn't over yet, she walked down in the direction the vendor had pointed, under string lights and streetlights that gave the place a vibrancy. Delaney eyed a booth of bright floral sarongs, another with gorgeous handmade teak bowls. She would've bought one or two under different circumstances—maybe later.

At first she didn't see the shoes, but then she spotted LD3 containers sitting on the bed of a semitrailer. The container nearest the end had its rear doors sprung open, and men were selling from the back of it.

A small stream of people passed by, headed into the marketplace. A few stopped to take a look, and a couple even bought some shoes.

"I found it," she relayed to the team. "Semi at the rear, selling from the back. Pretty busy . . ."

"Stay there," Garrett said, his breath huffing. "We're almost there."

Delaney watched, worried people were buying shoes with chemicals. Her heart raced as a mother slipped shoes on her daughter. A grandmother did the same with a toddler in stroller.

"Oh, Father . . ." Delaney felt sick, thinking that those might have chemicals in the butterflies. Chest squeezing, she fought the desperate panic, so badly wanting to tell them to leave the shoes. Don't buy them. So many doing the same, trying on the shoes.

Her breath caught in her throat when she saw that the vendor sported wire-rimmed glasses and slicked-back hair.

But when he turned, she could see his face. *Thank You, God.* It wasn't Tariq, whom she'd seen outside Shoemakers Extraordinaire in Singapore. He didn't have the same long, sharp nose. Or anything else. The other man unloading shoes wore a backward baseball cap. She didn't recognize either of them.

She shook her head. That semi had six LD3s. Six Sachaai logos. *Okay, let's just make sure . . .* Delaney led Surge along the

RONIE KENDIG & VONI HARRIS

truck, and he sat. A knot formed in her stomach. Then the next LD3 container. Same. And by the last one, the knot had tightened into a hard ball.

She started looking at the few jelly shoes they had on display, all purple. Absently, she picked up one and squished the butterfly, watching the glittery swirl of gel in the toe adornment, then let her gaze track over the rest of the shoes.

Suddenly Surge planted his rear on the ground. He alerted on the shoes in her hands. Then he turned and nosed another pair of shoes.

Stomach clenched, she stared at the sandals she held, jiggling the odd-shaped butterfly. Same as Caldwell's plastic . . . but . . . She felt it again. Yeah, each side of the butterfly's body was hard. She played with one side a little more, then it popped open a bit. That side gap—pocket? whatever—held a vial! Same on the other side of the body too.

Surge nosed her hand, hauling in stiff draughts from it. No wonder he'd even hit on Spook's purple plastic.

She blinked her eyes hard, put back the sandals in her hand. She knew what to do.

"These are adorable. I want some. Let me check my money," she called over to the vendors. She waved to get their attention. They looked over and waved back, continued chatting.

She took Surge away a few feet where the men couldn't hear her and keyed her comms. "The semi has six Sachaai LD3s," she said. "*Six*, Bear. Surge hit on all of them."

"Wow. We're almost there. Eagle Three's being jammed, so stay there until we can get eyes on you."

With his words, she felt the protective barrier around her vanish. "Think they know we're onto them?"

"Unknown. Stay there."

She swallowed. "Will do." She turned around and walked back to the vendors. Slowed her approach.

The men were in a panic, loading the boxes back into the last LD3.

Baseball cap guy wiped his hands down his jeans as they reached for another carton. "I can't believe he called. We're dead. He *threatened* us if we sold any."

"We didn't sell enough for him to even notice," the wire-rimmed guy scoffed. "Besides, he's paying us almost nothing. We deserve a little extra."

"He's going to rip us apart if we're late." More hand-wiping.

Wire-rimmed guy shrugged. "Let's lock up and get out of here." The hatch of the LD3 slammed shut, and the men trotted up to the semi's cab.

She pushed back the thought of all these kids with the contaminated shoes and how many Americans these terrorists wanted to kill with six LD3s full of chemicals. The poison could be headed anywhere nationwide, anyway. Maybe even to Dad.

Delaney's heart picked up speed. She had to stop this shipment from going anywhere—or maybe she should go with it. Yes, came a deep knowing. If she didn't and this got away . . . the repercussions would be large-scale lethal.

But she'd already crossed Garrett once. "They're leaving," she hissed. "Where are you?"

"Stay with them." The urgency in his voice ratcheted her heart rate even higher.

How was she going to stay with them? In her crouch, she pivoted in a circle and spied a woman climbing from the back seat of a car. "There's a Grab dropping someone off. I could catch it . . ."

A long pause. The truck pulled off.

"Snag it," Garrett said. "Stay with them and keep us updated. We'll track you via Surge. Right behind you."

When the Grab started pulling away, she ran behind it, waving her hands. The driver stopped, and she jumped in with Surge, wondering what to say. Well, that boyfriend phone story had worked last time. "My boyfriend forgot his phone. He's driving that semi up there."

"Sure," the driver agreed, and pulled out, following the semi.

As they merged with traffic, she had this nagging sense that her last line of defense—being close to Garrett and Zim—was gone. But they had to do this. Her concern didn't have long to breed doubts, because they were pulling into a train depot.

The semi drew up to the long silver train with eight cars so sleek they were aerodynamic. Both the engine and the caboose were shaped like bullets.

Driver paid, she grabbed the handle. "Thank you! C'mon, Surge," she urged as they slipped out of the car. Though she felt haunted by the last time she'd done this, she couldn't lie her way through why she didn't get out of the car. Especially since she'd told the driver her boyfriend was in the semi.

Keeping to the shadows of the depot building, hoping they would provide enough cover, she kept her voice quiet. "We're at a train depot." Her stomach plummeted, seeing that they'd already loaded most of the containers. "They're loading the last LD3 now."

A curse sailed through the line—sounded like Zim.

The semi's rig pulled away.

Oh no. No no no. Rig leaving, train closing up, and no Garrett yet. "What do I do?"

Silence crackled in the comms.

"Gar—" She winced. "Bear? Eagle Two, Three?"

Nothing. That's when she recalled Caldwell saying they were short-range comms. But she wasn't that far away.

So . . . what do I do?

Stay with them, Garrett had said. Pulse jacked, she scurried across to the track, verified nobody was aware of her, then tapped the grate landing for the caboose. "Hup," she ordered Surge, who sailed up. She hiked up after him.

She'd either just done the stupidest thing ever or the best thing. Time would tell.

Get in, get out.

Delaney led Surge into the half-lit sleek silver train car. She rubbed the back of her sweaty neck. They only had a few minutes before that employee she'd seen whistling would get to them as he walked down the train, checking each car.

She unclipped Surge's leash, stuck it in her hoodie pocket. She wished she had the baggie of chem vials. It didn't matter. At this point, Surge knew what they were looking for. "Surge, seek!"

He sniffed the air and jogged down the eighty-five feet or so to the end of the car, right up to a stack of silver LD3s, each with the purple Sachaai S logo. All six she'd followed here, in three stacks of two. But he didn't just sniff like before.

He sat and pointed his ears at the first shipping container.

"That was quick." Delaney ruffled his ears. "Thanks, buddy." She wiped the sweat from her forehead. She pointed at each of the rest of the six, and he alerted on each one.

She walked to the loading door and peeked out from beside it, saw nothing but the semi at the far end of the street. Back at the LD3s, she signaled Surge to turn and be her lookout. "Watch," she cued.

Standing at her side, he faced behind her, watching her six—the loading door—his whole body tensed, ready to defend her.

What would she do without this Mal? "Thanks, buddy," she whispered as metal against metal screeched through the air—the loading of other cars. She needed to hurry.

Delaney reached to slide open the bolt of the first container, but it was padlocked. She didn't have a key. Nor a saw or hammer. How would she . . . Wait—pocketknife. She pulled it from her jeans pocket and poked it into the keyhole on the padlock, jiggled it a little, twisted it a little. Heard a click. Opened the door.

Amazing. What she'd seen on TV had actually worked for her.

She glided her pocketknife through the tape on the first carton in the box to reveal shoeboxes. "Surge, seek." He immediately inched forward with a woof, ears pointing. Positive for the Sachaai lipids. She pulled out the top shoebox and opened it.

Glittery purple Mary Janes, each decorated with a purple butterfly, plastic tubes on each side of the body. Another Surge hit. She didn't have an FTIR, but she trusted her boy's hit on Sachaai lipids processed with toxic chems.

She quickly opened the next Sachaai container in the LD3.

More Surge hits on more boxes of shoes. Yes! "Good job. Give me a bop," she said, and he gave her fist a bump with his nose.

Get in, get out.

"Okay, Surge, watch," she said, pointing back at the loading door.

She took a couple pics with her SAT phone. All she had time for. She stuck one of the shoes from the first box in her pocket, returned the other to the shoebox, and scooched it into its spot in the carton. She closed the LD3s hatch and signaled Surge to stay with her. They headed toward the opening of the train car, but the whistling employee was approaching.

"With me, Surge," Delaney hissed, and they dove behind the stack of Sachaai containers. Surge's hackles rose from neck all the way down his back as he stood in front of her.

She'd jump out of the car as soon as whoever it was got past. Back to her and Surge just "taking a walk." She peeked out the container door just enough to see the whistling man wearing a railroad employee uniform. He walked toward the car they were in. She was ready to jump out the instant he passed and went around the back of the train. But when he whistled his way to the door, he looked in, made notes on his tablet, reached up, and clanged it shut.

Darkness fell over them. She was rooted to the spot. Frozen.

Oh no.

She leaped up and ran over to the door, tried to open it. Nothing. She pried with her pocketknife at the edge of the door, and the knife broke. Surge scratched at the bottom of the door.

How on earth was she going to get out?

14

JAKARTA, INDONESIA

"Surge's signal disappeared, and I can't get her on comms."

Garrett looked at the MWD Tracker app on his SAT phone screen as Zim negotiated the SUV through the crowded Jakarta traffic. *Rogue, where are you?* He closed his eyes for a split second, hoping he wasn't seeing what he was seeing. But when he opened his eyes, her signal hadn't appeared.

Delaney and Surge had vanished in the trainyard.

"Where do we need to go?" Zim sounded tight as he straddled the SUV on the line between the lanes to pass the motorcycle in front of them.

"Trainyard is all we know."

"Copy that." Zim kept zooming through traffic in that direction.

Garrett turned in the passenger seat and eyed Caldwell tapping away on his phone. Maybe his intel . . . "Got anything?"

The spook shook his head. "Some stuff about hydrogen cyanide," he answered without looking up.

Garrett clenched his jaw. Delaney gone, LD3s missing, and the spook looked for chem intel. Doing his own thing as usual. Eager to jump through his phone to Delaney and Surge, Garrett looked down at his screen. A slow smile spread across his face. "The tracking signal reappeared. Northeast, Zim."

The tires screeched as Zim steered around a car pulling out of an office parking lot in front of them.

He eyed his screen again for the tracker and stilled. "What . . . this can't be right." He frowned, watching Surge's tracker sliding across the screen. Fast. Too fast. "The tracker is going nearly two hundred miles an hour now! Southwest."

"That's strange." Zim squealed into a parking lot, spun the SUV around, and drove southwest.

"What is going on? It doesn't make—"

"Pull over," Caldwell said.

"Are you insane? Those chems, not to mention Delaney—"

"Nobody can catch a train going three hundred fifty KPH." Caldwell held up his phone to show a picture. "She's on Whoosh, the Indonesian bullet train they just extended all the way to Surabaya."

"You sure?"

"Nothing else in Indonesia goes three hundred fifty kilometers an hour."

"Augh!" Garrett banged the dash as he felt the SUV slow and pull to the curb.

A new problem to work. Garrett tapped fingers on the console. Delaney was with Surge. But they needed to find her now. It made sense that she'd followed the LD3s onto a bullet train.

"Wait. Passenger or freight train?"

"Freight," Caldwell said, reading from his phone. "They started a freight bullet train once a week last month. With security, but otherwise, only freight. A piece of technology worth more than seven billion dollars."

Garrett ground his teeth. The intel of that lone wolf Caldwell was . . . almost . . . perfect. He didn't trust the man. Hated to trust him. But he had to. He twisted in his seat. "Can you reach out to Damocles?"

"Of course. Why?"

Garrett grinned. "To catch a bullet train, we're going to need a helo."

"I think it's too high profile and high risk, but . . . we can't afford to let the chems get out of country." The spook grabbed his phone and punched speed dial.

Garrett turned forward.

Zim glanced back at Caldwell, who had reached Chapel, and shifted in the driver's seat. "You trust him, Boss?"

Garrett pinched his lips together, then gazed out the window as they passed the Merdeka Palace, lights starting to come on as the sun fell. It hurt to be in a position to rely on the spook. "Caldwell attacks a mission in his own way," he finally said in a low voice. "Holding the silicone evidence until he knew for sure what it was? That's not a team way of doing things."

"I see why you brought him with us. Keep your eye on him."

Garrett nodded, lowered his voice even more. "Trust is hard, but he is effective—"

"A helo will meet us at a nearby Navy base," Caldwell said from the back seat. "I'll send the directions to your phone, Zim."

Garrett started when it appeared on the screen of Zim's phone, propped up on the console. "That's Indonesia Navy."

Caldwell chuckled, shrugged. "This is the kind of thing Chapel does. I don't ask how. We meet the helo there in twenty mikes. Let's move."

Zim scrolled through the directions to the airport, then headed the car out, hit the gas. Nearly hit a car and steered crazily onto the shoulder of the road.

Garrett grasped the grab handle to keep from sliding as the SUV swerved back onto the road just as a motorcycle shifted into the same lane. Zim swerved back onto the shoulder, then sped past the motorcycle and finally got back onto the road.

"Sorry," Zim said. "We're almost out of downtown."

RONIE KENDIG & VONI HARRIS

The red color of the road on the phone's GPS map did turn yellow, then green just ahead. At the moment, he hated red. "But will we make it to the base in time?"

Tongue sticking out of his mouth in concentration, Zim nodded.

Silence reigned. For a second.

"By the way, the support team is bringing explosives," Caldwell said. "You're SEALs—you'll know what to do when we get to the bullet train. And that stuff will be off the planet."

Explosives? Garrett exchanged a look with Zim. "That's not the plan." He held his ground when Caldwell gave him a long look. "Not with Delaney and Surge aboard the train!"

Delaney had never planned on being in a freight car with containers full of potassium cyanide and sulfamic acid vials. In the dark. Only moonlight pushed past the black veil of night, slanting through the narrow window of the loading door.

How had she even ended up here, sitting between two stacks of Sachaai containers, her hands buried in Surge's fur? "I didn't freeze like at the store shooting," she muttered to him.

He reached up and licked her smack across her face.

She chuckled, wiped off his slobber with her sleeve. "Okay, okay. I admit it. I froze."

He snorted.

"But I didn't *stay* frozen. And I won't. I promise." *Please, God.*

He nudged her cheek and downed, his head on her knee as usual when she needed it.

Delaney ruffled the fur of his jet-black head that seemed to meld into the darkness and tried to call Garrett. Didn't work. Not in a speeding train, she guessed. Comms had stopped ages ago. He'd tracked her once via Surge's implant, and she hoped he could do it again.

God, keep Surge's tracker working. Please. Please. She rubbed the spot between Surge's shoulders where the tracker had been injected.

What would she do when the train stopped?

Delaney couldn't just sit here and pet her maligator, and she couldn't jump out and risk bumping into security. Wait. Hadn't she seen a door at the end of the train car? Yep. She walked over and pressed a button on the wall next to it. It slid open for her. Open sesame, right? She stepped through to the caboose, Surge right behind her, and found herself in a kind of foyer. The caboose, apparently, was only lit by the last rays of falling sun shining through the window in an outside door.

She could jump out with Surge, find someplace the SAT phone would work. Refusing to think how that jump would hurt, she looked through the window. Trees and buildings blurred by so fast it almost made her dizzy.

This had to be a bullet train. She couldn't survive a jump out of a speeding train.

"With me, Surge," she said, heading back to the LD3 stacks. Tension tightened the muscles in her shoulders, so she stretched her neck from side to side. Her hip brushed up against a piece of paper taped to the middle Sachaai container. She shone her SAT phone light onto the page with the flashlight app. A shipping document.

Wait . . . *coffee*? Seriously? What'd happened to the shoes and plastic butterflies? She glanced around the interior, trying to make sense of why these containers were headed to Cantika Coffee Farm, near Surabaya.

An uneasy thought churned through her—what if she'd somehow followed the wrong containers?

No. She hadn't. She'd never taken eyes off the semi from the time it left the market. So why on earth were these headed to a coffee farm? Not that she was mad—she loved Choca Cantika coffee, the coffee she and all her friends paid extra for at every opportunity. Her friends had posted about the new Choca Cantika Barbecue Sauce on their socials last week. She recalled once reading the "About" paragraph on the back of one of their coffee packages. The owners grew it and roasted it here in Surabaya, Indonesia . . .

Wait. Wait-wait-wait. She turned a circle, as if the wheels grinding in her brain were moving her body. But it all suddenly made sense. Crazy, stupid, evil sense.

Or was she the one with the evil mind? After all, at this point it was just a theory, but what if the shoe factory loaded cute plastic children's shoes with the chemicals, then shipped them to said coffee farm . . . then sliced open the butterflies and laced the coffee beans, shipped them across the Pacific . . . to where they were selling like wildfire across America?

She paled. That was the coffee she'd stopped for at Coffeeshop Nation on her way to the plane to Singapore. That was the coffee in the monthly coffee club she subscribed her dad to.

Terrorist Coffee.

She pulled the sandal out of her pocket, jiggled the vial in the right side of the butterfly body. It clicked and easily popped out. Knowing it was filled with either sulfamic acid or potassium cyanide, she didn't dare open the twist lid. She eased the vial back into the butterfly body, shoved it into her pocket.

Delaney had to hand it to the Sachaai—this was pretty genius. Terrifyingly so. After all, who'd ever think to look at cute kids' shoes? Then who would ever think that coffee, which Americans drank by the billions of cups each year, would be laced with a toxin?

An explosion could kill hundreds or thousands, depending on where it was set off, but if terrorists wanted to kill possibly millions of Americans, Sachaai just needed to put hydrogen cyanide in the number one favorite coffee brand in the US.

Merciful burnt beans! This was awful.

Garrett needed to know—*now*!

Again, she eyed her SAT phone. No signal at all. At least she'd told him there were six LD3 containers before she'd jumped onto this train. She scratched Surge between the shoulders. Garrett had the MWD tracking app. And without a doubt, even if he wasn't coming for her, she knew he and the others would be coming for the chemicals.

As long as *his* SAT phone had a signal. If the signal made it out of the freight car.

Oh no. She hadn't thought about that. Maybe she needed to get Surge into the open, onto the platform, but that . . . that seemed too dangerous. *Please, please, God!*

She sighed. Having no clue where the train was headed or how long it would be, she turned off and pocketed her phone. Surge's nose nudged her cheek again.

Was she foolish, or had she fearlessly—thanks to the peace and strength of God—leapt into action by jumping onto this train with Surge? She hadn't frozen but had been spurred into action by a deep conviction that losing sight of this shipment meant terrible things. That deep-down voice of Garrett's stayed with her . . . he had trusted her to follow these containers. *When you trust a man, you jump on a train.* She chuckled.

Since they'd started the mission, they had a few moments to review the Krav Maga self-defense, the shoulder grab from the front and the choke hold. Realization spread through her—God trusted him, had put him in charge of this mission, and it was God she ultimately trusted. And she'd learned to trust Garrett too . . .

What she knew because of that was that Garrett *was* coming after her and Surge. And of course the chemicals, but somehow accepting that he'd come for her spurred and inspired her. It didn't matter anymore how she was going to get off this train. What mattered was how she was going to destroy the Sachaai's plan and prevent the butterfly shoes bearing tubes of toxic chems from reaching Cantika Coffee Farm.

How exactly, genius?

Yeah, she wasn't a Navy SEAL. But the team wasn't here. She was. The weight of the mission's success was on her shoulders—

no wonder they were balled tight. Subconsciously, she'd known the responsibility she bore. But worse . . . what was the price if she failed?

Surge gave a low-throated growl. Looking up, she saw a flashlight bobbing around the front of the car as the sound of steps reached her. Could be help.

The beam bounced off a silver container and lit the face of a man as he looked around. Three-day beard, longish black hair, power in his every move.

A tremor went up and down her spine.

Hakim.

Surge's hackles rose.

Delaney drew him out of sight into the narrow space between the last LD3 stack and the door into the caboose. She signaled him into silence, then squatted behind him, letting him be the fury Hakim would meet if he came at them. Hands on the shoulders of her four-legged protector, his tense muscles rippling, she willed her own breathing to slow and quieten.

Hakim stopped and turned in the aisle they'd just vacated. He traced the area with his beam, then each of the six Sachaai containers before he pulled a radio from his belt.

"Everything looks good back here, Tariq," Hakim said into his radio. "We're underway, so once the engineer knows our exact arrival time, contact Alina. Her team will need to get busy with the vials at Cantika."

Tariq was on the train too? *God, now what?*

"Are you sure?" crackled Tariq's voice. "Rashid and I can handle the exchange. Don't need her."

Delaney's stomach clenched. Rashid too? Good heavens! The three men were so dangerous Garrett had almost made her remain at the safe house. So dangerous that she was sitting here, hiding behind LD3s. Frozen.

What do I do, God?

Hakim snickered. "Alina has more passion for Pakistan leading the true Muslim world in her little toenail than the two of you have together in your whole bodies. She will get it done, and the widespread damage will let America know we do not need or want them! That's why I put her in place there— maximum damage!"

The door between the two cars opened and shut.

Easing back against the vibrating hull of the train car, Delaney kept Surge close as she listened for any sign that Hakim was still in the box with her. Smooth strokes along Surge's spine kept Delaney's nerves from fraying any further . . . for the first five minutes. But her mind worried over the things she'd overheard and what she'd learned. Who was Alina? Hakim had said he had her in place—for maximum damage.

And the chemicals in the containers . . .

When Surge stretched forward, swiveling his head around the corner of the container stack, she realized she'd been sitting here for quite a while, ruminating. Since no shot or shout erupted when he'd eased out, she released him.

Surge rose to all fours, seemingly confident and calm instead of muscles tensed, ready to attack. That was good, right? She peered around the stack and, finding it empty, sagged against the wall of the freight car. *Call Garrett!* She yanked out the SAT phone and groaned . . . still no signal. And sweet mercy—the power bar was fading.

Tears welled, and she pressed her hands to her eyes. No tears now. Mission. She had to get word to Garrett, but the phone wasn't working. *What do I do?* Her heart screamed for help, but then in whispered the still, small voice . . . reminded her to trust.

She'd just said that, hadn't she? That she trusted God, that she trusted Garrett? And where was that trust and peace now that her SAT phone wasn't working?

Still there. She drew in a deep breath, reaching for the inner quiet stillness. Let it guide her.

If the SAT phone wasn't working because of interference with the train somehow, how could the tracker possibly work?

Nerves thrumming, she tightened her jaw. *God . . .*

Mentally, she stepped back, drew in a breath. She couldn't do anything other than be here. She more-than-ever believed God had her exactly where she needed to be—but *her* limitations didn't limit God. Or Garrett.

He knew she'd gotten on the train. As a Navy SEAL operator, he could easily discover it was a bullet train. Probably already had. And he knew where they'd last been before boarding the train. So with Caldwell's intelligence help, he could ascertain the destination, which she knew only because of the label.

But the coffee beans . . . She eyed the containers. Was this shipment important? Or did they already have more chemicals at the coffee bean farm? No . . . she doubted that simply because she recalled Zim saying this was enough to wipe out thousands. What worried her second-most, after the spread of this horrific chemical mixture, was when the train stopped. How would she get out of here without being seen? How would she follow them to this farm?

Okay. That seemed next to impossible. So . . . yeah. She needed Garrett here. Now. And she *wanted* him here. Even if he got in her face about being a rogue and found her frustrating to no end. He was likely the best guy she knew . . . after Dad. And Surge.

But would he make it in time?

Augh! Stop stop stop.

"'God is my refuge and strength. An ever-present help in time of trouble . . . '" Psalm 46:1 infused her with more peace, staying the panic that threatened her. "I know you don't have signal interference God, though sometimes it seems like it, but, uh, yeah—I'm in trouble here. Please, help."

15

MEJAYAN, INDONESIA

"Anything?" Garrett demanded.

"Negative," Caldwell bit out. "The Whoosh is nonstop to Surabaya. She'll be fine. It is still moving and—if it wasn't, I would've told you—"

"Do you get that she's not an operator, that she has no idea about tactics or hand-to-hand?" One lesson in Krav did not an MMA fighter make.

"Do *you* get that she has a dog capable of ripping out throats?" Caldwell scoffed. When Garrett growled, the spook held up his hands. "Bear. You let her go, told her to stay with the chems. We know where that train is headed, and it's nonstop." He scanned the intel.

Garrett wanted to kill the guy. But he was right.

Hold up. "It's nonstop to where?" Garrett asked, checking the tracker app for the thousandth time. Still no active signal from Surge.

"Surabaya."

Surabaya . . . Why was that familiar? "What's in the area?"

"Surabaya is a big, thriving city. It's known as the City of

199

Heroes after a great battle during Indonesia's independence revolution." Caldwell ducked closer to his device. "Top companies include Next1—a mobile services company. A blood donation center called Reblood, and PT PG Rajawali—a sugar factory that produces maple, sweet maja—"

"Shoe factory . . . sugar factory . . ." Garrett chewed through those names. "Zim, any of those work for mixing the chemical? I'm thinking about the sugar factory."

"Uh . . . wait—negative. The sulfamic acid in Sachaai's formula is an ingestible poison—a nightmare for a sugar factory owner."

"Okay, so not the sugar factory," Garrett muttered. He glanced back at Caldwell. "What else is there?"

"You realize," Zim said, "any of these companies could simply be a front."

Garrett grunted even as he realized the spook was still listing companies.

" . . . eTraining Indonesia, Cantika Coffee Farm, Belajar—"

"Wait!" Garrett whipped around in his seat. "Cantika . . . Choca Cantika—Delaney loves that coffee."

Negotiating traffic, which had let up, Zim eyed him. "You think . . ."

"Favorite coffee has nothing to do with the chems," Caldwell countered.

Man, Garrett wanted to punch the guy. But he was right. Again. "I know . . ." But what were the chances that Delaney had talked about this coffee right before they ended up headed straight toward it?

"However," Zim said as they pulled up to the Indonesia Navy base, "coffee would combine well with hydrogen cyanide, thanks to Tariq's non-dissipating oil spray . . ."

Garrett hesitated, eyeing the guards around the gate, who were well-armed and giving other entrants a hard time.

"Evening, sir," the guard said in a thick accent. "ID?" Once he had Zim's ID, the guard checked a clipboard, then nodded.

"Very good, sir. Straight down. Two rights. You'll find the airstrip."

"Thanks," Zim said, easing the vehicle forward.

"That was easy," Garrett said. Too easy.

"That," Caldwell said, "is the power of Tyson Chapel."

As they headed to the chopper, Garrett refocused. "So, Cantika . . . think that's where they're headed?"

Zim bumped his arm. "With all those chems in all those shoes, Sachaai could contaminate a whole crop of coffee beans at the roastery."

"It's genius, really," Caldwell said. "Lace coffee beans with the chemical, ship it overseas with nobody the wiser, then let Americans drink themselves to their death."

"Sick . . . we have to stop them."

Ping!

Garrett snapped his gaze to this SAT phone. "Yes! Finally, got a signal on the tracker."

"Which tells us what? That they're still going three fifty klicks an hour?"

"One day," Garrett said as they climbed out and grabbed their gear, "you're going to smart off and have my fist in your teeth."

"And I'll have your career."

He shouldered into the ruck and jogged toward the helo, noting they didn't have a support team.

"Bear?"

Garrett grinned. "Yeah."

The pilot struck out a hand. "Frank." He thumbed over his shoulder. "This way and we'll get you in the air."

"Where's the rest of the team?"

Frank smirked. "Copilot is all we have," he said, indicating toward the gear. "Chapel sent some weaponry and gear but sends his apologies. They got spun up on an op to save an HVT."

So, we're on our own, Garrett thought as he hiked into the bird and planted himself in a seat, grabbed the onboard headphones. Once they were airborne, he decided to make use of the local asset. "Frank," he said over the din of the engines and rotors. "What can you tell us about Choca Cantika?"

"Cantika Coffee Farm is on the Mount Bromo volcano slope," Frank said, sounding like a tour guide. "The farm is about ninety-five klicks out," he added, sounding much more serious.

Holding up a data pad, headphones on, Caldwell shone it at Garrett. "It's not far from the bullet train station in Surabaya."

"True—you can smell them roasting it every night from that platform."

That coffee farm had to be it . . . Garrett looked out of the helo at the sky darkening over hot, humid Indonesia. The thought of preschool shoes decorated with butterfly shapes filled with lethal chemicals. Those chemicals being consumed across the States. Ice dumped into his gut. Maybe he'd never have Cantika coffee again. But . . .

Caldwell shifted in his seat. "Just checked shipping manifests for Cantika. Next shipment is going out first thing in the morning. Factoring in timing for delivery, unloading . . . processing . . . they could be gone by morning."

Chest tightening, Garrett shook his head. "With no assets to support us, no way we can raid a whole factory."

"Agreed," the spook said.

"We have to stop that train." Okay, time to work out a plan. Garrett rubbed his hands together. "Bullet train is going roughly three hundred fifty klicks an hour. Can we catch them, Frank?"

Frank messed with the controls for a second. "Train will slow as it approaches Surabaya, but we're flying two hundred." He tapped at his screen, and Garrett strained to see what Frank was showing them . . . the speed dial and the map. He clicked his tongue. "We're ten mikes from the train."

Garrett reached up and clapped his shoulder.

"Then in six minutes," Caldwell said, "we bomb the train, explode the chemicals off the planet. Success!"

NEAR SURABAYA, INDONESIA

The train was slowing. They had to be coming up on a train station.

Delaney knew that while Garrett was en route, he wasn't *here*. Hakim was on board, and if they stopped, they could get these containers to the farm and make their deadly chemical. That didn't even take into consideration that Hakim was here. *Hakim!*

She needed a plan.

Plan A: Send Surge to each car ahead of her, then take on Hakim when they found him. But that wasn't solid, because if she sent Surge, she had exactly zero ways to defend herself against the others.

Plan B: Leave Surge here to protect the LD3s full of Sachaai chemical vials while she sought Hakim herself. Still left her with no way to defend herself. As well as she had learned the technique from Garrett's lesson in martial arts, she knew she wasn't up to a three-on-one.

Plan C: Drag the LD3s to the caboose and dump them overboard. Huh. Could she? She stood up and pulled at the LD3 on top of the stack as hard as she could. She couldn't even budge it. They were way too heavy. Yeah. Plan C was terrible too.

Plan D . . .

She didn't have a Plan D.

Plans A and B had the same problem—she'd had quick self-defense classes that didn't amount to anything against three armed terrorists. Even with Surge. And while he could solve the Hakim problem, that would leave her to solve the Rashid and Tariq problems. Not to mention it wouldn't tell her how to stop the chemical attack.

Surge nudged her leg, and she slid down to the floor, wrapped her arm around him.

Dad was right. She was useless when it came to the most important moments in life. Not that he'd ever said that—he was too nice to actually voice it—but how could he not think it? He'd lost his leg because of her. She'd hid instead of stopping the shooter.

Now this mission was also going to fail. Because of her. The chems were going to make it to the coffee farm.

Because of her.

She wasn't a SEAL. She was just a girl on a train with an MWD. She reached down and scratched the Mal under the chin.

Yes, climbing into the rideshare to follow had been her choice. A maverick move, but . . . *Garrett* had told her to stay with the containers on the train with Surge. Her team would save her.

Except, what if Garrett was right in what he'd said yesterday? That she refused to be seen as incompetent—so she just rushed into wherever she wanted, to do whatever she wanted.

Her breath hitched.

The truth was that whenever she barged into a situation to "prove herself a hero," what she really ended up doing was *testing* God.

Ouch.

She'd been so determined to prove herself at the middle school that she hadn't watched—*really watched*—Surge. She had barged into it. The whole embarrassing public overwhelm could've been avoided. Her heart skipped a beat. She was bold all right. Bold for *herself*. Because she didn't want to be seen as weak or afraid or . . .

Or a little girl caught in a robbery, watching her world fall apart.

She'd frozen. Because what was she supposed to do as a child? Delaney scoffed. Garrett said she'd probably saved her life, and her father's. By freezing. Yeah, right.

Delaney, you were eight. Dad's voice bubbled up in her memory. *You couldn't stop the shooter. But it was you in the store with me. It was your hands pressed against my gunshot like the 911 operator told you. Because of Christ.*

She had forgotten he'd said that back when she was a teen, so tied up in a push to prove herself a hero—which was how she'd ended up serving community service at A Breed Apart.

The truth of that stung deep and pushed a tear down her cheek.

Surge licked the tear.

"Thanks, boy," she whispered, burying her hands in his fur.

It was true she'd mavericked her way through life for herself. But it was not Surge, Heath, Garrett, America, or even Dad she owed an apology to. She sank her chin to her chest.

God, please forgive me. I thought I was doing Your will. But I was doing nothing more than trying to be a hero. To show off, really. To protect myself, so I didn't have to trust You or anyone else to protect me. But I do trust You. And I need your help.

"Situational awareness" echoed in her mind—Garrett's voice during their self-defense training session. And it was Garrett who'd surprised her when he'd called her "bold" for taking off after Rashid and Tariq outside the Shoemakers Extraordinaire.

Garrett was bold himself, in his own way. Yeah, lots of guys had biceps and wide, strong shoulders. Bright brown eyes. But they couldn't lead a team to stop a terrorist attack. They didn't all laugh at a Mal chewing on their underwear. Nor were they willing to learn how to work with said Mal. Most weren't trustworthy like Garrett.

His hands on her shoulders during that first Krav Maga self-defense lesson . . . she could still feel them. Garrett was all man.

She'd seen his strength, his confidence, his willingness to own his mistakes and apologize . . . all those things had helped her be a better version of herself. It'd helped her to stop being a rogue and instead focus on the mission. Which was how she and Surge had ended up on a bullet train with six LD3s of potassium cyanide and sulfamic acid.

Delaney scruffed Surge's thick neck fur. When he licked her

whole face, she chuckled. Then hugged him tighter, realizing how it'd all come together. Maybe it wasn't over, and clearly she would still face the darkest battle yet, but she could see how God had orchestrated all the pieces of this puzzle to confront and stop these terrorists. First . . . a year ago, God had stirred her to not give up on Surge, who had the aggression and scent training needed for this mission. And God had let Heath not give up on her, teaching her how to train dogs and believing in her. Then word had gotten back to Garrett through a series of connections and he'd come to the ranch.

Because of all that, God's merciful hand, she and Surge had detected the chemicals . . . gone to the market, discovered the shoes . . . now, they were here.

And Garrett was coming.

She refused to believe otherwise. Neither would she believe she was frozen. Or helpless. God was with her.

Okay, God . . . help me do what I can because of You.

She freed her hair from its ponytail, smoothed it, then put the elastic band back in.

Now. So she couldn't get LD3s full of chems off this train by herself. She needed to know what was in the boxcar. She patted Surge's chest and stood, looked around the dark interior. With her head on a swivel, she shone her SAT phone flashlight around and walked the car with Surge at her side, snuffling all over the place, especially at containers marked "Good Job Dog Treats."

She grinned. "Not yours, buddy. C'mon."

They finished the tour of the car in about two minutes. No hits. She returned to the six Sachaai LD3s and slid back to the floor, and Surge rested his chin on her leg.

Wait. What was that black lump on the floor by the container in the corner?

She got up and walked over. "Surge, check it."

He sniffed at it, then looked up at her. If he were a person, he would've shrugged.

"Let's see what it is, then." She drew closer. Oh. It was a black rock. Hand-sized. Hefty. Her mouth twitched.

If they'd been here with her, Garrett and Zim would have been doing one thing—checking their weapons. At least one of the three Sachaai would return to check on the LD3s, for sure. If there weren't even more Sachaai aboard.

She picked up the black rock. It wasn't an official weapon at all.

At least it was weapon-like. She grinned. *Thank You, God.*

This was apparently Plan D.

BETWEEN MEJAYAN AND SURABAYA, INDONESIA

"You out of your mind?" Garrett growled. In his mind's eye he saw Delaney and her fearless, swingy ponytail, the way she tilted her head at him . . . flying into a million pieces. "No way. We aren't bombing a seven-point-three-*billion*-dollar bullet train."

Caldwell held his gaze.

There was something in Caldwell's gaze that silenced Garrett, though he wasn't sure what it was.

"You have to trust me," Caldwell continued. "We'll just hit the engine. Precision. That will knock only the front of the train off the rails. Rogue will be fine."

Garrett couldn't believe the spook was that dumb. But one thing kept ringing in his head—well, two. First, the most obvious, that Rogue would be killed. But second, he'd never trusted anyone. Trusting Dad had taught him that painful lesson. And maybe his anger at Caldwell and his misplaced irritation with Delaney had a core base: also Dad.

God probably wanted him to work on that. He would. After this mission.

His breath stuck in his throat, knowing that if he didn't resolve this and didn't make it back alive . . . Wasn't there something in the Bible about if you withheld your forgiveness, God would withhold His?

Like he needed anything else bad in his life right now.

So. Deal with it. Anger and rage had been his tack in life.

Truth sizzled through his veins. His anger toward Dad came from his anger toward God for all He'd "let" Dad do to Garrett. Let their family go through.

Yet . . . he saw now how God had put teachers, friends in his life. The SEALs. This team. Delaney. Wow. Yeah. God had always been building his life. *I'm so sorry. I really do trust You. I really do.* His gaze focused back on the spook. He didn't have to agree with Caldwell's idea, but he could deal with it in a legit manner. "One, that is a seven-point-three-billion-dollar mistake, because if we bomb it while it's going at a high rate of speed, that whole thing will fly off the tracks. With Rogue and Surge in it. They won't survive." He shook his head. "So that's out. Besides, I don't have that in my bank account to pay back. Do you?"

Caldwell nodded. "Point taken. Guess you want to punch me again."

Actually . . . no. Strange. But that familiar rage that drove his life . . . it wasn't there. What was there, however, was a keen awareness. Forget not hitting him. Forget control. *This man was wrong, all wrong.* When they got to the ground . . .

He took a deep breath. "Explain the logic behind what you want to do."

Caldwell gave Garrett a tight smile. "One: Surabaya has over three million people. We need to stop the thing before it's near the station and people get hurt. Two: it's just the three of us right now, so if there are more Sachaai at the station, we won't have a prayer of stopping them."

Garrett's mood went grim. He looked out of the bird. Nobody wanted innocents dying. Hang it all if Caldwell wasn't right again—it was smart to destroy the chems before Sachaai could grab them. But there was another option. "We slow it down."

"How?" Caldwell demanded.

Good question. "Modern-day trains don't have cabooses. Bullet trains have operation cabs at the front and back, so fast-rope down to the train, anchor onto the roof, shimmy down to the roof hatch, and drop in."

"At three hundred fifty kilometers an hour?" Caldwell balked.

Garrett lifted a shoulder in a shrug. He really appreciated the shock in the spook's expression. "We're SEALs. We've done worse."

"You're insane."

"Me? You're the one who wants to bomb a seven-billion-dollar bullet train." Garrett rubbed his jaw. "Look, we don't need to destroy the train. We just need to stop it. So, we get aboard. There's a driver, so we either make him slow it, or we slow it. That'll keep the US on good terms with Indonesia and give Damocles time to assemble a team to help locals interdict the chemicals."

"That's . . . a lot of uncertainty."

"Right now, it's the best we have. We cannot let them get the chemicals to Surabaya." Garrett watched Zim packing some C4 and detonator wires into his tac vest.

"Just in case," the guy said with a shrug.

"Zim and I fast-rope down to the Whoosh. Frank falls back"—he caught the pilot's eye —"but stays close enough for a quick exfil. We get Thompson harnessed up, and you bring her to safety. Tricky and dangerous, but if this goes south, it's better that she's not aboard. Then Zim and I work our way to the engineer and force him to stop the train outside Surabaya."

Caldwell puffed a breath, looked to the pilot. "Can you do that? Lower them to a speeding train?"

The pilot shrugged. "I'm a go if you are."

"Let's do it," Zim said.

Garrett still didn't trust Caldwell—not sure he ever would—but he did trust God. "Let's do it."

"Five mikes to the train," Frank answered.

Garrett shifted to the edge of the bird and moved to the jumpseat, the terrain blurring beneath his boots.

Caldwell climbed next to the door, holding his position, shouting to be heard. "Once we get to the train, you'll have twenty mikes to stop it."

"Three mikes!" the pilot shouted.

Nodding, Caldwell readied the fast-rope. "If you fail, the hydrogen cyanide coffee beans get to the States. Then you can face Chapel and thousands of families whose loved ones died."

"Thanks for the pep talk." Stuffing his hands into the thick gloves, Garrett nodded. "Warn Chapel." He pinned Caldwell with his gaze. "We'll need a team to intercept the LD3s before the Sachaai realize what happened and send their people for them."

Caldwell reached for his SAT phone.

"Two mikes!"

Zim looked Garrett up and down and patted his shoulder, assuring him his gear was ready.

"Wait till Rogue is ready, then come down with a harness for her. I'll get Rogue off, then you come," Garrett said.

"Copy that, Boss."

With a nod, Garrett shifted his glance. Held the rope, coiled his right leg around the part whipping in the wind. He swiveled around, gave one more nod, and hopped out into the dark night and let gravity yank him downward.

16

AT LEAST THEY HAD A LITTLE AIR CONDITIONING ON THIS BULLET train. Delaney supposed there were products on board that wouldn't do well in Indonesian heat. Still, she was getting hot, and her legs were falling asleep underneath Surge's seventy pounds. She massaged his shoulders, shifted her weight.

They sat against a shipping container right across from the loading door—the rock-weapon right next to her—so they could slip out immediately when the train stopped. Somehow. Somebody from Sachaai would be picking up the LD3s, right? Could she follow them to Cantika and not be seen? She hoped so. She wasn't sure what else to do.

Delaney looked at her SAT phone. Still no bars, and that power bar was slowly but surely dropping. The team would know the train she was on, where it'd left. But what if they were delayed? So many things had already gone wrong that she couldn't count on it to be simple.

She turned off the phone and slipped it back into the pocket of her denim jacket.

Once at the coffee farm, what would she and Surge do about

the chemicals before they became hydrogen cyanide? She had no idea.

I'd appreciate an idea, God, but please get Garrett there.

Surge popped into a stand, his hackles raised. He gave a low-throated rumble.

"What's up?" she whispered, suddenly very alert.

His rumble turned into a growl. What had gotten his attention? She pushed up, but her toe accidentally sent that rock rolling across the floor. "Oh n—"

The doors of the car slid open and shut.

Sucking in a breath, she jerked back. Carefully peered around the containers to see if it was Hakim who'd entered the boxcar.

From behind, arms hooked her back into a choke hold.

The feral snapping and barking of Surge blended with her own panic as rough fabric scratched her cheek, as her air cut off.

She felt the impact as Surge lunged into the guy, clamping onto his only available limb—a leg. Though the guy cried out, his grip on her did not release. Air cut off, she panicked. Knew Surge was doing all he could.

Her vision started blurring, veins pulsing against her temples. Hearing started going.

God, help. The time Garrett taught her how to defend the choke hold wasn't enough. She didn't have any muscle memory to work from.

Or brain memory. Hands . . . something else . . . crotch, then eyes . . . Shoot. There was more. Where was her brain?

Hands, gravity, crotch, eyes, twist, ground.

She pulled down on his arm as hard as she could. Gave herself a little room to breathe. She dropped her center of gravity.

He stumbled, and though he still held her, the grip had lessened. She could breathe. Enough to remember what to do next. She leaned to the side, dropped an arm, and threw her elbow into his crotch. No pretending this time.

Amid a strained, pained groan, he dropped low. That's when

she saw his sleeve tugged up . . . and peeking out from it, the Sachaai S tattoo.

Moonlight through the narrow window gave her a look at the man. Bald. Thick, trim beard. Rashid! The man who'd passed her in the alley during Garrett's second undercover operation.

A chill crashed down her spine.

Delaney used the moment to scrabble out of reach. "Surge, on me!" She patted his side and steadied herself.

"You stupid woman!"

Heart in her throat, Delaney flipped back to face Rashid, found him aiming a weapon at her. She sucked in a hard breath. Realized too late that she was blocking Surge from reaching him. Then again, she wasn't sure she wanted him in the line of bullet fire. But that's what he was trained for, right?

Firming his grip, Rashid took aim.

Choice made for her, she held out a hand. Then at the last minute, angled aside. "Surge, attack!"

The sleek black body of her Malinois sailed through the air. The report of the shot echoed in the space. She could only pray there was enough noise on the train that the others didn't hear. That the shot hadn't hit Surge.

Shock forced the Sachaai to rely on instinct—his arm raised to protect himself gave the perfect anchoring point for the maligator's powerful jaws. Surge hung onto Rashid's arm. Though the guy thrashed and fought, he couldn't keep the hold on his weapon. And Surge wasn't letting go.

Staggering around, Rashid lifted his arm, swung it around, hard. Thrashed Surge into a container. That normally wouldn't have worked—MWDs were trained to lock and hold until their handler gave a command to release. But the confined space and the angle of the hit dislodged him.

With a yelp, Surge dropped and crashed to the deck.

Her heart stopped. Delaney struggled for air. "Surge!" She started toward him.

But he roused, shook his head, dazed as he climbed back to his feet.

Thank You, God! Able to breathe again, she marveled as her four-legged hero whipped around to once more face and take on Rashid. Head down, he bared his teeth in a low snarl.

She really wasn't sure who was more determined to kill the other. Her bet was on Surge any day of the year. She rounded to face the bald man too. But what could she do? She had no weapon—her gaze drifted to the rock nearby.

Rashid clenched and unclenched his hands.

In a real battle, you have to flip on a combat mindset, Garrett had taught her. But she had no idea how to do that. Not in this situation. *I don't know how to get out of this, God.*

Eyes fixed on her, Rashid stomped toward her, his bloody arms at the ready.

She took a step back and felt the press of the container digging into her shoulder blades. Shoot.

The train banked around a curve, jerking all of them—even the rock. It didn't seem Rashid had seen it or noticed her. He was now locked onto Surge and his now-bloody canines.

She dove for it and felt heavy weight crash into her spine, knocking the air from her lungs. Her fingers coiled around the rock.

Rashid drove a punch into her side and blinding pain erupted.

"Augh!" Arching her spine against the agony, she felt and heard the vicious snap of Surge as he careened into Rashid. The two battled and she worked to free herself from beneath Rashid.

She twisted around. Reared back and, with all her might, brought the rock down on Rashid's head. *Crack!*

With a moan, he dropped to the ground and went limp.

But her military working dog was ticked. With a snarl, he dove in for another lock.

"Surge, out," Delaney said, holding her stomach. The

sickening crack of stone-on-skull had made her want to vomit. On all fours, she breathed deep, eyed the terrorist.

Unconscious.

So *that* was Plan D.

She pulled Surge into a hug. "Thank you, boy." She kissed his silky, narrow skull. As she hugged him again, she noticed something rocking on the train floor, bumping into a container.

A radio. She bent toward it—but the whirring vibration of the train and the high speed seemed to pull the radio beneath the pallet slats. Shoot.

Time to move. She turned to her Malinois and slid her hands over his sleek fur, half to inspect him for injuries—none—and half for the reassurance she found in him. "Okay, boy. Stay close. I need to make sure . . ." Nerves quailing, she inched toward the prone form. Avoided the halo of blood around his head and focused on the body. Lowering herself into a crouch, she reached toward him. Pressed her hand to his side. Felt no rise or fall. That's when she spotted the weapon holstered at his side. And the black grip of a gun. She slid it out of the leather brace and stuck it in her jacket pocket. She wasn't trained in firing weapons, but at least he couldn't use it against her if he suddenly resurrected.

Surge snuffled away . . . at blood around Rashid's head.

"On me, boy," she said, drawing the sleek, powerful Mal to herself. No idea what to do next or where to go—she did not want to stay here with a dead body—she struggled. Buried her face in Surge's fur. "We need Garrett here, don't we, Surge?"

Mercies, how badly she wanted him here. His arms around her. To hear him say that perfect phrase that would make everything better. Or at least not terrible. "I really need him." Her stomach twirled, bringing a startling realization. "I'm in love with him I think . . ."

Surge huffed.

"I know, I know. You'll be my first love . . ."

Another huff.

Delaney tousled the top of his head. They really did need Garrett. Surely he was already on the way, right? She pulled out her SAT phone. Did they even have service yet?

A clank came from the car ahead. Was she hearing shouts? Oh no.

OUTSIDE SURABAYA, INDONESIA

Gloves heating beneath the friction of the rope, leg coiling to control his momentum and keep him from being flung away, Garrett spiraled in the open air, the rotor wash stinging his face. Concentrating as wind spun him, he homed in on the end of the bullet train tearing across Indonesia. Aimed toward the operation car.

This will be interesting . . .

As he neared the end, he used his boot to slow himself and released a hand to grab his dagger. He'd need something to stop himself from flipping off under the force of the headwind. Three . . . two . . .

Garrett let the rope go and pitched himself at the barreling bullet train. He careened into it and bounced. Shoot! Dagger in hand, he was ready when he landed, though he felt the fury of the elements tear at him, the wind a violent enemy trying to slam him into oblivion. The dagger dug into the fiberglass hull. But with the rate of speed, the forces of gravity exerting themselves against him, the dagger didn't stop him. He slid, the blade gouging a line . . .

"Augh!" Garrett two-handed the blade. Scrambled for a toe hold on a ledge. Wedged himself cockeyed. Saw the five-inch scar he'd inflicted on the roof. Eyed the hatch that was to his left, close to his waist. Man. A few more inches and he'd have been hamburger meat. He gritted his teeth, holding the dagger, and pressed his hand to the hull. Tracked it toward the hatch.

He worked the cover free, then dug into the small well and flicked up the handle, then twisted it. Felt the pop of its release. Pulled it up, but the headwind battled him. It ripped out of his hand and slammed shut. He bit back an oath and tried again. This time, he managed to pull it up—but the angry wind tore it from the hinges and sent it flying.

Garrett dragged himself to the hole. Since nobody was shooting, he guessed the operation car was empty. Hoped so. He hauled himself down into it, snapping his submachine gun to his shoulder and scanning the darkened interior. He preferred this weapon in close quarters, as opposed to his holstered Sig, because having it set against his shoulder provided stability, and the fact it used handgun bullets meant he wasn't sending lead through several cars in overpenetration. Interior clear, he keyed his comms. "I'm in. Moving to freight car," he said, glancing at his watch. "T-minus nineteen and counting."

Delaney, where are you?

Garrett advanced. Stepped into the sealed juncture between cars, marveling at the pull of gravity on the high-speed train. He readied himself to breach the first freight car. Prayed and hoped Delaney was there. That'd be nice and quick. Get her topside and one less thing for him to worry about.

He released the latch and slid open the door, easing into the large open car filled with crates. Cleared left, then angled right, moving slow and smooth, submachine gun tucked to his shoulder. He cleared one stack, then a second, continuously moving forward and too aware of the seconds falling off the clock.

C'mon, Rogue . . . where'd you go?

A head popped up above a stack of LD3s, then popped back down.

"Hands! Hands!" he shouted, angling in that direction and hustling toward it.

The unknown stepped out from behind the stack. "Garrett?"

Her voice and worried visage were a sucker punch to his

chest. "Rogue!" Three long strides carried him to her. Instinct had him pull her into his arms. He tightened the hug. Then eased back and cupped her face, studying her eyes and expression. "You okay?"

"Yes! I am now."

Before he could tell himself otherwise, he set his mouth to hers. Kissed hard and quick. He pulled back.

Her eyes were wide, but she pressed her cheek to his chest and hugged him. Surge came up behind and pressed his shoulder into Garrett's thigh. "I knew you'd come. I kept asking God to help you find us." Though he heard his own relief mirrored in her words, she didn't sound right.

"You sound off." He surveyed her head to toe, as much as the moonlight through the narrow window would let him. "What's wrong?"

Her eyes went melty in the dim lighting. "I killed him," she whispered. "I killed him."

She'd killed someone? "Who? Where?"

"Rashid!" She pointed around the corner of the LD3s.

His pulse jacked. "*Rashid*'s on the train?" Her first kill—and Rashid to top that. "Good. You did good."

She opened her mouth to object.

"Not now. We'll talk later." He moved to the dead body and checked the pulse.

"Hakim and Tariq are here too."

That complicated things. A lot. He tightened his jaw and eyed the puncture wounds in Rashid's arm, leg, and shoulder. He smirked at Surge. "Good job." From his tac pants, he drew out zip cuffs and secured the hands. Wouldn't be the first time someone'd had a miraculous resurrection on the combat field.

"He isn't breathing—he's dead, right?" She was shaking.

On his feet, he guided her back toward the operation car. "Don't think about it. You did what you had to do. Time to get you off this train." They stepped into the juncture between the two cars. "Helo One, send the rope." He nodded to Delaney and kept moving. "Tell me what happened and what you know."

"These containers have the butterfly shoes with chem vials. Intel told us from the start they wanted to poison America's food supply, and given the coffee farm labels on the containers, I guess—"

"Coffee-drinking America."

"Yeah. And I saw Hakim. He was talking to Tariq on his radio before he left this car."

"Anyone else?" he asked, accessing the operation car.

"I . . . I don't know. I didn't see anyone else."

As he stepped into the operation car, where the roar of the wind swallowed sound, he looked at his watch. His gut roiled. Sixteen mikes. Closer to Surabaya. "Chopper's waiting—they'll draw you up in a hoist."

"Hoist me? Don't you want me down here handling Surge?"

Rogue's fearlessness made him smile. "There's going to be more fighting, more shooting. More dead bodies."

Her gaze drifted in the direction where Rashid had lain, and though she couldn't see him, it was all over her face that she couldn't do that again. "I . . . Okay . . ." She paled for a minute then pierced him with her eyes. "Surge can help you. He trusts you. We do."

"Trust God."

Light flickered, and clanging drew his attention topside. He saw boots toeing the edge. He grabbed Zim's boot and guided him inside.

The scrawny guy dropped to the deck with a nervous laugh. "That was insane!" He pivoted, extending the harness. "Caldwell's ready and waiting."

Garrett turned to her. "Here. Step in." He keyed his comms. "Package ready for exfil." When she did, he tightened the straps, his knuckles grazing something in her jacket pocket. "What—"

"That was Rashid's," she said, holding her elbow up and out

as he adjusted the harness. "My other pocket has the butterfly shoe I stole out of the top LD3—and I took pics."

"Show them to Caldwell." He tugged on the harness to make sure it was tight, then opened the door.

Hand on his shoulder, she nodded, her smile wavering as their gazes connected.

If they weren't in a life-and-death fight, he'd give her a longer, more meaningful kiss than the snatch-and-grab version he'd given in the container car.

"Okay." Garrett snagged the carabiner end and with his free hand caught the harness hugging her hips, drawing her toward the opening. "Hold on tight," he instructed over the wind and roar of the high-speed train. "When you lift out, you're going to swing out and possibly spiral. Just don't let go. Caldwell will bring you up."

Blinking, she held his gaze, but the fear crouching at the corners of her eyes tugged at him.

"You can do this."

"Didn't know I'd have this much adventure when Heath told me I was coming," she said in his ear with a grin.

"Never do." He tugged again to confirm she was set. He moved into view and peered up, finding the belly of the bird holding steady as Caldwell stood in the open door. Garrett waved the readiness.

With a quick jerk, Delaney was lifted off her feet. She gave a nervous laugh.

Surge barked, hopping at her.

"Stay, boy," she said, then looked up. Guided herself through the opening. Hair whipped free of her ponytail. She pitched forward. The harness snagged on an anchor.

A scream tore his heart from his chest. That and the sight of her anchored between a high-speed train and a helicopter struggling to keep pace.

"She's stuck!" Zim shouted as he caught her feet.

Garrett hopped up onto the control console and fought the snag.

"Cut her loose! Cut her loose," Caldwell barked. "Powerlines! We have to veer off."

God, help me!

Garrett fumbled with the harness, snagged on the handle. There was too much torque to free it. He crammed his hand between her stomach and the rim of the hatch. "Hold her legs!" he shouted to Zim, who anchored her with a carabiner to himself and wrapped his arms around her legs.

Garrett found the release and squeezed the D ring. Felt the nylon rope between the chopper and train straining.

"Bear—now!" Caldwell roared in his ear.

The stupid ring fought him, but he finally wiggled the catch. Freed it. And grabbed Delaney by her waist and dropped down. She flopped back inside, whacking her head against the hatch before she crashed to the deck on top of him.

Her body was trembling.

Garrett held on tight for a second, then shifted and laid her on the floor.

Delaney pressed her hands to her face, breaths coming in snuffling gasps.

"Hey." He rested a hand on her stomach. Gave a shake. "You're okay."

"No," she said beneath her hands. "I'm not." She lowered her arms, and tears streaked her face. But her breathing was steadying out, and Surge was there, snout stuffed in her face, sniffing, licking the tears. She hooked her arms around the fur-missile's neck and held on.

Garrett was kinda jealous.

"Boss, sorry . . . but we're losing time."

"Copy that." Garrett sat up, resting a hand on his knee, realizing they didn't have time to get her back up to the helo, which had to clear off. He looked at her. "Guess you're with me."

17

OUTSIDE SURABAYA, INDONESIA

Refocused and geared up, Garrett briefed Zim as Delaney shifted to sit in the operator's chair, her legs still wobbly. She smoothed her hair back into a ponytail.

"Hakim and Tariq are aboard." Garrett jerked his thumb into the car portion. "Rashid too, but Rogue neutralized him. Unknown if there are civilians up there, but we'll also have the train driver to deal with."

"Understood."

Garrett eyed her. "Think you're up to handling Surge as we clear the train?"

Wariness crowded her expression, but she slowly nodded. "I think . . ." She shuddered a breath, and the ghost of a smile hit her eyes. "I'm here, so I might as well do what I know to do."

He liked that. Liked that she'd rallied, that she had the grit to get back in the fight when things got hard. "I'll take lead, you'll stay behind me, and Zim will bring up the rear. Use a shoulder tap to signal in position each time we stop. Zim will tap yours, you tap mine. It'll tell me you're both ready. Clear?"

Clipping a lead to Surge, she nodded.

Weapon in a low-ready position, Garrett eased through to the connecting freight car. He moved past Rashid's body and pointed out the LD3s for Zim to mentally catalog for later use.

As they shifted past the body, Delaney let Surge sniff it again, as if maybe hoping she hadn't really killed the guy. She met his gaze and swallowed. "There, uh, wasn't anyone else in the car, so we should be okay."

"Always check," Garrett said as he pivoted and advanced with lethal determination. "We'll let him lead in the next car."

They moved steady and smooth to the next juncture. "Wait," he subvocalized, hand on the door. When she gave a nod of understanding, he flicked open the door and stepped in, doing a quick look-see, sweeping from the corner around to the right. He stepped forward and motioned her, keeping his weapon up and trained forward. He shifted to the side and looked to her. "Let him take point. Stay with me."

She nodded and extended the lead, staying just behind his shoulder as they moved through the crates of freight packing the car. They made it to the other door with no hits and no contact. He called that a win.

"Same thing. Slow is smooth, smooth is fast."

A wry look creased her pretty face, but she again inclined her head.

Again, he eased in, cleared left then swept around to the right. More of the same—crates packed to the ceiling, leaving little walkway. Delaney extended the lead and let Surge again do his thing. Same result—no hits, no contact.

By the seventh car, they'd fallen into a steady rhythm that made things comfortable. Yet he knew this was like Russian roulette—the more they cleared, the more likely that the next door concealed trouble. The metal-on-metal sound of the train wheels on the track drummed a cadence as they continued to advance.

"Only two cars left, plus the operation car," he subvocalized before entering the juncture. "We're going to make contact soon."

"Not soon—*now*," Delaney said, indicating to Surge.

He frowned at her, but then saw the maligator had locked onto the next door, staring through it as though he had X-ray vision. The muscles in his body rippled, and his hackles rose. A low rumble sent chills up Garrett's back.

Garrett met Zim's gaze and gave a firm nod, which the guy returned. "Once in and clear, stay close, Rogue."

"I trust you."

He twitched his gaze to hers, appreciating that but also well aware that her life and Surge's were on his shoulders. Just like Djibouti. Like Samwise. And Tsunami.

God, have mercy!

Stress pinched the nerve at the base of his neck. She stared at the door, knowing this was it. Surge had a hit, so there were either unfriendlies on the other side or the chems. Maybe both. Which meant they'd face opposition.

"Trust God." Delaney's whispered words skated down his neck.

He shifted and saw her face very close, appreciated her confident nod. Wasn't sure how he felt about her throwing his own words back at him, but she was right. Bouncing a nod, he angled to the front. Hit the release button and eased open the door.

Ping! Ping! Crack!

Garrett jerked back and threw himself to the side. "Contact! Down!"

They huddled there, and he eyed Zim and Delaney. "New plan," he hissed. "Tariq is by the far door. I'll go in and lay down suppressive fire. Rogue, stay with me. We'll go right with Surge, and you can take cover when needed. Zim, work your way toward Tariq on the left."

"Copy that," Zim said, his hand firming around his weapon. "I want Tariq."

And Garrett wanted Hakim, the man who'd taken on his evil father's goals . . . Fahmi Ansari, who'd killed himself to take out Samwise and Tsunami. Garrett gave his partner a curt nod. Rather than being paralyzed by fear, he'd use determination to drive him.

Repositioned to insert, they stacked at the door, this time with Zim flanking it. He held up his fingers. Three . . . two . . .

Zim hit the access panel and flicked open the door.

Submachine gun tucked into his shoulder, Garrett squeezed off rounds, advancing to the corner of the container. Though Tariq fired off a couple of rounds, he was forced to take cover as well. A double pat came to his shoulder, and Garrett jerked back and pressed his spine to the containers. Switched to the other side and did a quick look-see. Clear. In a crouch-run, he moved, noting the way Delaney was on her hands and knees, drawing Surge into a low crawl. The dog slunk along with them. Hakim had to be somewhere.

"*Apna hathyaar pheink do, Amrici!*" Tariq yelled in Urdu.

"Drop your weapon!" Zim yelled at the same time, closing in on him.

The mad scientist took a crack shot at Zim, but the operator ducked out of sight, then swung out and fired a short burst as he moved.

Garrett seized the confrontation to gain the front of the car. He peered around the corner and muttered an oath. A container stood between him and Tariq, who was in a standoff with Zim. "No line of sight," he subvocalized to Zim.

Where on earth was Hakim?

A light shift beyond the last sealed juncture between this car and the operator's cabin drew Garrett's attention. Had to be Hakim. He drew up his weapon, knowing Tariq was occupied staving off Zim, and advanced to the door. Accessed it and stepped in—

A blur rushed at him.

Awareness of Delaney with him flared through Garrett. He

shifted back, blocking access to the juncture. Felt the door whisk shut even as a dagger came at him. He stepped forward, reaching for his Sig as the door between the cars shut out the noise—and the team—behind him.

Hakim lunged with a knife and a feral scream.

Darting toward the man, Garrett deflected his knife hand. Caught Hakim's wrist while simultaneously sliding his own right hand up and behind the guy's neck. He gripped it tight and drove it down and around, enabling himself to get the guy's knife hand twisted up behind—

With a roar, Hakim dropped hard and released the weapon, then drove upward with a violent thrust, breaking Garrett's lock. He shoved Garrett backward, driving him into the wall. Garrett skidded around, drawing his Sig.

But Hakim rushed him.

Garrett raised his left arm at an angle, and Hakim rammed into his forearm, chest height, punching the breath from Garrett's lungs. He strained around the move and pushed his left shoulder forward to force Hakim back. Struggled to bring the weapon into a firing position, even as the breath choked out of him.

Hakim shifted suddenly.

A searing cut blazed across Garrett's forearm. He gritted through it, still determined to bring the Sig to bear. End this guy. With a roar, he shoved the terrorist backward. Got a foot between them. Snapped up his weapon and eased back the trigger. Once. Twice.

Gaping as blood slid between his eyes, Hakim slumped to the ground. Dead.

A scream came from the interior of the freight car.

"Delaney!" He snatched the knife and slapped the access panel. Shouldered into the door, weapon at the ready.

To the right, he spotted a flurry of activity that moved out of sight. He angled that way as he heard Delaney shout for Surge to attack.

Around the corner of the container, he spotted—

A blow to the back of his head pitched Garrett forward. He stumbled. Air rushed out of his mouth in a cough. But he drew up his weapon and came around—only to feel a bullet graze his shoulder. "Augh!" He wasn't going down. Not with Delaney here. He fired a round as the guy rushed him again.

But this time, Surge appeared over the container. Barreled at the guy. Broadsided him, slamming him in the door of the juncture. He chomped into the tender spot of Tariq's clavicle, eliciting a howl of agony.

It bought time for Garrett to get on his feet just as Delaney rounded the corner, her eyes wide. "Call him off," he said, aiming the submachine gun at the guy.

"Surge, out," Delaney said, the command fierce and controlled.

As soon as the maligator worked his teeth out of the shoulder and pushed away, Tariq lunged for his gun.

Garrett double-tapped the guy. Motioned Delaney to the side with Surge as he swiveled to Zim, who was panting hard. "You okay?"

The kid nodded. "With that guy down, yeah. At least he can't use science for evil anymore." He jutted his jaw. "Gotta stop the train."

"Copy that." Garrett headed back to the juncture and eyed the access panel. Hit it and the door popped open. He stepped in, weapon up.

The driver was hunched over the console and wheel, blood spilling across the white surface.

Garrett felt for a pulse. "Dead." He eyed the console and huffed—set to autopilot. "They didn't want anyone stopping it."

Coming in with Delaney, Zim dropped his ruck to the floor, moved the chair back, and played around with the controls. He sighed. "I have no idea how to slow this."

"Look it up," Garrett grunted as he peered out the long, sloping window. "We have six mikes before this thing enters the

RONIE KENDIG & VONI HARRIS

city. Takes five to slow it. You have thirty seconds to figure it out."

"Pressure, pressure," Zim muttered, scanning the dials, switches, and screens. "Okay . . ." He flicked a switch. "Autopilot is off. This . . . is almost like a video game."

"Except this one has real, deadly consequences."

"Right," Zim muttered and tapped on some screens.

"Twenty seconds."

"Rogue, kiss him so he'll shut up." Zim reached for the throttle. "At least I've played enough games to use a joystick. What if . . ." He pulled it down slowly, the train slowing from bullet speed. "Ah, there we go . . ."

"Thank You, God," Delaney whispered, stepping toward Garrett with a shuddering breath. He slumped into the seats as the train dropped out of warp and slowed.

Peering out the window, Garrett saw Frank's chopper and a few others now. "And here comes the cavalry." He stood, ducking to see better out the window as the train screeched to a stop. "I think we did it . . ." He laughed. Clapped Zim's shoulder. "Good job."

"Hey." Delaney shifted toward him. Touched his arm.

"Yeah?" He turned to her.

She pointed at the blood on his shirt. "You were shot. Are you okay?"

"Just a graze."

And she moved into his arms.

He stilled as her gentle brown eyes looked up into his, telegraphing exactly what she wanted. What he wanted. He caught her waist and snugged her into his hold. The citrus smell of her hair whirled into his nose. She tilted her head up at him, a full-hearted smile on her soft lips. A smile started across his own face. But he set his mouth to hers and kissed her. A long, deep one. One they both deserved, they'd both longed for. He crushed her to himself, and as he deepened the kiss, her arms hooked around his neck.

Hoots and claps sounded. "Get a room!"

Garrett broke off and grinned down at her, tucking her hair behind her ear.

Surge let out a moan-groan of protest.

"Hey," Garrett said, smiling down at the Malinois. "I think she has room for two operators in her life. One with two legs, one with four."

Surge huffed, then sneezed right in his face.

18

"Congrats, Bear!"

Garrett hopped down from the train, the fields around it swarming with local authorities and still-landing choppers delivering not just locals but a handful of Damocles guys. He hesitated, waiting for Delaney and Surge to join him.

Caldwell had a wide grin. "Knew you were the right guy for the job."

Was it his imagination, or did the man sound respectful? And despite Garrett's hesitation about the spook's loyalties, his intel had worked out this time. "Appreciate it." He nodded. "You've done good, Caldwell." He extended a hand.

Caldwell dipped his head and accepted the proffered handshake, then got called away by someone.

Delaney edged into view next to him. "That seemed a little nicer than all your other convos with him."

With a nod, Garrett shrugged. "Bygones . . ." He took her hand and drew her nearer. "You really stepped up to the plate in there." He shifted closer, ignoring the chaos around them. "I know you weren't prepared for that. Taking a life is never easy,

230

and if it is, then you have big problems. But give yourself time to work through that."

"Thanks. I will."

He cupped the back of her head and drew it closer, planted a kiss on her forehead. "I'm proud of you."

"Walker."

At the barked voice, Garrett pivoted. Felt himself start at the guy stalking toward him, flanked by a couple of operators. Chapel. Holy . . .

"Good work," Tyson Chapel said as he reached him and thumped Garrett's good shoulder. "Sorry we couldn't be of more help, but I knew you could handle it."

Stunned, Garrett wasn't sure what to say. "Yeah. Thanks. That means a lot."

"We're going to coordinate with Indonesian law enforcement and get things cleaned up. Think maybe it's time for you to bug out and get some well-deserved rest."

"Again, I appreciate it." He felt more than saw Delaney behind him. "Oh, hey—the real hero of the day—Surge, the Malinois you contracted from Ghost."

Appreciation shone through the legendary operator's hazel eyes.

"And this is Delaney Thompson. Without her scent work, we would've been up the proverbial creek."

Chapel extended his hand to her. "Thanks for stepping into the fray." He indicated the containers being offloaded by teams in HAZMAT. "Without you, that would've been all over our country and people. You're a hero. Thank you."

With another clap on Garrett's shoulder, he jutted his jaw to the chopper. "Frank's going to get you guys out of here. We've already got arrangements in play to get y'all stateside ASAP."

"Thanks."

He wanted that nap but couldn't stop thinking of the woman next to him. Without her, they wouldn't have known about Tariq and Rashid. Or the bullet train. He'd trusted her, and she'd gone off by herself from that Jakarta street fair to find it. When they'd first met, he hadn't trusted her at all. Hadn't even wanted her on the mission. But she had been eager to start that self-defense training with him and to teach him to work with Surge. Except for ABA's Mal, she'd been in over her head on this trip. No training. But she was fearless.

Plus, she reminded him to trust Christ. They'd actually reminded each other that's where trust needed to be—faith.

And there was that red-hot kiss on the train.

A guy could go a long way on a kiss like that.

EPILOGUE
SIX MONTHS LATER

HILL COUNTRY, TEXAS

Delaney climbed into Garrett's burnt-orange Jeep and shut the door. "Thanks for picking me up. Made it easier." She glanced back to say hi to Zim, only he wasn't there. Nobody was. So . . . he'd just picked her up? But he'd said this was a team event at the quarterly Navy SEAL Foundation fundraiser at Fox's Barbecue.

Only her.

She shifted in the passenger seat as they made their way to the restaurant. "So, is Zim meeting us there?"

"Can't," Garrett said, adjusting his ball cap as they sat at a red light. "He was deployed. Africa, I think."

"Oh." She watched as he pulled onto the county road leading to the ranch. "Caldwell?"

"He's in DC, busy with some spook business or another."

So how was this the "team event" he'd told her about last week when they'd met for one of their near-weekly meetups since returning from Indonesia? She'd enjoyed their alone time. Long talks. Real talks.

But that had been coffee, and this wasn't that. It felt . . . different.

"Team" with just Garrett?

She riffled through her brain, trying to find something to talk about. She could ask how his contracting was going now. Or how his new golden retriever pup was doing with the training advice she'd given him over coffee.

She looked over at him. The way he drove with one hand, the way his muscular arms just perfectly stretched his solid black T-shirt . . .

Delaney gulped. She thought about his arms way too much. She ripped her eyes away.

Um, God? What's happening?

They passed one of the signs announcing the fundraiser and she read it aloud. "Our quarterly SEAL Foundation fundraiser in December features the Choca Cantika Barbecue Sauce! Their coffee too! Today from four to closing." She smiled, satisfied their work had made that possible. "It's awesome they can still offer Choca Cantika."

"Right?" he agreed with a nod. "Between the US Army and the Indonesian police at the train explosion, Sachaai is gone," Garrett said. Then he *hmph*'d. "But really, coffee with barbecue? I mean, Choca Cantika is great, but it's Dr. Pepper with barbecue, dude."

Coffee. There was a decent topic. "You sure you want to try the Choca Cantika Barbecue Sauce? I heard about a poisoning or something?"

The corner of his mouth lifted. "More flavor. Are you sure?"

"Well, I do know the guy who saved the Cantika Coffee Farm . . ."

His grin spread wide.

"Supposedly. So maybe I better not." Delaney laughed, and he took the turn into the barbecue place.

Someone pulled out of the parking spot right next to the

entry to Fox's Barbecue. He pulled into it and turned off the Jeep. She reached for her purse and would've opened the door for herself, except Garrett appeared there, helping her out.

She hopped out and found herself right next to him. Liked the way she seemed to fit beside him. Felt her insides go giddy at his proximity. And the warm pressure of his hand on the small of her back.

Country music spilled from Fox's, and she just naturally danced her arms a little as they walked up to the restaurant. The smoker stood beside the door, smoke furling gently into the air. She screeched to a stop as the aroma of the meat smoking over mesquite made her mouth water. "How have I never eaten here?"

"No idea. There is some of that food to eat, inside." He grabbed the pocket of her burgundy jacket and gently tugged toward the door.

She laughed, and they walked in and joined the line. Brisket, ribs, pulled pork, chicken quarters. She read the menu but couldn't decide. She threw her hands in the air. "Just order for me."

"So you actually trust me, huh?"

She laughed. "So much I'll let myself be hoisted off a bullet train at full speed."

He groaned and shook his head, moving along in line. "Don't remind me."

A woman in a Fox's Barbecue apron approached, bearing a tray with mini plastic cups. "This is the famous Choca Cantika Barbecue Sauce that we're featuring today. Would you like to try it?" She leaned toward them, talking in a fake whisper. "Don't tell Mrs. Fox. I tried one. This sauce is so good. You're going to like it."

She and Garrett wouldn't have laughed if they hadn't made eye contact.

"I do," Garrett said, and grabbed a mini cup.

The lady hesitantly held the tray toward her.

Delaney bit her lip to stop the laugh and smiled as she took one. "Of course. Thanks." She tipped the barbecue sauce into her mouth. Her knees dipped. "Oh! Oh! That is so good," she groaned in pleasure. "I knew it would be good, but not *this* good. It's so . . . sweet and deep."

"Told you so," the lady said holding out a trash bag.

Delaney and Garrett tossed their mini cups into the bag.

They reached the front, where the cashier greeted them. "Hey, Mr. Walker. I suppose you want the usual pulled pork sandwich basket?"

"Two please, Charley. With fries and . . ." He narrowed his eyes in thought. "Dr. Pepper."

Delaney dug in her purse for her wallet, but Garrett was already paying for it. Like he'd paid for all their coffee.

He leaned up against the counter as they waited for their order. "How was Surge's last scent work contract with the Houston Police Department?"

"He found a very big drug stash."

The employee brought the two baskets on a tray, which Garrett retrieved and headed to the condiment trough. There he piled pickles and onions on his sandwich.

Delaney frowned. "Why do you cover up the awesome smoky meat with all that stuff?"

With a wink, he grinned. "Pickles and onions make the sandwich." He handed her one of the bowls of banana pudding. "And this makes the meal."

She stared at the banana pudding. "Deal." When they finally found the only empty, clean table, she sat down and snatched the Choca Cantika sauce from the sauce basket on the table and pointed it at him. "This. Sauce is what makes the sandwich."

He pulled out the sriracha smoke sauce and squeezed it onto his pulled pork.

"Let me guess. You always eat the same thing here."

"When it's good, it's good." He took a bite. Practically half the sandwich.

"Walker." Heath approached, his own basket laden with items from the trough and Crew trailing him with his own pile of barbecue. "Delaney. Mind if we join y'all?"

What was ABA doing here?

Crew took the seat next to Garrett. "Hey, Delaney. Garrett." He indicated the Choca Cantika she was holding. "Done with that?"

"Sure," she said with a laugh.

He took it and squeezed some onto his brisket. "Been wanting to try this."

Heath chewed, then took a gulp of water. Jutted his jaw at Garrett. "You ready to start tactical training with our handlers?"

Delaney almost spat out her Dr. Pepper.

Garrett nodded at Heath. "I'm good to go. When do you want me?"

"Monday too soon?"

"Negative."

"Ten-hundred every Monday, Wednesday, Friday, right?"

"That works."

"You—" Delaney's voice hitched, and she cleared her throat as she gaped at Garrett. "You're going to teach tactical training? At the ranch?"

"I am," he said with a slow smile. "Ghost and I talked about it and came to an agreement."

"How will that work out with you doing contract work?"

"I . . . I was going to talk to you about that. I'm done."

"Oh." She couldn't believe it—that meant he'd be here, around . . . a lot. That was good. Wonderful, even. Their relationship . . . Nerves thrummed, so she took a bite of her sandwich. Set her hand on the table, thinking through what he was saying, that he would stay . . . Did he feel what she felt?

He and Heath chatted about the different techniques and the

possibility of finding a location for Garrett to train locals in self-defense for added income.

Delaney felt the whisper of a touch against her pinky and glanced down. Garrett's hand rested there, and he was apparently oblivious. So she slid her pinky closer, hooked his.

His gaze flicked there, then back to Heath with a laugh about something. She'd lost track, too focused on them. Could they have a future?

"Thompson," Crew said as he swallowed some food. "We've procured more dogs and want you to put them through scent training."

"Oh, wonderful. Nice to have some job security." At least she still had a career at the ranch, and apparently Garrett did too, so he'd be around for a while. "I hope to get in on Garrett's class too. That okay?"

"That's what it'll be there for," Heath said. "Classes are free for staff."

They ate in silence for a few more minutes, then Garrett stood. "We'll check y'all later. Ready, Rogue?"

Startled at his rapid change of topic, she faltered. "Uh, yeah. Sure." What was up with Garrett? She scooted out and stood, hung her purse on her shoulder. "See you guys later."

Crew and Ghost gave their farewells but kept eating.

On the way to the exit, Garrett dropped a large bill in the mason jar set out for donations. He stood by the passenger door at the Jeep, but instead of opening it, he leaned up against it. Definitely a bear face. But she trusted this Bear.

"That was a quick exit. You okay?"

"Yeah," he said with a huff. "I like Heath and Crew. Good guys." He sighed and opened the door for her. "Just wasn't expecting them today."

"You said today was a team event . . ."

He frowned and scruffed the back of his head. "Yeah, thought it was a good idea, since we saved Cantika and Fox was offering that Choca Cantika Barbecue Sauce. But when Zim and Caldwell had to cancel . . ." He gave her a sheepish look.

"You didn't want to cancel." She cocked her head at him. "You could've just asked if we could make this a date. We've been on a few. Remember, before your last op . . ."

"Right." He took her hands into his. "I've been praying, and, well, after all we went through together in Southeast Asia . . ."

She considered him.

"I want something more than a coffee date. I want a future with you."

Heart racing, she smiled. "Me too."

"Sorry I didn't talk to you about the self-defense thing. I . . . I want our lives to align. And while I was on that South America contract, I was praying about what was next for me, for us."

Oh, that made her heart swoon.

"Then last week, when Heath and I were talking, the self-defense training thing happened, and I realized it made a way for me to stay, to provide . . . and I got to thinking about us."

"Go on," she said, hooking her arm around his neck. "I'm liking this natural progression."

"I know with your dad here, you want to stay."

She smiled. "He really likes you, especially since you helped me get that leg for him."

"Seems I'm winning on all counts." Garrett stepped forward, pulled her into a bear hug, a hug she didn't want to ever step away from.

She laced her hands behind his neck. "So it would appear."

He eased back a fraction and looked into her eyes, then lowered his mouth to hers. His kiss was warm and gentle. Strong.

She loved his kiss. Wanted more.

"Put a ring on her finger, Walker!" came a barked laugh.

Garrett glanced over his shoulder as Crew and Heath laughed all the way to a big black dualie. He shook his head, but then looked at her, something deep in his brown eyes. "What do you think?"

Confusion skidded through her. "About?"

"Me, marriage."

She drew in a quick breath. "I . . ." Holy wow, was this really happening? "I think it's a sound tactical plan."

As they pulled out of the parking lot, his pinkie lapped over hers.

Be sure you haven't missed any of the high-octane romantic stories in this epic series.

A BREED APART: LEGACY UNLEASHED!

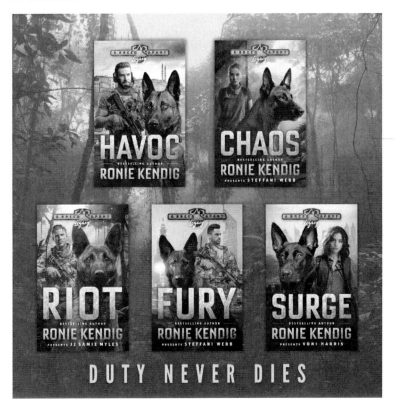

Get your hands on all of Ronie Kendig's
A Breed Apart: Legacy series.

HAVE YOU READ RONIE KENDIG'S ORIGINAL A BREED APART SERIES?

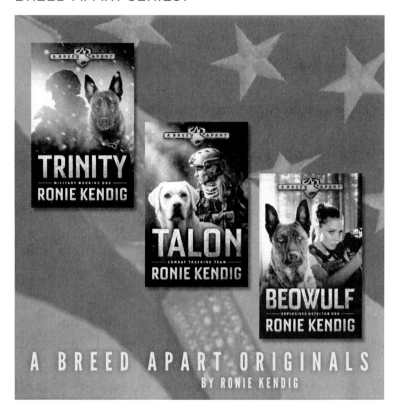

Dive into Heath Daniels' origin story now!

GET READY . . . THINGS ARE ABOUT TO GET HOT!

With heart-pounding excitement, gripping suspense, and sizzling (but clean!) romance, the CHASING FIRE: MONTANA series, brought to you by the incredible authors of Sunrise Publishing, including the dynamic duo of bestselling authors Susan May Warren and Lisa Phillips, is your epic summer binge read.

Immerse yourself in a world of short, captivating novels that are designed to be devoured in one sitting. Each book is a standalone masterpiece, (no story cliffhangers!) although you'll be craving the next one in the series!

Follow the Montana Hotshots and Smokejumpers as they

chase a wildfire through northwest Montana. The pages ignite with clean romance and high-stakes danger—these heroes (and heroines!) will capture your heart. The biggest question is . . . who will be your summer book boyfriend?

This exciting series is available in ebook, print, and audiobook. What are you waiting for? Read the complete series now!

Keep reading for a sneak peek at *Flashpoint* by Susan May Warren, the first book in the thrilling Chasing Fire: Montana series.

FLASHPOINT

CHASING FIRE: MONTANA || BOOK ONE

CHAPTER 1

Clearly, his last hope at a comeback was about to crash and burn.

Maybe he was being a little melodramatic, but Spenser Storm knew a good story.

Knew how to cater to an audience, knew when a script was a disaster.

And this one had flames all over it.

Yes, the screenplay had all the right ingredients—a winning western retelling of a widow and her son who leaned on the help of two strangers to save her land. And they were shooting on location in Montana at a real abandoned western town rebuilt and redressed for the movie, complete with a jail and a church.

They'd even hired an up-and-coming country music star to write original music.

The problem was, the producer, Lincoln Cash, picked the wrong man to die.

Not that Spenser Storm had a say in it—he'd been given all of sixteen lines in the one-hundred-twenty-page script. But he wanted to ask, while waving flags and holding a megaphone—

Who killed off the hero at the end of a movie? Had no one paid any attention to the audience during the screening of *Sommersby*?

He didn't care how many academy-acclaimed actors were attached to this movie. Because everyone—even he—would hate the fact that their favorite action hero ended up fading into eternity. And he wasn't talking about himself, but the invincible Winchester Marshall.

Perfect. Spenser should probably quit now and go back to herding cattle.

"Back to ones!" Indigo, the first Assistant Director, with her long black hair tied back, earphones around her neck, raised her hand.

Spenser nudged his mare, Goldie, back to the position right outside town. Sweat trickled down his spine, and he leaned low so a makeup assistant could wipe his brow.

Yeah, something in his gut said trouble. It didn't help that all of Montana had become a broiler, even this early in the summer—the grass yellow, the temperature index soaring, turning even the wind from the pine-saturated mountains into the breath of hades.

But saving the movie wasn't Spenser's job. No, his job was to sit pretty atop his horse and smile for the camera, those gray-blue eyes smoldery, his body tanned and a little dusty, his golden-brown hair perfectly curled out of his black Stetson, his body buff and muscled under his blue cotton shirt and a leather vest.

He wore jeans, black boots, and could have walked off the set of *Yellowstone*. No, *swaggered* off the set. Because he wasn't a fool.

They'd cast him as eye candy. With sixteen lines and the guy who got the girl at the end. Spenser was the sizzle for the audience who was too young for Winchester Marshall, the lead of the movie, although Spenser was just a couple years younger.

But, like Lincoln Cash said when he signed him, Spenser had a special kind of appeal.

The kind that packed the convention floor at comic cons around the world.

Wow, he hated comic cons. And adults who dressed up as Iwonians and spoke a language only created in fanfic world. If he never heard the name Quillen Cleveland again, he'd die a happy man.

He hated to mention to Lincoln that the fans who loved *Trek of the Osprey* might not enjoy a western called *The Drifters*, but a guy with no screen credits to his name for five years should probably keep his mouth shut when accepting a role.

At least according to his agent, Greg Alexander.

Keep his mouth shut, deliver his lines, and maybe, hopefully, he'd be back in the game.

"We need a little more business from the extras." Director Cosmos Ferguson wore a *Drifters* T-shirt, jeans and boots, and his own cowboy hat. "Feel free to cause more havoc on the set."

Behind him, Swen, from SFX stepped out of the house, checking on the fire cannons for the next shot. The set crew had trailered in an old cabin for today's shoot—a real structure with a porch and a stone chimney that rose from the tattered wooden roof—and plunked it down in a valley just two hundred yards from the town, with a corral for the locally sourced horses. It was a postcard of bygone days.

Was it only Spenser, or did anyone else think it might be a bad idea to light a fire inside a rickety wooden house that looked already primed for tinder?

"Quiet on the set!"

Around him, the world stopped. The gaffers, the grips, the second team, the stuntmen, even, it seemed, the ripple of wind through the dusty one-horse ghost town-slash-movie set.

Not even Goldie moved.

"Picture's up!" Indigo said.

At least Spenser could enjoy the view. The sky stretched forever on both sides of the horizon, the glorious Kootenai mountains rising jagged and bold to the north, purple and green wildflowers cascading down the foothills into the grasslands of the valley.

"Roll sound!"

A hint of summer night hung in the air. Perhaps he'd grab a burger at the Hotline Bar and Grill in Ember, just down the street from Motel Bates, where the cast was staying. Okay, the lodging wasn't that bad, but—

"Action."

The extras, aka cowboys, burst to life, shooting prop guns into the air just before Winchester Marshall, aka Deacon Cooper, rode in, chasing them away with his own six-shooter. They raced out of town, then Deacon got off his horse, dropped the reins, and checked the pulse of the fallen extra. "Hawk, C'mere. I think this is one of the cowboys from the Irish spread."

Spenser's cue to ride on screen, dismount and confirm, then stand up and stare into the horizon, as if searching for bad guys.

Seemed like a great way for a guy to get shot. But again, he wasn't in charge of the script.

So, he galloped onto the set, swung his leg over Goldie's head, jumped out of the saddle, and sauntered up. He gave the scene a once over, met Winchester-slash-Deacon's eyes with a grim look, and nodded. Then he turned and looked at the horizon, his hands on his hips, while the camera zoomed in, trouble in his expression.

"Cut!" Cosmos said as he walked over to them. "I love the interaction between you two." He turned away, motioning to Swen.

What interaction? Spenser wanted to ask, but Winchester— "Win" to the crew—rose and clamped a hand on Spenser's shoulder. "One would think you grew up on a horse the way you rode up."

"I did," Spenser said, but Win had already turned away, headed to craft services, probably for a cold soda.

"Moving on. Scene seventeen," Indigo said. "Let's get ready for the house fire."

Spenser jogged over to Goldie and grabbed her reins, but a male stunt assistant came up and took hold of the mare's halter. "I've got her, sir."

Spenser let the animal go and headed over to the craft table set up under a tented area, back from the set, near the two long connected trailers brought in for the actors. The Kalispell Sound and Light truck was parked next to an array of rental cars, along with the massive Production trailer, where the wardrobe department kept their set supplies, including a locked container for the weapons.

"That was a great scene." This from the caterer, a woman named Juliet, whose family owned the Hot Cakes Bakery in Ember. She wore her brown hair back in a singular braid and handed him a sandwich, nodding to drinks in a cooler. Not a fancy setup, but this far out in the sticks, they were beggars. Cosmos had also ordered a hot breakfast from the Ember Hotline every morning.

"Thanks." Spenser unwrapped the plastic on his sandwich. "This bread looks homemade."

"It is. The smoked chicken is from the Hotline, though." She winked, but it wasn't flirty, and continued to set out snacks—cookies and donuts.

The sandwich reminded him a little of the kind of food that Kermit, the cook for the Flying S Ranch, served during roundup, eaten with a cold soda, and a crispy pickle.

Sheesh, what was he doing here, back on a movie set? He should be home, on his family's ranch…

Or not. Frankly, he didn't know where he belonged.

He turned, eating the sandwich, and watched as lead actress Kathryn Canary, seated on a high director's chair, dressed in a long grimy prairie dress, her blonde hair mussed, ignored a makeup assistant applying blood to her face and hands. She held her script in one hand, rehearsing her lines as Blossom Winthrop, the heroine with Trace Wilder, playing the role of her husband, Shane Winthrop.

Who was about to die.

He hadn't seen Trace since his last movie, but the man seemed not to remember their short stint on *Say You Love Me*.

Spenser would like to forget it too, frankly. Another reason why he'd run back to the family ranch in central Montana.

It all felt surreal, a marriage of Spenser's worlds—the set, busy with gaffers setting up lighting, and the sound department fixing boom mics near the house, the set dresser putting together the scene. And then, nearby, saddles lined up along the rail of a corral where horses on loan from a nearby ranch nickered, restless with the heat.

Cowboys, aka extras, sat in holding with their hats pushed back, drinking coffee, wearing chaps and boots. All they were missing were the cattle grazing in the distance. Maybe the smell of burgers sizzling on Kermit's flat grill.

Bandit, the ranch dog, begging for scraps.

They did, however, have a cat, and out of the corner of his eye, Spenser spotted Bucky Turnquist, age eight, who played Dusty Winthrop, chase the tabby around the set. His mother, Gemma, had already hinted that, as a single mom, she might be interested in getting to know Spenser better.

Now, she talked with one of the villain cowboys, laughing as he got on his horse.

"You guys about ready?" Cosmos had come back from where the cameramen were setting up, the grip team working to shade the light for the shot, on his way to Kathryn and Trace, who were rising from their chairs.

One of the SFX guys raised a hand from where they set up the cannons that would 'fire' the house. Not a real fire, not with the burn index so high in this part of crispy, dry Montana. But enough that it would generate heat and look real.

And enough that they'd asked the local wildland fire team on set to keep an eye on anything that might get out of hand. He'd caught sight of the handful of firefighters dressed in their canvas pants, steel-toed boots, yellow Nomex shirts, and Pulaskis hanging out near the fire. They'd brought up a fire truck, too, with a hose ready to deploy water.

"Get a hose over here, Emily!" A man wearing a vest, the word Command on the back, directed a woman, her blonde hair in a tight ponytail, to pull up a hose nearer the building, and hand it over to another firefighter. Then she ran back to the truck, ready to deploy.

According to the script, the cowboys would fire at the house, and then a stuntman would run out, on fire, and collapse to the ground. Cue Kathryn, as Blossom, to run in with a shirt she'd pulled from the hanging laundry to snuff it out while the cowboys attempted to kidnap her.

She'd panic then, and scream for Dusty, and only then would the kid run from the barn. They'd be surrounded, swept up by the villains and taken away while poor Shane died.

At which point the guy would go down to the Hotline for a nice cool craft beer and a burger, then tomorrow, catch a ride to Kalispell and head back to his air-conditioned apartment in LA.

"Ready on Special Effects?" Indigo shouted. She'd reminded him that this wasn't *Trek of The Osprey* and that he wasn't the star here when he'd headed to the wrong trailer on day one.

Whatever. Easy mistake.

"Ready!" This from Swen, who stood away from the house. The cowboys were already in place and Blossom stood at the clothesline in the yard, away from the house.

"Quiet on set!" Indigo shouted. She glanced at Cosmos, who nodded. "Roll Camera. Roll Sound."

A beat. "Action!"

And that's when he spotted little Bucky, still chasing the cat, scooting under the house on his hands and knees.

At the front of the house, a window burst and flames licked out of it.

"Wait!"

The next window burst. More fire.

251

"Bucky's in there!" Where was his mother? It didn't matter. He took off for the back of the house.

The cowboys in the front yard whooped, shots fired, and of course, the stuntman stumbled out in his firesuit and flopped onto the front yard.

Blossom screamed and ran to put out the fire just as Spenser reached the back of the house.

The fire seemed real enough, with the roof now catching. "Bucky?"

With everyone's gaze on the action, no one had seen him wriggle under the porch. Spenser hit his knees. "Bucky?"

There. Under the middle of the house, curled into a ball, his hands over his ears. "Bucky, C'mere!"

He was crying now, and Spenser saw why—the entire front porch had caught fire.

Sparks dropped around him. The grass sizzled.

Aw—Spenser dropped to his belly and army crawled into the center of the house, coughing, his eyes watering. He grabbed Bucky's foot, yanked.

Bucky kicked at him, split his lip. Blood spurted.

"C'mon kid!"

He grabbed Bucky's arms and jerked him close, wrapping him up, holding him. "It's okay. C'mon, let's get out of here." Smoke billowed in from where the porch fell, a line of fire blocking their escape. But out the back—

Then, suddenly, a terrible crack rent the building, and with a thunderous crash, the old chimney tumbled down. Dust and rock crashed through the cabin, tore out the flooring, and obliterated the porch.

Blocked their exit.

Spenser grabbed Bucky and pulled him close, holding his breath, then expelling the dust, his body wracking with coughs. And Bucky in his arms, screaming.

When he opened his eyes, fire burned around them, a cauldron of very real, very lethal flames.

"Stop! Stop the film! There's someone inside there!"

Or at least Emily thought so. She still wasn't quite sure if that was a person or an animal she'd seen dive under the burning house.

In truth, she'd been stationed by her fire truck, watching the house burn, trying not to let her gaze drift back to the beautiful and amazing Spenser Storm, standing near craft services.

The Spenser Storm.

From *Trek of the Osprey*. Quillen Cleveland in the flesh, all grown up and ruggedly handsome, dressed in western getup: leather vest, chaps, black boots, and a Stetson over his burnished golden-brown hair, those gray-blue eyes that a girl could get lost in. He even wore that rakish, heart-thumping smile. The man who saved the galaxy, one world at a time, there he was...

Eating a sandwich.

She'd spotted him almost right off this morning when she'd arrived with fellow hotshot Houston James and her fire boss, Conner Young. The Special Effects department had called in the local Jude County Hotshots as a precaution.

Not a terrible idea given the current fire index.

The SFX supervisor, Swen, had briefed the hotshots before the event—squibs of dust on a lead that would explode to imitate bullets hitting the building. They'd walked through the system that would create the explosion, a tank filled with propane, rigged to burst the window and release a fireball.

She'd expected the bomb, but when the squibs detonated, Emily nearly hit the dirt.

Nearly. But *didn't*. So, take that, panic attack. No more PTSD for her, thank you ten years of therapy.

Except, the explosion hadn't gone quite like they'd hoped. Sure, the gas dissipated into the air, but somehow cinder had fallen onto the porch.

The entire old wooden porch burst into flames.

Black smoke cluttered the sky, and if she were a spotter, via a fire tower or a plane, she'd be calling in sparks to the local Ember fire department. Which would then deploy either the Jude County Hotshots or, if the fire started further in, the Jude County Smokejumpers. The first and last line of defense against fire in this northwest corner of Montana.

About as far away as she could get from her failures, thank you.

Not anymore. This was a new season, a new start, and this time...*this time* the shrapnel of the past wasn't going to eviscerate her future.

So, she'd stood by the truck, waiting for the signal from Conner. Tall, brown hair, calm, he'd been brought in to command the team for the summer while Jed Ransom, their former boss, now crewed the Missoula team.

And that's when, in her periphery, she'd spotted—was that a *person* diving under the back of the house? Black boots disappeared under the footing of the cabin.

Were they out of their *mind?*

Maybe it was an animal—cats sometimes ran toward a fire instead of away.

"Boss!" —She had nearly shouted, but that would carry, and with the house on fire, the director only had one take. Instead, she'd headed to the house—

The chimney simply collapsed. A crack, then thunder as the entire handmade stone chimney crumbled. She dropped to her knees, her hands over her head, as dust, rock, and debris exploded out from the house.

From the front came shouts and shooting, the cameras still rolling. She lifted her head, blinking as the dust settled. The inferno now engulfed the front of the house, moving fast toward the back, the roof half-collapsed. "Boss!"

And then a thought clicked in—*black boots.* "It's Spenser! Spenser Storm is under the building!"

No one heard her over the roar of the fire, the shouts from the street.

No one died today. Not on her watch.

C'mon, Emily, think!

She ran over to the truck, grabbed her Pulaski, and then opened the cab door and hit the siren. It screamed over the set as she scrambled toward the house.

Flames kicked out the side windows now, the heat burning her face. She pulled up her handkerchief and dug at the rubble.

The siren kept whining, sweat burning down her back, but in a second, she'd created a hole. She dropped to her knees. "Hello? Hello?"

"In here!"

Smoke cluttered the area, but she made out—yes, Spenser Storm, and a kid.

Oh no, the little Turnquist kid, the son of one of the locals in town.

Emily's eyes watered, but she crawled inside the space, pushing the Pulaski out in front of her. "Grab hold!"

Hands gripped her ankles. "Emily! Get out of there!"

Conner's voice.

"Grab the ax!" she shouted.

Spenser's hand gripped the ax, his other around the kid.

"Pull me out!" this, to Conner.

It was everything she could do to hold onto the Pulaski as they dragged them out from the crawl space. She cleared the building, then launched to her feet even as Conner tried to push her away.

Spenser Storm appeared, like a hero crawling from the depths of hell. The child clung to him, his face blackened, his wardrobe filthy and sooty, his eyes reddened, coughing as he kicked himself free.

"Bucky!" His mother ran toward him, but someone grabbed her back.

Instead, superstar Winchester Marshall, aka Jack Powers, aka whatever hunk he was playing in this western, was right there, pulling the kid from Spenser's arms.

Cosmos pushed through to grab Spenser, helped him to his feet. Spenser bent over, coughing.

"Water! Make a hole!" Cosmos yelled, leading Spenser away.

The movie star didn't even look at Emily as he stumbled to safety.

"C'mon—we need to put out this fire." Conner took off for the hose.

She ran to the truck, still coughing, turned off the siren, then, seeing Houston's signal, she hit the water.

The hose filled, and in a moment, water doused the house, spray saturating the air.

She leaned over, caught her knees, breathing hard. Watched as the fire died. Listened to the roaring on set, and in her heart, subside.

Felt the knot unravel.

No, no one died today. Especially not Spenser Storm.

She stood up, still hauling in breaths. She'd *saved* Spenser Storm. Holy Cannoli.

No, no she wouldn't make a fool of herself and ask for an autograph. And certainly not tell him, ever, that she'd had at least two *Tiger Beat* centerfold posters of him in his Osprey uniform—a pair of black pants, boots and white shirt, leather vest, holding a Vortex Hand Cannon. Never mind mentioning that she'd once attended a Comic-Con just to stand in line for a photo op. He wouldn't remember her, right? Or her status as a Stormie—a member of his official fan club?

"Hey!"

She looked up. Froze.

Spenser Storm was headed her direction, holding a water bottle, his eyes watering, looking like he'd just, well, been pulled from a fire. "You okay?"

She nodded, her eyes widening. C'mon words—

"I just wanted to say thanks." He held out his hand. "You saved my life back there. And Bucky's."

She nodded again. *C'mon words!*

"Maybe I can buy you a drink down at the Hotline sometime?"

"Mmmhmm." *That didn't count!*

Then he smiled, a thousand watts of pure charisma, sunshine and star power, winked, and walked away.

And right then, right there, she nearly died.

CONNECT WITH SUNRISE

Thank you so much for reading *Surge*. We hope you enjoyed the story. If you did, would you be willing to do us a favor and leave a review? It doesn't have to be long- just a few words to help other readers know what they're getting. (But no spoilers! We don't want to wreck the fun!) Thank you again for reading!

We'd love to hear from you- not only about this story, but about any characters or stories you'd like to read in the future. Contact us at www.sunrisepublishing.com/contact.

We also have a regular updates that contains sneak peeks, reviews, upcoming releases, and fun stuff for our reader friends. Sign up at www.sunrisepublishing.com or scan our QR code.

ACKNOWLEDGMENTS

Ronie Kendig, I had such fun playing in your fictional world of A Breed Apart in Texas. It has been pure joy to my heart, thanks to you. You are very much an encouragement and a challenger. I love that. Thank you, Susan May Warren, for turning this project into an advanced, Masters-level class in fiction writing. I love that. Thank you, both of you, for bringing out the storytelling in me as I worked on this story.

Thank you, Crystal Caudill, Liz Brezinski, and Angela Carlisle … my writing partners. Somehow, it's not just a writing partnership, it's a deep friendship. Thank you, my friends.

Then there is, without doubt, all the help I received from Coast Guard Military Working Dog handler Daniel Alati and Air Force dog handler Sgt. Bruce MacWatters, to former Coast Guard helicopter rescue pilot Zach Koehler. Each of you helped me achieve my goal of authenticity to make the world of a novel seem real to readers …even though it's totally fiction.

Thank you!
Voni

ABOUT THE AUTHORS

Ronie Kendig is a bestselling, award-winning author of over thirty-five books. She grew up an Army brat, and now she and her Army-veteran husband have returned to their beloved Texas after a ten-year stint in the Northeast. They survive on Sonic runs, barbecue, and peach cobbler that they share—sometimes—with Benning the Stealth Golden and AAndromeda the MWD Washout. Ronie's degree in psychology has helped her pen novels of intense, raw characters.

To learn more about Ronie, visit www.roniekendig.com and follow her on social media.

With a law-enforcement instructor father and a newspaper editor mother, it's no wonder Voni Harris grew up to write suspense novels. Voni writes from the home she shares with her legal-eagle husband on the beautiful and mysterious Alaskan island of Kodiak, where her creativity abounds. She belongs to American Christian Fiction Writers and has been published in two short-story collections: Heart-Stirring Stories of Romance, and Spiritual Citizens at http://drawneartochrist.com.

Connect with Voni at voniharris.com.

MORE A BREED APART NOVELS

A Breed Apart: Legacy

Havoc

Chaos

Riot

Fury

Surge

A Breed Apart

Trinity

Talon

Beowulf

Made in United States
Cleveland, OH
16 January 2025

13443560R20162